# NO PLACE TO CALL MY OWN

# NO PLACE TO CALL MY OWN

ALINA GUFRAN

Published by Tranquebar, an imprint of Westland Books, a division of Nasadiya Technologies Private Limited, in 2025

No. 269/2B, First Floor, 'Irai Arul', Vimalraj Street, Nethaji Nagar, Alapakkam Main Road, Maduravoyal, Chennai 600095

Westland, the Westland logo, Tranquebar and the Tranquebar logo are the trademarks of Nasadiya Technologies Private Limited, or its affiliates.



ISBN: 9789360454814

10 9 8 7 6 5 4 3 2 1



Typeset by Mukul

Printed at Thomson Press (India) Ltd

# CONTENTS

# 1

# DELHI

'REMEMBER ME?'

I'm unsure why I sent the text or where the shameless bravado came from. Like Farhad had any other choice. Years ago, in Dubai, he would be unceremoniously kicked out of the bedroom he shared with his brother on the nights we returned to his. He would pick me up when I was wasted outside clubs, too high to hail a taxi, out of phone credit, trying to stay away from the random boy I'd kissed a few hours earlier. We'd drive back to his parents' home in silence and spend the remaining hours of the night playing pool at the empty community hall, where he avoided my questions about Azhar before buying me breakfast at the local McDonald's.

I dulled my hangover with buckets of orange juice as he watched me with pity and fascination. He was the same person I met for coffee on sober winter mornings in Delhi, back when he was visiting his brother, who was by then busy dodging my calls. He pleaded with me to stop being in touch with Azhar. *He's got a wife now. You're a good girl, Sophia, if a bit stubborn.* I nodded along to his assertions, thanked him for his time and the mental energy he spent on me and gave him a wooden hug; at some point, I suspected he might have wanted me.

My time with his brother ended a few months ago, but it feels much longer. It comes back in bits and pieces—the clinic, the last time I met Azhar, the migraines, the inevitable shift between Medha and me. With every loss, I clung on to the possibility of what could have been, the memory of what was, until it chipped away at any understanding I might have of the present, of my actions and how they whittled down those who loved me. I'd become an expert in not acknowledging my emotions; I could only feel something when somebody close to me was hurting. Usually, I engineered this hurt to prove to myself I was still alive, my sense of self only apparent to me through the expectations and judgements of others.

The relationship that spanned two countries left me alone in a city I'd followed Azhar to. The memories pounce on me when I'm doing something ordinary like brushing my teeth, reading a book, fake-laughing at some tasteless joke, kissing some boy with the chemical tang of mouthwash on his breath, or staying silent on phone calls with my father. I believed if I went on with life—a combination of drug-addled evenings, greasy hangover breakfasts and sleeping around with zero restraint—then I would move on from the fact that the person I am in love with is now married.

At the clinic, the impassive nurse thrust an innocuous white pill into my hand. *Any side effects?* She nodded but before I could ask her what they were, she sashayed into her corner, attending to the pregnant women and crying babies milling around me as a small TV, taped to the wall, played videos on ovulation. I watched the gulmohar tree outside the clinic's window, its leaves swaying gently in the wind, a familiar respite from the anxiety building steadily in my throat as I chewed on the bitter pill that tasted industrial. I looked around meekly—quite unable to meet anybody's eyes, knowing what they thought of girls like me. I thought about whether it was a boy or a girl. I had this feeling in my bones, as sure as the change of seasons, that it was a girl.

When Azhar and I sat across from each other, naked in a hotel room, a tab of acid on our tongues, I insisted that it wasn't kicking in. He smirked while he leaned against the bedrest and rolled a joint. Later, I heard his wife paid for the room. I remembered her from a few years ago, from the time they chatted on a phone call at 4 a.m. and he passed her off as his colleague. Something never added up—the decade-long age gap between us, his stony silence about his past relationships and a cruel dismissal of my questions about our future. But he was an escape from everything I knew to be familiar, an escape from home.

My parents aren't inherently bad people. They fucked me up as much as any other set of parents. Ma taught me how to keep things back where they belong, to brush my teeth before bed, how drinking chai with somebody every morning is better than drinking it alone, how successful relationships are underpinned by compromise, and how doing what I love is more significant than chasing money. I believed everything she told me. My father taught me that any bad day could be turned around by a cold shower, by wearing freshly laundered, ironed clothes and stepping out to a five-star hotel for a coffee, to sit in the lobby and believe you deserve to be there even if you only have a hundred rupees in your pocket. When I got hurt, he wiped my tears and knee scrapes and taught me how to go back to school with my head high.

They respected my independence and privacy—perhaps, a bit too much, at times.

Did they notice a change in my behaviour when I started seeing Azhar? They could've nipped it in the bud. Grounded me. For once, acted like how parents are supposed to. They taught me that religion is a weakness before Ma changed her phone wallpaper to that of Hanuman, and Dad began spending his Friday mornings at the mosque. They said I could be who I wanted, live where I wanted, and do what I liked, underpinned with the belief that Dad's move to Dubai had afforded me a kind of privilege that had escaped my parents. But they never taught me how to cook or love my body or build relationships or even accept pain so it won't stick to everything I say or do until it erodes me. Maybe I was born rotten. Maybe I even loved Azhar. Although, it's harder and harder to believe that with each passing day.

At some point in our affair, Azhar's wife called me. I remember the slow Delhi afternoon like it was yesterday. I deepened my voice and spoke in a stiff monotone—a trick I'd picked up from Azhar. I felt euphoric, triumphant—she knew who I was. I wasn't just a speck on his horizon, a girl he picked up at a bar and called weekly for a mind-bending fuck and my ability to punctuate his sermons with well-timed laughs. His wife tried to appeal to my sense of humanity, to get me to admit my transgressions, but I didn't budge. She disconnected the call.

Why couldn't she have just asked her husband instead? I suppose, since we were little girls, we were taught not to question the men in our lives too much.

When I told Medha, she insisted that I needed to be a better ally to women. But her constant insistence on imposing morality on real-life emotions and their inherent messiness was irritating.

I first met Medha when she was dating my college flatmate. She was an obvious 'it' girl—flat midriff, silver studs dotting her ears, tattoos snaking along her arms and long eyelashes eclipsing large eyes. Something about her dark, chaotic energy simultaneously attracted and repelled me. For the first few days, I was jealous of her—her presence pervading every corner of my home, her strong perfume mixed with the acidic scent of turpentine lingering in corners, the cups of coffee she'd whip up with dexterity and the plates of toast and eggs that would materialise on the table every morning. When she and my flatmate fought, she slept on the single futon in our hall and sometimes, in the middle of the night, on my way to the kitchen, I'd find her lying awake, staring at the ceiling and the grey-blue sky changing colour outside.

One night, she drank too much rum and barged into my room, slurring while narrating stories from her childhood, her relationship with her parents, and asking me questions about my life. I was as irritated as I was flattered, and when she threw up in my bathroom, I held her hair back and ignored the bits of vomit clinging to it.

She had an infuriating habit of slapping my hand whenever I bit my nails, refused to talk to people she didn't like even for the sake of politeness and terrified even the professors with her temerity. She broke up with my flatmate eventually, but we stayed friends; our time together was spent experimenting with drugs, indulging in random streaks of rebellion against our hapless teachers, having each other's back in any new, strange social situation and, at first, tip-toeing around the edges of a new, vulnerable friendship before diving into it headlong.

I'm not sure when we decided that we were each other's ride or die.

Maybe it was around the time I first heard from Azhar after a long spell of silence, after which I decided to fly to Dubai to surprise him. My friends from back then, no longer in my life now, dissuaded me from doing anything impulsive, whereas Medha told me I should go, so I don't have to worry about the 'what ifs' later. Or, perhaps it was around the time we skipped class to take an impromptu trip to a music festival in an isolated Rajasthani village. It might've been the moment she admitted to being clairvoyant under the stars in the desert. She was lying, but I didn't care. I accepted it like I had accepted many such stories she told me in the hope of winning my confidence. About how her parents convinced her she had Jewish roots as a response to an affair her mother had early on in their marriage. The teenage Medha threw a Hanukkah feast complete with fried briskets, a lit Menorah and copious red wine. In her adult years, Medha had done away with the habit, but I knew she had a contentious stand on the Israel-Palestine issue. Still, I wasn't going to be the one to question her.

So, when I learnt that it was Medha who had reached out to Azhar's wife via Facebook and informed her about the affair, I thought I could understand. Medha was fiercely protective of me and got a manic look in her eyes when I was in pain or hurting. I thought I could appreciate her good intentions and self-righteousness wound up in her spindly limbs and reserved smile, occasionally breaking into gurgling laughter at my antics or my failed attempts to make her happy. But I'd underestimated my own anger. I wasn't ready for anybody to clarify the delusions I held about Azhar and me. A part of me wanted to text her from the clinic. I knew I needed her, but another part took pleasure in shutting her out.

I tried to catch the nurse's eye at the clinic, but she avoided looking at me. *I'm not feeling anything.* Another attendant placed a warm hand on my back and guided me to a seat. A snot-nosed kid came and sat across from me, his head blocking out the meagre view of the tree. He stared at me, the edges of his nose crusty and hardened, and I couldn't decide whether I wanted to roll my eyes or weep. The afternoon sun made me drowsy, and I closed my eyes. I'm not sure at what moment the cramps kicked in—all I knew was I wanted to vomit, take a shit and faint, all at the same time. When I felt like I was about to lose consciousness, Medha burst through the clinic entrance—whiff of flowery perfume and strong mint. She gripped my wrist, and we slipped into the backseat of a cab. I saw flashes of trees and smelt musky sweat and pine freshener. I wasn't sure if she'd intuited the date of the appointment or if I'd messaged her in my pill-induced haze.

In the cab, I thought of Azhar's brightly lit apartment, cruising down the highway in his beat-up Maruti, our knees inches away from one another, silences piling up as the radio blared and he shifted into fourth gear.

Once I knew about the pregnancy, I called him, only for him to pick up and snarl—*What do you want?* Medha had snatched the phone from my hand and disconnected it. We turned up at the nearest gynaecologist—three days spent in the haze of doctor visits, quacks trying to pinch money from us for something that should be free. She immediately transferred thirty grand into my account, assuring me I didn't have to worry about paying it back. Google found me a sweet doctor willing to carry it out for five. I'm not sure where I spent the rest of the money.

I visit Farhad in his penthouse at the Hilton. The room he's booked for a month is in disarray. He gets the same room every time he visits from Dubai. Formal clothes lie strewn across the floor with little regard for the expensive labels; the soft mattress is littered with weed stems and stray rolling papers; and a bottle of hash oil sits on the bedside table. The room reeks of expensive cologne, socks that haven't been washed in a week, half-eaten plates of burgers with soggy fries and beer. The force of the uncanny similarities between the two brothers, most prominent in the shape of their hands, are enough to make me turn around and walk out. Instead, I stay and draw the curtains apart. I kick his dirty clothes into one corner of the bathroom, turn the faucet, tip bath salts into the tub, light some insipid candles and sit next to him to roll a joint. His eyes remain glued to the FIFA game he's likely been playing for a month, a fact he confirms.

Meeting Farhad feels like some sort of an approximation of revenge on Azhar but it doesn't feel delicious or sacred like secrets usually do. Instead, I feel heavy with remorse.

At Medha's, as I bled, I considered the bottles of cold water and orange juice she placed next to stacks of sanitary napkins (plastic ones, not the hemp ones that I prefer). After thirteen hours of bleeding through what became two mattresses stacked on top of each other, I drank the juice and made distasteful jokes about what, to an outsider, would seem like an abject state but, to us, was a blood pact. I remembered flashes of the punching bag hanging from the ceiling at the other end of the room. On particularly overwhelming days, Medha and I would strip down, play some grimy drum and bass and throw sharp punches at the bag while crying out simultaneously until, heaving but satiated, we collapsed on top of each other. That night, when Medha and I lay beside each other, hands clasped, eyes wide open, watching the gulmohar trees sway outside her window, I told her I want a child when I am thirty. She held my hand tighter even as I felt a deepening chasm between us.

I'm not sure why I've carried the feeling of betrayal with me wherever I've gone—my expectation of it acting as a self-fulfilling prophecy. Maybe it first began in sixth grade.

We'd just shifted to Dubai, and my misery in having been uprooted from my life and planted in a strange, new city on the verge of being a teenager was exacerbated by how I was a magnet for bullies. I responded not by caving but instead seeking out the popular girls, only to be ultimately rejected by them. Or perhaps, that sense of betrayal went deeper, back to the first fights I witnessed between my parents, the feeling that the threats I perceived weren't outside, but within my own home.

And, sometimes, it's the capacity for self-betrayal that cuts the deepest. On my twenty-third birthday, a few months earlier, Azhar obliged me as if he were humouring a petulant child. We sat across from each other at a posh café. I downed too much wine in the middle of a hot day, gracelessly finding his lips and clinging on to them, the unforgivable summer sun slipping through the cracks in the trees, waiters averting their eyes. Unabated kissing and crying and the aghast looks from the gaggle of rich wives congregating for their weekly kitty parties, him shaking me off like a mild irritant before leaving without paying the bill. Happy Birthday to me.

Soon after, he stopped calling. I'm unsure if this is when the self-destructive impulses kicked in or if they'd always existed, lying dormant. I recall reacting to one of the many ugly fights my parents had by downing half a bottle of the vodka Ma had stashed in her cupboard and throwing up right after. For those few hours, my parents were a single unit, focussed on me and my 'problems with puberty'. It helped me buy time before another Tuesday- or Friday-night family outing devolved into something more sinister.

Were these incidents a cry for help, the only way to continue living, or simply a way to drown out the noise? On a downward spiral after the news of Azhar's marriage, I successfully managed to push everybody out of my life and Medha, who stuck around, was amazed at the abandon with which I began spending my time. She had my back better than anybody else I knew in the city. Waiting until ungodly hours to make sure I got home safe while I was cutting lines of low-grade cocaine in some random bathroom with ceiling mirrors, waking me up as she dropped me to the office, my head teeming with a terrible downer, spittle down my formal shirt. She was disapproving but not judgemental, quiet but loyal—and her loyalty was exactly what disgusted me because I needed it so much. She had her own way of retribution where, after a heavy night of drinking, she swerved on the wide roads of the Delhi-Gurgaon highway, making sharp turns until I wildly beckoned her to stop, so I could vomit by the roadside. She leaned against the car and watched me with grim satisfaction, holding a bottle of water that she didn't extend to me. I don't blame her. I know if it wasn't for Medha, I'd be dead.

I did think I was dying the first time the migraine kicked in. A star-shaped white light flashed in front of my eyes and I thought I heard my neck crick. I asked Medha to drive me to the nearest hospital before passing out completely. I regained consciousness with an IV drip hastily taped to a greenish, exposed vein on my hand, blinding tungsten light bringing blurry shapes into focus; Ma's worried face—she looked like she'd aged five years in the last half hour—next to a genteel doctor called Amit (or maybe Amar) drawing a pencil back and forth in front of my eyes. I felt a pang of relief immediately overtaken by irritation—I didn't want to be fussed over. I wanted to return to my sterile job, my brief texting windows with Azhar when he wasn't at home with his wife, to lines in random bathrooms with strangers. But Ma brought me home and sat by the bed while I alternated between sleeping and eating. When I came around from the painkiller-induced sleep, I looked into her brown eyes, aged with wisdom and empathy, her usually cold demeanour cast aside for a warmth she reserved for moments like these.

Ma left Dubai years ago because she didn't want to live with a man she couldn't question anymore. Now, she lives in a quiet suburb of Delhi where everyone goes to bed at 8 p.m., bats hang in the trees lining the outskirts and tall gulmohar trees swish outside her window. The seasons turn four times, and the water tastes sweet. I ask her if she gets lonely, but she tells me she finds solace in a routine that is entirely hers—a cup of chai precisely as she likes it, with two crushed cardamom pods and three peppercorns, in the early hours of the morning unbroken by somebody else's demands, the empty stretches of time enveloping her body and coalescing into reading, sleeping, watching TV, until the years of aches and pains recede from her muscles, filling her with renewed strength. I imagine she gets tired often, but not as tired as when she was with my father.

Through the large French windows in Farhad's hotel room, I watch a young child pull out tufts of grass in rapture before his mother scoops him in her arms and scurries away. Farhad and I are connected by nothing except a pain that feels common and the pull of memories. It feels less like a friendship, more a eulogy to the people we once were.

The automated roars of the audience and the commentator echo in the room as he scores a goal, and I lean against him. He shifts his arm to accommodate my weight against his body.

I'm not sure what I'm chasing, but it's nice to be held.

At Medha's, the more I slept, the more my time with Azhar felt like a distant memory, snippets from somebody else's life. I debated telling Ma about the pregnancy but eventually didn't. I'm not sure at what point in my childhood I stopped sharing anything intimate with my parents. Over the years, when Ma called me up, beset with tears—over yet another fight, some new object smashed, over my father blocking her number or disappearing for days altogether—I stayed quiet and listened. Every attack at him, a lament about their fractured marriage, or a frantic call to an urgent death lodged inside me, jamming up my insides until language itself felt like a disservice to the magnitude of grief. I understood what happens to feelings when they're left repressed or unexplored, how they bubble up like muck rising to the surface, infecting mind, body, lungs with their force: *I'm here, reckon with me.*

In my studio apartment in the southern part of Delhi, with one tiny window that opened out to a back alley full of cows, a makeshift shrine against the holy basil plant, sandalwood incense wafting through the windows, Ma committed herself to my recovery with a kind of protectiveness I only experienced when things were dire. She bought bitter gourd and beans, ginger and lemon to be mixed in honey, several packets of orange-flavoured oral rehydration solution, fresh coconut water and waxed apples glistening in the morning sun. She cooked simple, hot fare that I ate with a martyred expression. She monitored my phone to ensure I wasn't attempting to call Azhar.

Medha texted and called several times until I finally succumbed, and she visited, armed with a pack of cards. While we played bluff, the only card game I knew how to play, I tried to defeat her with pointed viciousness. I'm not sure if she noticed my simmering resentment, but if she did, she didn't say anything.

---

Farhad tells me that Aisha, his wife, has left him, that she's gone back to Karachi. I look at him and don't say anything; everyone leaves Dubai eventually. He beats me at the FIFA game. Later, I force him to swim with me.

I close my eyes in the pool and notice how strong the chlorine is. Farhad doesn't seem to care and tells me how he'd angered his entire family by going to Karachi and marrying Aisha and how his Indian parents, although Muslim, would never have agreed to his marriage to a Pakistani girl. What does it really mean to be Muslim in India or Dubai? I cling onto the pool wall as the sun descends; my eyes glaze, watching the stubborn streak of pink break across the horizon. Farhad tells me the pain of his marriage collapsing feels like physical stabs through his body. I stay quiet.

Is the pain the same as I felt the last time I met Azhar? After a long stretch without contact, a call from him—*I'm going to be a father.* In the cab, I wanted to call Medha, but instead, I texted her about some vapid sitcom I'd been watching. The only way I could understand my last meeting with Azhar was if I could view it as something that happened to everybody, that all women were walking around with giant secrets lodged inside them and on most days, they collapsed with the weight, but on some days, they could laugh it off over a glass of cheap wine.

The taxi stopped at a gated community with leafy driveways and round-the-clock security meant to alleviate the fears of the rich. I found Azhar and a freckled, blond guy at the exclusive community club, replete with a swimming pool and identical row houses. Once the car exhaust dissipated and the horns died down, it felt like a suburban fever dream.

The bar smelt of expensive cologne and cheap leather. The two men were already down half a bottle of whisky. I was nervous, so I sipped neat vodka with a single cube of ice from a glass. A lone bartender poured drinks as the 84-inch TV blared Wolves versus Arsenal, 2–1. Arsenal was losing again. Azhar masked his depression with larger-than-life assertions. There was soft jazz emanating from one end of the bar. Everything seemed hyper-realistic, like a video game, like I was an avatar Azhar had conjured to claim a new life.

'Michael,' the Frenchie introduced himself.

I didn't give a shit. I was more drawn to Azhar's Timurid eyes, absolutely impenetrable, his olive skin and aristocratic nose, the swagger that comes from the curious mix of money and good looks, arrogance playing around his decidedly cruel mouth. Throughout our affair, I'd witnessed Azhar cycle through several personalities—each more aggressive, dogmatic and attractive than the previous one. He could rattle Biggie's lyrics to make his point about the Dalit-Muslim nexus while quoting Gibran and playing '88 Detroit techno. Each assertion would've been more ludicrous than the last, but his conviction was sweeping; he was a man most affected by things that had never happened to him.

At the bar, he spoke about his conspiracy theories and grandiose plans for the future. I listened more than I talked. I stared at him with impunity. I thought of the last time he was inside me. I grabbed a cigarette, and Michael and I stepped out of the stifling bar with its purple velour seats studded with large gold buttons, wide-set wooden tables and rounds of vodka I wouldn't be paying for.

'Where's his wife?'

'She's asleep.'

'Do you think we're in love?'

What would he know? He'd met Azhar a few months ago and immediately been sucked into his orbit. I asked why Azhar wasn't at the hospital, where his child was likely just delivered. Frenchie shrugged.

'I don't know, but I think he needs you as much as you need him.'

Before I could respond, taken aback by his unexpected observation or maybe his well-timed diplomacy, Azhar staggered out of the bar, grabbed me by the waist, and we spiralled into the swimming pool, feet first. All the vodka drained out of me in one swift go. Azhar had already swum away from me. The gulmohar trees were tall and imposing, like furious black dashes against the sky. The road was hushed outside—no animals, not even a firefly. Frenchie watched us impassively, with a distant look in his eyes. Maybe he missed home, maybe he didn't feel included. I didn't know or care. Azhar swam up to me and took me by the waist before his lips parted mine. I let him kiss me.

Later that night, I spat in his face as I came. He said he liked it.

I spend a listless week in Farhad's hotel room. One night, he gets drunk and tells me how I'd be in his bed if I wasn't the girl his brother was in love with. The following day, I buy him candles that smell like the ocean and leave.

On my way out, men in stiff suits with well-groomed moustaches avoid meeting my eyes as I walk through the hotel corridor. Crossing the coffee tables, I smell expensive cologne and hear important business chatter. I can tell all eyes follow me as I walk out. Maybe they think I'm a prostitute. Do I look expensive enough for the Hilton? Do people think similar things about Ma? The burly watchman with a handlebar moustache that hides half his face smiles at me warmly as he holds the door open. I can feel Delhi's dry heat already settling in my bones. I smile back at him.

# 2

# BEIRUT

I TRY TO LIGHT MY CIGARETTE IN THE SMOKING room at the airport through the weird contraption where I press a button for a few seconds, leaning forward with the cigarette placed precariously between my lips, attempting to make contact with the rusted coil glowing bright red. Smoking rooms make me sick to my stomach, and my last meal was a few hours ago, so the cigarette makes me retch. The room's full of men—a flight steward watches a review of a sports car in Hindi, another man with a threatening moustache slurps from a can of Coke as he glares at me, probably wondering what business I have smoking. Like clockwork, Ma calls and tells me about a bombing in the northeast region of Lebanon and asks me to be safe. Then, she tells me how her leg, the one with the limp, has been hurting, but the doctor can't detect anything wrong. She asks me to say the Gayatri mantra before the flight takes off. I thank her for the sixty-fifth reminder and leave the room choked with smoke.

I have the details of the hotel, an hour's drive from the airport. I'm soon greeted by a man in a brown leather jacket with a faux fur neckline who smiles at me broadly as he secures my suitcase atop his cab. After exchanging the usual salutations and addresses, he tries to converse with me in Arabic. I nod along, only understanding snatches as we ride along the highway through Beirut to one of its border districts, Jounieh.

'Shia or Sunni?'

'Sunni.' I half-whisper my response, and his face breaks into a bigger smile.

We stop at a kiosk along the highway, and he buys me black coffee and offers me a cigarette from his pack. I'm shown to my room at the hotel, enveloped by the Mediterranean Sea. It looks like a relic from the past, surrounded by stores selling cigarettes, shisha and kiosks selling fresh, hot pieces of bread drizzled with olive oil and plates of lamb kebabs. The meat smells fragrant and is a far cry from the scents of home.

From the hotel balcony, Beirut wears a forlorn look. A sea of muted colours, women with impeccable make-up and men with groomed beards, gelled hair and pointed shoes. Arabesque Ottoman buildings stand alongside modern ones, and the grey November skies cast a dull, uninviting look. I feel so far away yet strangely at home, with names similar to mine and a language I grew up with.

As I go through the check-in formalities, I think of how it all started with Savitri, my landlady whose outhouse I'd been renting in Delhi since the abortion. She turned up unannounced at my doorstep at 6:30 a.m., as the sun rose and her husband fed stale roti to cows collecting in homogenous groups in the alley behind my house.

My paramour du jour and I were asleep, and he had to scramble around the bedroom for his underwear, groggy and uncoordinated, as her voice rose an octave higher with indignation. Savitri was everything you'd imagine a South Delhi landlady to be. She would rent to an unmarried girl who smoked and frequently came back home late at night, and she would do it to fan her God complex. She studied anybody who visited me with probing eyes, attempting to sniff out who I interacted with, where I went and at what time I returned home. I'd just started a new job and hadn't saved up enough to afford an independent flat, so the outhouse, or the servant's quarter as it was infamously referred to, had to do. Rent was cheap and the flat was fairly private. I was working on my script and I needed little more than frequent sex to keep creative frustration at bay.

Life since the abortion had taken on a strange colour. My body was out of whack. My breasts immediately returned to their usual size, thank god, but the rest of me wasn't quite the same. My moods were more erratic than before. I'd burst into tears anywhere, anytime, especially when doing something banal like washing my face in the morning, riding the metro to work, or looking at paintings in museums. I preferred crying in public places because people staring eventually compelled me to suck the grief back in, as opposed to crying at home, which felt untethered. I floated from one work gig to another, writing social media posts for bars and food delivery apps, sometimes meeting odd men at parties, pretending to be a screenwriter, and assisting them on film sets in Old Delhi. Sometimes, I even worked as a tour guide, taking groups of annoying American students or confused French vacationers through the streets of Old Delhi. As much as I found solace in not being restrained to one thing, the unpredictability was also creeping into my personal life.

I ignored Medha, making flimsy excuses for not meeting her, and instead got bombed alone at home while binge-watching shitty reality TV. My savings were running out and the rent was still due, so soon, I landed a job scripting reality TV for a travel channel. For the first time since college, I had a steady income, a home to myself, albeit one with plumbing issues, but mine nonetheless. Irrespective, I slept poorly, drank too much, didn't call Ma back and flirted with increasingly dangerous situations.

So that morning, when Savitri burst in and asked me to get out of her house, I only half reasoned with her. It felt like a cosmic wake-up call; perhaps being homeless would help. Ultimately, I knew I was too unsanskaari to continue being her tenant.

'We cannot have you polluting the minds of kids in the neighbourhood,' she yelled.

'Aunty, I saw Mukesh watching porn the other day.'

'He's barely ten years old.'

'Exactly. And aunty, uncle plays poker and eats chicken tikka when you go to your mother's.'

Soon, my bags, with my belongings somehow thrown into them, were lying at the entrance. As I surveyed the hot, dusty road, the cigarette-wala slipped an overdue bill to me, then handed me a lit cigarette for my nerves. The unforgivable Delhi smoke stung my eyes, and cars whizzing past kicked a cloud of dust in my face. It really wasn't turning out to be a great year.

My Iranian hotel mate, Amal, and I take a walk along the ocean. There's a cabaret bar advertised by a photo of a middle-aged Lebanese woman with red lips next to a shop selling hijabs, Islamic swimming costumes and dokha—tobacco blended with herbs, spices and dried flowers. Rusted metal gates wrapped in barbed wire seal the walkway to the ocean, and as we walk, I cross what used to be a beauty salon, in complete ruins. Bits of the ceiling, mirrors and half-blown-up salon chairs still litter the floor, covered in dust. We pass some men who stare at Amal, and some women in hijabs beckoning us to enter their stores or cafés. Signboards in French and Arabic hang at various entrances. The entrance of a deserted red brick building is overtaken by wild shrubs and vines; it's impossible to tell what the building used to be for. The city bears signs of life but has a strange seaside sleepiness to it. At an outdoor café, we're served chilled beer and grilled lamb with bread as Amal tells me about her dual life in Iran—how being a woman and shooting a film means hiding from authorities, how Facebook and Instagram are banned and women rarely allowed to step out without a male chaperone.

'My AD directed the film while I instructed him via a FaceTime call, sitting in a car parked outside,' she says with a laugh.

I marvel at her bravery and a kind of elusive wisdom in her eyes that she explains comes from growing up around war and loss. She doesn't ask me any questions about my life; I don't have much to share either way.

My problems felt trite in comparison. How would I even begin to tell her about Nihal? When I was evicted, he approached me carrying a plastic bag containing one

Kingfisher 500 ml, a packet of roasted peanuts and one orange, which I ate.

Nihal was a stand-up comedian who lived in a sketchy building close to the outhouse. His neighbours were a flight stewardess, another comedian from Ahmedabad struggling to stay afloat in Delhi, a woman with brown hair and coloured contact lenses whom I only glimpsed sometimes. I was unclear about where she worked but I often spotted her speed-walking to the nearest parlour or getting into a dusty sedan with bird poop dotting its rear windshield.

Nihal and I first met outside the Nirula's at our local market. I'd been staying at a two-star hotel near the outhouse since the eviction and having checked my bank account at the ATM close by, I was at the precipice of a panic attack. The numbing goodness of a hot chocolate fudge would help me self-soothe, and I found that he was doing the same at a table across from mine. We shared a knowing smile and over a cigarette outside, we chatted about me being a screenwriter-filmmaker without having written scripts or made films, his refusal to get on YouTube and the risks associated with doing political comedy in the capital. We hung out the entire day, ending up at the zoo, watching langurs swinging from metallic railings and parrots fluttering around in their rusty cages. At one point, while watching a hippopotamus splash around in the mud, he told me I could bunk with him for a few days.

Living with him was fun in a vague sort of way. Initially, his anti-establishment approach, extended to turning down corporate gigs, and disdain for organised comedy, evident in his refusal to mingle with fellow comedians backstage, was very attractive. His material was dark and absurdist—a reflection of his personality. A Scorpio, he shared his birthday with Kurt Vonnegut, which made me more eager to place him on a pedestal, however briefly. We smoked really tasty hashish, watched videos of cult American comedians and discussed writing. He was pretentious in a way that I enjoyed. He was also capable of a searing loyalty. His English was rusty, sprinkled with Punjabi cusses and terms of endearment, and his bear-like hugs, suited to his large body, were warm and made me feel like no Savitri aunty could evict me again. To him, I was a brilliant filmmaker to-be, a woman unconcerned about the rat race, a minimalist with charm and grace, an artist complete. He looked at me in ways I'd never looked at myself and so, soon enough, I slipped into his bed. I attended some of his shows. I even enjoyed the spectacle of being his girlfriend in the green room, aware of the other dorky comedians watching us. Often, I felt like his arm-candy so I made my jibes sharper and my jokes darker as a desperate attempt to be something more.

On a day trip to Byblos, a picturesque hill-station about an hour from Jounieh, I become friends with Fatima. She is from Afghanistan, has cat-like eyes, and her hair is coiffed in a stylish bun at the nape of her neck. Her thick eyebrows move expressively as she chats in a familiar voice. She's decked in expensive heirlooms adorning her wrists and neck. I'm so taken with her beauty that I feel slightly ashamed about it, but she says she enjoys the attention, that it's a rare commodity for her. She shows me a photo of her with male chaperones, covered head to toe in hijab, only her eyes peeking out from the black cloth.

'My family thinks I'm doing a research project in Qatar,' she grabs my hand and squeezes it while looking around to make sure nobody is within earshot. She tells me about the pains she had to go through to produce her movie in secret, that she was liable to be stoned publicly, even sentenced to death if her government found out.

'It's about a girl who gets arrested for venturing outside without a man. And yours?' Feeling slightly ashamed, I mumble something unintelligible about Asur's film.

My reply is drowned by the sound of a faraway drone strike. From this distance, it's impossible to determine what the drones are looking to target. Syria's border is one and a half hours from where we are. I look around at the table, a bit panicked, but everyone smokes, laughs and chats about the films they're directing, the funds they're waiting on, and the hottest festivals they've been invited to. I feel dizzy, unsure of how to keep up the conversation. I worry I've had too much to drink.

I whip my phone out to connect it to the WiFi. I figured Medha and my cold war could be let up for a minute now that I was in another country, and surely, Beirut could be considered neutral, but instead, I notice a series of furious texts from Nihal—mostly screenshots of hateful tweets he's posted on his profile. I log into my account; the notifications are pouring in—likes, quotes, retweets and the gleeful comments of other comedians. *The only way for my ex to win a peace prize is posthumously. My ex thinks networking is very important because your name should be out there, even if your work isn't. One day my ex looked at my WhatsApp and said, wow, there are no girls on your chat list. The same can be said about her. My ex thinks comedy is not art, and as somebody who used to work in an office and is now unemployed, she probably knows these things.*

I reply to one of his tweets; *You're welcome for the clout.* Immediately, a new tweet rolls in. *Nobody can make a fake account of my ex. She's already the best fake version of herself.* I know my chin wobbles in the ugliest manner when I'm about to cry, so I excuse myself and begin walking down to the hotel.

On the way, I stare at the message Medha sent me a few days ago and think about how leaving her on 'read' lent me a sense of power I was sorely lacking in every other area of my life. *What time's your flight? Get a drink before you leave? Hello?* I make up my mind to get to the hotel and call her; being mad is one thing, but not sharing juicy gossip is another altogether.

But when I return to the hotel, I find Jack, an Irish filmmaker, in my room, blithely chatting with Amal. Amal, it appears, has taken a luxurious shower, and the room is bathed in the scent of frankincense. Jack has tattoos running down both his arms—from his time in prison, he clarifies. Word is that he's one of the hottest new directors on the block and his film about a working-class kid losing his virginity to an older woman has producers salivating. He seems enchanted by Amal and asks her if women are allowed to wear pants in Tehran. I try not to roll my eyes as I scribble notes about Asur's film in my diary. At some point, she stretches out in his lap, and he strokes her hair like she's a child. She closes her eyes and curls up, tucking her knees under her chin. I leave the room and decide to head to the crowded café downstairs. In the lift, I start typing a message to Medha but stop myself; I have no words to describe all that's come to pass in the last few weeks. Watching Jack and Amal cuddle reminds me of my last few sexual encounters with Nihal.

---

At some point, I realised Nihal could only get an erection while watching porn. I took it upon myself to get him to have one. I was unsuccessful. He could feel me slipping away, and one night as I lay in bed, half-naked, not expecting much from the evening, he made a move. We had clumsy, uninspired sex; his eagerness to please eliciting an acute contempt in me.

'Promise me you won't be mad if I tell you something. I took Viagra today.'

I felt violated even though I knew all he was trying to do was win my love. I yelled at him mindlessly, humiliating him to the point of tears. Then, I took him in a hug. I felt terrible. After all, I did love him in my own begrudging way. He apologised, tears glistening on his face, a picture of pain and longing.

Soon after, it became clear that the relationship was on its last legs. After residing in the endless material and emotional comforts he provided, I ventured back into the world, even as I continued living with him. My eyes wandered around at the local bar and performance space, and I chatted with numerous random men—small talk that didn't amount to much more than a free drink. New Delhi's men were beginning to bore me with their entitlement, negging couched as witty banter and trust funds. I shifted focus and combed bars, libraries, parks and South Delhi parties for inspiration, but none came through. On most days, I was the cliché of a failed artist.

I sent my script to a colleague, who hated it because it was formatted wrong. But when I showed it to Nihal, he waxed poetic and I felt temporarily okay. Scripting reality TV didn't exactly match the artistic vision I had for myself and barely covered rent, so with Nihal's space caving in on me, I lapsed back into a life of too much alcohol, drugs and general debauchery. It was better than thinking of the future. Nihal didn't mind the hedonism; what he did mind was me spending my time with others.

'I imagine we are this couple who only ever needs each other. You're all I need, and I'm all you ever need.' He clasped my hand in an unforgiving gesture of pathos, and all I could muster was vague disdain.

Medha and I occasionally met for drinks. Now, the distance seemed marked, tainted by something unspoken. We shifted focus from our fraught friendship to Nihal, cackling at his unfortunate sexual performance and the nickname he earned himself because of his threatening protectiveness: *papa.*

Medha, a talented artist from one of the top art schools in the country, hadn't done much since graduation. Her one-bedroom apartment-turned-painting studio, passed down by her grandfather, who worked with the civil services, was filled with expensive paints, empty canvases, coffee table books on art history and subscriptions to global art magazines. Mostly, she spent her time on the internet listening to playlists, making tofu bowls or figuring out parties for us to attend. Sometimes, she landed an interview for which she turned up late and if she managed to get the job, it didn't usually last for more than a few weeks. But who was I to judge? We tried to act like adults and attend networking events but usually got too trashed on the free booze.

---

At the café, I make friends with a student at the university hosting the festival.

Noor is the daughter of the third wife of the founder of the El Din Dance Theatre, a unique Lebanese dance philosophy that blends Eastern and Western traditions. Noor is Catholic and supremely rich, making her a double minority in Lebanon. She's only nineteen but sounds much older. She drives around Beirut in an 8-series convertible and dresses nondescript—black jeans, black nail paint, an oversized grey sweater and twinkling diamond studs, the only nod to her pedigree. Everybody around me glitters with their looks that prove they won the genetic lottery, their notable film credits and the right influences. I feel lost among the multitude of certified artists, and Noor's indifference to the circles of influence, even if curated, is attractive to me.

I'm not sure what lies at the end of finally being approved as an artist. Or why that's important to me at all. I could've done my graduation in marketing or public relations, or any of these marketable degrees that don't necessarily require a high level of intelligence or some obscure talent that's hard to define. Maybe I suffered from the 'gifted child syndrome'. Ma routinely embarrassed me by telling her friends and extended family members, most of whom I hadn't spoken to in years, about how the first poem I wrote was when I was eleven years old. The poem was about keeping my neighbourhood 'clean and green'. How could she, with her triple degrees, mistake rhyming skills for actual talent? And how could she overlook that I barely passed in science despite hours spent in tuition?

Everything I held cool and sacred in school felt like it was coming to a head in real life. I wasn't an activist, nor was I an artist, nor was I rich. The career of leisure I imagined for myself, where I could swim for hours, sleep deeply, get high, get laid, make art and write poetry, was a career for the rich. I couldn't even afford to live in an apartment with no mould or views other than that of dogs pooping in narrow alleys. In Delhi, the changing circle of people I found myself hanging out with varied from uninteresting to downright toxic. There was the expat crowd, junior-mid level staffers at the French embassy, small-town European boys working with local biking companies, rich kids from private boarding schools, kids with industrialist fathers with a drinking problem and too many hands waiting on them at home, struggling musicians from Janakpuri. I could either be a party girl, somebody who got around a lot, or I could date somebody older and successfully 'sugar baby' my way into positions, parties and conversations. I failed at both, being too egotistic to cater to anybody else's expectations and soon, the excessive partying snowballed into a growing addiction to amphetamines.

After a distant friend ended up in the hospital for taking LSD laced with mescaline, Ma called, 'I'm worried about you, first the bad grades, then running around with several men. I'm praying for you.' Too livid to point out the hypocrisy to her, I started spending an inordinate amount of time with Nihal. I may have been using him, but I tried hard not to be a shit companion. It's hard to tell precisely when and why he started hating me or how accurate or justified his victim complex was.

The filmmakers are called in to watch a series of films at the university's main screening room with seats fitted with wine holders and an intense intermingling of various fragrances. After a live orchestral performance, an Iranian film about a hospital bombed, a Saudi Arabian film about domestic abuse, an Argentinian film about a student revolution and a Lebanese film about an underground radio station follow. I think of the trauma of growing up in war-torn countries, the creativity that forces its way out under restrictions, and my script about two schoolgirls looking for their missing teacher sitting in the recesses of my computer, collecting dust. I feel like a complete sham. When Asur's film is screened, I step out of the hall to avoid anybody who might track me down for questions or feedback.

My chance meeting with Asur happened at a random Delhi party filled with producers and veteran filmmakers. Asur, a premier Indian film institute graduate, was immediately taken by my opinions on Kamal Swaroop's cinema, even though I knew I was spouting the information I'd gleaned from hanging out with film students. I didn't particularly care for or even understand his films. Kind of like David Lynch. Or Tarkovsky. I made lists of directors I should be obsessed with, movies I should be watching but never really understood the creative genius, the curated irony or the fuss about the Western canon. Still, it made for good party conversation.

'Kamal and I are good friends. He finally asked me to write for him,' Asur said with no hint of irony.

She didn't express much interest in what I was writing, but everything about Asur intrigued me. Her broken English, reminiscent of my father's tenor, eyes that darted with nervous energy, rock-hard confidence in her own abilities and disdain for everybody else. I suppose managing to grab the industry's attention when you're an indie filmmaker from Assam with no particular privilege or connections is its own cause to celebrate. So, I chatted with her, eager as a puppy, and we went our separate ways, having exchanged phone numbers.

The following day, I tried to stay awake at work, reeling from the previous night's hangover, when a gaudy bouquet of flowers was delivered to my desk; *with love, Nihal.* I wanted to scream.

Later that day, Robbie, my boss with a penchant for Friday night poker and cutting bonuses, called me out to the balcony. He looked pretty nervous as he fiddled with a cigarette.

'Rob, I understand. I'll do the handover, pack my things and be out by 6 p.m,' I said while handing him my lighter, half-terrified of the abyss of free time that lay before me, half-relieved for it.

Coming in late, vehement disinterest in the work's demands and my contempt for reality TV had finally registered on his radar. Medha texted me to see if I wanted to join her for drinks post-work. I procrastinated but eventually agreed on the condition that she spot me.

At the sticky club where people mingled with one another, name dropping unabashedly and gassing up their new start-up, Medha flitted about her cool design friends as they chatted about upcoming exhibitions and what galleries look for when commissioning a young artist. Somebody else introduced themselves as a curator, which I knew was code for 'my dad owns the gallery.' I thought of my derailed career and dwindling finances. My only real option was to move back home, but I was unclear on where exactly home was. Continuing to live with Nihal was untenable; the more I regarded him with contempt, the harder he tried to secure his place in my life. Maybe I could move in with Ma and start a home catering thing. Although, I could barely make boiled eggs. Perhaps that could be the business proposition: average boiled eggs with an average cup of chai for mediocre people like me, at mediocre prices. Or I could look for yet another job, but something about the idea of spiffing up my résumé, blast-emailing it to companies, or hitting up vague faces from parties for jobs repulsed me.

Medha took a break from chatting about lunar cycles, the Kundalini and how native American women practised bleeding into the Earth in a process called 'earthing' and turned to me.

'I can practically see you clenching your butt.'

'I don't know how I'm going to spend another minute in his company. He's stuck to me like a leech.'

'Just come stay with me.'

'You know I can't.'

'Is this about Azhar's wife?' She moved in closer, swaying with the liquor, her eyes widening.

Luckily, I was saved by a call from Asur, who I'd forgotten all about. Instead of rolling her eyes and letting it go like any normal person, Medha ordered another round of drinks and put her ear next to my phone. I shrugged her off and walked away to hear Asur better. I thought I heard Asur ask me how I felt about representing her film at a film festival in Beirut, a trip that was entirely sponsored and I wanted to be sure.

'What's the catch?'

'There's no catch. I'm busy with another project so just represent my film well in front of all the other delegates.'

I wanted to ask her to read my script in exchange but felt that could be considered transactional. The visa was easy enough to arrange. One phone call, a trip to the Lebanese embassy and a few polite salaams. After the ambassador's consul offered me some Sulaimani tea, my passport was stamped.

Nothing good had ever really happened to me of its own accord, even after my own attempts, discipline or plain prayers. It always felt like I had to hinge on the men in my life—Robbie for my salary, my father to supplement my meagre income at the end of the month, Nihal for a place to stay, Rajesh at the Gulmohar Park club, who allowed me to play badminton despite no membership. I had an opportunity, and I was going to make the most of it, even if it meant lying. Fake it till you make it; isn't that how the refrain goes?

In the parking lot, I find Noor smoking in her car. She offers me some. I accept, and under the sharp haze of excellent Cascade Cream with a THC content of 40 per cent, I ask her about her plans after graduation. She tells me she's next in line for marriage, which means getting out of Beirut. How do choices remain the same across borders? I remember failing my eleventh-grade exams and my father's email arriving with its usual air of menace in my inbox. *If you continue to perform so poorly, we'll just get you married. What's the point of spending lakhs?* The mental gymnastics I performed to simply contend with his power over me changed me for good.

Noor asks me if I want to come out for drinks. In the car, she tells me she watched the film I'm representing and asks me if she can be honest. I nod; I'm curious. I watched Asur's movie on the flight here and couldn't understand why it was so exceptional. It was shot on film, in black and white and was about a farmer searching for water in an Assamese village. So, essentially, festival fodder abroad.

'It's really pretentious, isn't it?'

'I met the director at a party and she was too paranoid to fly down to Lebanon so she sent me instead,' the words fall out of me in quick succession and the momentary relief of speaking the truth is immediately replaced by a sharp embarrassment. Noor smirks as she drives into a bohemian quarter of Beirut.

'Don't worry, everybody's posturing here. Fatima returns to the festival every year. Her parents are rich builders.'

'She seems sweet enough.'

'You don't have anything to be embarrassed about.'

'I love how you speak to me like I'm not older to you.'

'Everybody in Beirut is older than they look.'

We arrive at a street dotted with al fresco bars, street vendors selling flowers and offering to shoot polaroids of the smiling tourists. Noor and I loop our arms around one another and pose for one. Clutching the grainy polaroid, we slip into a bar where some Euro trance emanates from a barely lit room, and she falls into a table full of other young Beirutis. An American producer, Rory, with soft, brown curls and a great laugh, chats me up. At some point in the night, I lose Noor to the bodies writhing on the dance floor while Rory and I kiss. I smell the shawarmas on his breath, and it makes me hungry.

I walk away from the bar to look for a shawarma vendor. Beirut feels like an exciting possibility, a gift from God, Allah or Jesus. In Delhi, I was partly excited by the pop culture impressions of Beirut—the pearl-blue Mediterranean Sea, the confluence of students and filmmakers from the rest of the Middle East and the hummus. When I had floated the news of my trip on social media, I got hundreds of messages—some asked me to stay safe, and others asked if I planned on joining the militants.

As I watch the man slice succulent, delicately spiced lamb, he tells me about how he illegally entered Beirut from Syria several years ago, at the peak of the war in Damascus. As he hands over my shawarma, he talks about Lebanon's corrupt ruling class and the lost dreams of Syrians, how things are not different for them in other Arab countries, and how Syria became a scapegoat in the larger political game. I listen with hot lamb juice running down my hands when I see police cars with loud sirens rush into the crowded street. Tens of policemen packing serious heat tumble out. I hear something about a bomb threat and notice Noor and Rory sprinting across the street. Noor grabs my arm and steers me towards her car. Rory slips into the back seat. I try to breathe as she swerves through the almost empty streets and realise I've lost the polaroid.

Once we reach the hotel, she grabs me by the arm and takes me downstairs to a bar without windows I didn't know existed. A man with a bushy beard and long, tangled hair mixes drinks behind the counter. Rory orders us more drinks. The sounds of the police sirens are soon drowned out by the Arabic pop emanating from the radio.

Before long, the other filmmakers trickle in, including Amal and Fatima, and we all fall into a drunken circle, singing along to the Arabic cover of 'I Will Survive'. Amal climbs atop a chair, whirling and moving her hips to the music. Fatima breaks into a song, and her voice is beautiful, fruity and deep, like Dinah Washington's. I can't understand the lyrics, but I feel sad all the same. The gravity of the evacuation seems to be directly proportional to the sheer amount of substances being consumed. I feel a sudden urge to call Medha; life is much too short to hold grudges, when I hear Rory waxing poetic about James's film.

'Of course *you'd* like his film. He ticks all the boxes,' I say. My head sways with my seventh drink of the night, and the disillusionment is really hitting home.

'Someone's had a lot to drink.'

He grabs my glass and downs it in one go. I feel a thick annoyance spreading through me.

'Would you sign any of the directors who're female and brown?'

'Everything isn't a political stand. Sometimes, a film is just a film.'

Rory looks around at the other filmmakers for approval. In the warm light of the bar, he appears much older, with the crow's feet around his eyes and his pigmented temples. The woman next to him laughs uncomfortably. Seething, I move to the bar, where the amused bartender hands me another drink.

'It's like this every year. If it's silent for too long, we can hear the war brewing at every corner.'

I get a call from Nihal that I disconnect.

The night Medha and I gyrated on the dance floor to pulsating hip-hop, wearing too-tall heels and glitter, she poked me hard in the ribs, her large eyes staring at the profile of a man with something akin to fear. *Papa*, she whispered. I turned around to find Nihal looming over me.

'What the fuck?'

He insisted vehemently that he wasn't stalking me. I didn't own the bar and he was free to do as he pleased. I remember shoving him in his chest, watching him trip backwards into a group of men moving stiffly in front of the massive speakers, and the look of wild fear and anger in his eyes, before Medha grabbed my arm, and we stepped out into the sweaty night.

From the corner of my eye, I see Fatima grinding up on Rory as the music switches to rap. I don't feel jealous, just irritated. Then, I see them slip out. Like clockwork, Noor approaches me.

'I think they're having a threesome. Let's go find out,' she slurs.

We stand outside their room while Noor grabs a glass from a stray trolley and places it on the door. Unsure, I hang back. She beckons me towards the door and shoves the glass in my hand. Placing the glass on the door, I listen. All I can hear is the sound of the TV I move towards the elevator when Noor hisses my name. She's listening again. I put my ear to the door, and I can hear heavy moans. I'm amused and slightly sad, but I laugh and wish her good night. Noor looks like she regrets bringing me here.

Back in the safety of my room, it's harder to drown out police sirens and the terrifying buzz of the drones. I knew through Google that the militancy was concentrated along the Lebanese-Syrian border, but in Delhi, this reality seemed faraway, largely inconsequential.

I look out of the window, half-expecting to see a plume of smoke but see nothing but the pointed emptiness of the street and the clear November night sky. There's a knock on my door, and it's housekeeping. A man in a coat with embroidered lapels walks in, apologising for disturbing me at this hour and goes straight to the windows. He pastes strong black tape in the shape of an 'x' and leaves the room, nodding at me respectfully. I try to sleep but my mind is abuzz. Regretting it only slightly, I rummage through Amal's stuff and come across some sedatives. I'm unsure about their reaction to alcohol, but I pop one anyway.

---

I wake up to life in the city like nothing's amiss. I've drooled on my pillow, and my hair looks like a racoon's made its way through it. I check my phone, and a series of irate texts from Nihal pop up on the screen like confetti. My eyes focus, and a lump forms in my throat; my heart pounds so loudly, I can hear it in my ears. I scroll through the accusatory texts, each more unhinged than the last. *You're going to die miserable. I gave you everything when you had nobody; home, food, money.*

*Nobody in your life loves you except me. Why do you think your parents left you? Your friends use you. When you return, I have a gift waiting for you.* Then, a shaky video of a pile of clothes on a familiar terrace. His hairy hand pours viscous liquid on it, and a flame lights up, crackling and swirling before he holds the lighter to the clothes. The pile catches fire, slowly at first, and then all together. He tosses the lighter into the inferno, and the entire pile rages with a small explosion. The camera flips around to his face, his pupils dilated with rage and adrenaline; he hisses with froth clinging to the side of his mouth, *This is what you deserve, cunt.* He spits on the ground next to him, and the screen goes blank. I lie still for several minutes before I sit up and crack the window open, breathing in the air. The buzz of the hotel lobby travels upwards. The shop shutters are thrown open, cars honk at intersections, and hawkers yell out to tourists. The sea is calm and I spot children building sand castles at its edge. I see Amal hasn't slept in her bed. Did I hallucinate the whole last night? I send the video to Medha with a message: *Glad I didn't get strangled in his bed.*

In the courtyard downstairs, a group of schoolgirls in colour-coordinated hijabs and large gold hoops glinting in the sun snap gum as they stare into their cellphones. The strong smell of roasted coffee beans from the silver top counter wafts towards me as portly men in business suits, bellies threatening their waistband, take hurried sips and switch between calls on multiple cellphones.

The filmmakers from Nigeria sit at a table, chain-smoking and playing cards. Everything looks innocuous, feels commonplace, like I've transported myself to a functioning city that wasn't exploding with the threat of bombs at techno raves last night, that it was completely normal to have hidden bunkers in the basement of beach resorts, that it was appropriate for a man I'd dated for a few months to burn my clothes and other belongings most dramatically and send me a video of it. That almost a year was going to pass since I last met Azhar, and while I was sure I didn't love him, I fucked other men with ferocity and detachment like they were all approximations of the kind of man Azhar was. Perhaps if I was a different girl, living a different life, growing up in a home where moral codes weren't determined by a convenient sense of religiosity and punishments not meted out according to my parents' personal vendetta, my life would be different. Perhaps if I hadn't annihilated my soul by continuing to sleep with the man who treated me like a plaything, a shiny toy that was only good for its first few years, if I hadn't lied my way into a film festival I had no business attending; maybe then I could feel a sense of justified anger, the kind that could solidify and propel me into action instead of coagulating in me like poison.

I pour myself a coffee and sit at the corner table when Fatima picks me out from the crowd and takes determined strides towards me, oversized sunglasses obscuring half her face. She falls into the seat across me and groans intermittently as she drops an aspirin into a glass of water.

'Did you know Rory's on the jury?'

'Did he say that before you slept together?'

She tells me she's leaving for Afghanistan earlier than planned because her family has grown suspicious. The radio switches to the news of militant activity at the border. She takes a sip of my coffee, puckers her lips at how sweet it is and plugs in her earphones.

'I think you should stay for your screening.'

She smiles at me but doesn't say anything.

It's closing night. A red carpet, loud flashbulbs and local news reporters. Quick conversation in soft Arabic floats through the evening air. I meet an older German producer, surrounded by a bevy of beautiful actresses in shimmery satin dresses and red lips. He tells me about how some filmmakers make films and others make statements. I feel he's hinting at Asur's film and want to ask, but he is engulfed in the sea of women after a quick wave my way.

Actors network with ferocity, young Arab filmmakers pitch to European producers, and everybody gets drunk on copious amounts of wine. The main delegates sit at a long table lit with fancy candelabras, rounds of kibbeh and red wine. The glamour and the vapid chats remind me of Delhi parties, and I feel extremely out of place. I don't really belong here. I don't have films, even pretentious ones, to speak of. I don't even have my own home. I am thinking of slinking away when a guy wearing nail paint and several rings taps my arm lightly.

'Are you okay?'

I put on a fake smile.

'Want to get out of here?'

I grab a kebab on my way out.

We turn up at somebody's garden shed. It is decorated with fairy lights, and several young people sit around a small fire. Somebody plays the tambourine, and two women drink wine from the same bottle while the stereo plays funk. Everyone greets Amin like a regular and welcomes me with warm hugs. I realise I'm in a sharing circle of some sort. People pass a glass of arak from one person to the next. A beautiful woman, Aliza, with blonde hair and starry blue eyes, takes a sip of the strong liqueur.

'I came here illegally from Aleppo. Last week, cops arrested me at the café downtown and took me to the police station. They stripped me and tortured me.'

A grim silence falls across the circle.

'All for being, for lack of a better word, trans.'

The moonlight catches her face, and she looks like a sacred sculpture for a brief moment. Another guy with gentle eyes starts talking—about how he was taken into police custody, and an egg-shaped device was inserted in his anal cavity to determine whether he's experienced seizures. I feel numb listening to them talk. Eventually, the glass passes to me. I take a sip, and the taste is sharp and burns my throat before settling into my chest. I tell them about the eviction, Nihal, the insipid sex, the Viagra, the stalking, feeling like an imposter and having my belongings burnt in a revenge bonfire. Everyone blinks and looks around. Aliza breaks into a tinkling laugh that soon turns guttural and loud. Others join in. I crack an awkward smile too.

'*La taqliq habibti*, we all make do with whatever we can get here.'

Another woman tells us how her olive farm in Beqaa valley, northeast of Beirut, has been overtaken by militants, and she's relocated to Beirut since, making do with odd waitressing and cashier jobs. As everybody gets progressively drunk on the arak, the music gets louder, and everybody falls into each other's arms as they sway and spin. I overhear somebody talking about how their boss, an orthodox Shia Muslim, displays a kind of radicalism where he believes suicide bombings in specific scenarios are justified, but also vehemently supports gay pride week for however long it lasts before the police mercilessly cracks down on the attendees. Another person talks about how they're sick of the West's singular gaze on Beirutis, how it's exhausting to be suitably exotic while living up to the hedonistic reputation Beirut carries on its shoulders. I find solace in the disillusionment, in the quiet bitterness, everybody one step away from throwing their arms up in defeat, in indifference.

Life is and has always been exhausting, and looking for salvation in an artistic pursuit or in the arms of a lover or friend is a fool's errand.

Before leaving, I hug everybody tightly. As we drive back to the hotel, I thank Amin.

'I didn't work on the film I'm representing.' I watch the buildings of Beirut whizz past.

Amin throws me an amused look.

'People believe what they want to believe. If they really opened their eyes, they'd see that the son of one of the biggest Lebanese politicians is gay.'

I smile at him, and he grins, speeding up on the highway, overtaking white Toyota taxis and second-hand BMWs.

Later that night, I'm awoken by soft sobs emerging from Amal's corner of the room. I lie with my eyes open, staring at the ceiling, unsure what to say.

Finally, I turn to her in the darkness, and my eyes find her hazy shape on the twin bed.

'Amal?'

'I'm sorry, I don't know what to say. I'm losing my mind. Sometimes, I just start crying and I can't stop. I could be dancing and next, I'm crying. It's too much,' she says, between sobs.

'What happened?'

'Nothing. That's why it's so much worse. There is no reason.' She hiccups. I grab a bottle of water and extend it to her. She takes a few hurried sips.

'Can I give you a hug?'

I immediately regret asking. She comes over to my side. She rests her head on my shoulder, and I can feel the dampness from her cheeks on my collar-bones. Soon, she nods off to sleep while I stay awake in the dark.

I watch Amal prepare for her flight back to Tehran. Transferring all the photos, videos, conversations from the trip onto iCloud before deleting them from her phone, stashing her make-up away, stuffing the glitzy short dresses and stilettos at the bottom of the suitcase, ironing her hijab on the flower-patterned ironing board. Before leaving, she hugs me and promises to stay in touch via email.

From the café, I watch Fatima get into a taxi in a niqab for the first time. I grab a yellow sunflower perched in a vase and hurry to her cab. I inhale the sharp scent of Oud and nicotine when I hand it to her. She smiles at me and blows me a kiss. The taxi starts, and I watch until it disappears around the corner. I spot Rory and Noor drinking coffee across from one another. Neither of them looks at me.

I go for a walk by the sea. It's calmer today, as the water collects in pools and froths at the rocks. The sunshine breaks in patterns across the clouds, and pocket-sized white crabs move sideways haphazardly. I ignore Asur's texts asking me about the festival and call Medha instead. She picks up on the second ring, her face shining through the FaceTime screen.

'Termite infestation. Ate into at least twenty sketches of mine. Poured boric acid. Pest control's too expensive. I saw the video, though. What a total psycho. How's Beirut?'

The lock at the beach entrance seems broken into two halves. I push the gate, and it swings opens easily. I walk in.

# 3

# PRAGUE

'I HAVE A PROPOSITION FOR YOU.'

David approaches while I'm in the middle of wolfing down a cream cheese bagel and a bodega coffee, the only lunch I can afford today. His manner isn't nervous or overbearing. He is just there. The barista with shrewd eyes and blue hair continues to brew coffee behind the counter, and a couple canoodling on the couch don't move away from each other's lips.

Without asking, David sits in front of me, his hands gripping his coffee cup. I notice how he's chewed his nails down to stubs. Conscious of the similarities between us, I reach for my gloves.

'Will you do the sound for my thesis film?'

He tells me about how it's an experimental film, only one scene, perhaps two or three lighting set-ups, we'd knock it off in a day's shift. The sound has to do most of the storytelling as he doesn't subscribe to expository dialogue or trite narrative set-ups. I nod, excited at finally being asked to be on somebody's film set.

'You're the only one who can handle how headstrong I am.'

He stands up and sticks his hand out. I clasp it, surprised by how clammy it is even in the –2° C weather.

I'm flattered. Ever since I moved to Prague a few months after I turned twenty-five, I have imagined myself to be this sort of mysterious, unassailable sound recordist with cool tech, the kind to hike through the Black Forest in Germany and capture sounds the frozen lake makes when ice skaters glide on it. I could have a cool pseudonym; maybe I can create such an aura around me that if I record a single synth tone and release it on Soundcloud, it'll get a million listens. I doubt anybody in school, or even back in Delhi, feels the same way.

Asur never really got back to me on the script, although the film festival credit did help me get into school. The next few months were spent figuring out the bewildering visa application form, arranging money which meant borrowing from Dad, while casually sidestepping his disappointment at me formally pursuing filmmaking. I guess he had always hoped that one day, I'd finally get tired of working dreadful hours and having nothing to show for it, except deteriorating mental health and a dwindling bank balance, and switch to a more sustainable career. As if money was the only barometer of worth. After a few weeks of the silent treatment, he finally gave up and transferred the money. I had inflated the figure the embassy required, but he didn't ask me any questions. I wasn't proud of it, but I was convinced I wouldn't be returning to Delhi and wanted to leave having made an impression on my smattering of friends; whether that meant buying drinks I couldn't afford or going parties I had no business attending.

I'm not sure why I was drawn to recording sound in school. It's not like I learnt how to play an instrument or even had an enviable collection of records, cassettes or CDs. I'd only ever owned Walkmans that gave way to iPods to illegally downloaded songs to streaming websites, my sensibilities lost in a clutter of predetermined algorithms. I didn't have a noticeable aptitude for technology or science, and working in sound required both. Then again, I wasn't really sure of any one kind of ambition or direction. Nobody around me encouraged diverse interests, although a curious entrepreneurial spirit seemed to have gripped my friends. Around the same time I was preparing to go to film school, quite a few of them quit their mediocre jobs and were assimilated into their family businesses or borrowed money from their parents to open luxury e-commerce websites, pet grooming stores and wood-fired pizzerias. Medha, too, started working on a maximalist collection she hoped to exhibit in a few months. When I asked what she was attempting to depict through her work, she shut me down by branding my question as pedestrian.

The coldness between Medha and me could be attributed to her disappearing into her studio, spending hours with canvases, listening to Korean composers on repeat, and smelling of turpentine and sweat whenever we met. But it was mainly because most of our hangs were marked with a vague distance and painful misunderstandings.

One Sunday evening, as we painted in her studio, she asked me to channel the strongest emotion I possibly could. I painted the canvas with broad strokes of purples, pinks, blues and whites in acrylic.

'I feel the love you've poured into this. What were you channelling?' she asked me, standing close, arms akimbo, flecks of paint dotting her white dungarees.

'Pain.'

'You're so dramatic.' She dipped her brush into an empty can filled with water and plugged her earphones back on as she returned to her painting that she refused to show me.

'You're so lucky you're into women,' I lay down flat on her wooden flooring, and her neighbour's puppies pattered around me, sniffing my armpits, licking my nose. She didn't react to what I said, but I knew she'd heard me. After that evening, I saw her less and less.

While I waited for the visa to come through, I sent cold emails into the void, hoping to land work while fantasising about leaving the country. I would drown out my anxiety about the visa status by watching every film I could illegally download and reading books required for the course I'd spent twenty-five thousand rupees on. For my twenty-fifth birthday, I got myself a basic zoom recorder and began using it discreetly at parties, the metro, cafés, parks and beauty parlours. The eventual results were mostly garbage, with snatches of interesting conversations that I tried to stitch together on a free editing software I learnt how to use from YouTube tutorials. I don't know what triggered this interest; perhaps it was Ma's radio every morning that had prompted my father to refer to our family home as a 'paan ki dukaan', when they lived together, or maybe it was his collection of Mohammed Rafi, Bhupen Hazarika, Fatima Begum records, before he gave up on music altogether, switching the records out for Qu'ran recitals on the local radio. It was hard to pinpoint exactly where this desire to find meaning in everyday noise stemmed from, but I grabbed it with both hands and refused to let it go—it was something new and yet to disappoint me.

Today, we are learning Photography for Cinematography. The professor is a sixty-something lady with conspiracy theories and colourful insults she likes to hurl when unimpressed with our answers. Her bright eyes are enlarged behind her glasses as the projector beams images from the American Famine on the whiteboard. She gives me an accusatory look and calls on me.

'You! Tell me what you see.'

I am not used to this sort of attention. I usually slink in and out of school, trying to attract as little notice as possible. A lesson from my days in Delhi, perhaps. On the off-chance that somebody addresses me directly, I immediately assume a tone of superiority, a cadence only those who know better can afford, to avoid further conversation.

I'm not sure why I feel so out of place—maybe because I am one of the few brown faces on campus or because I feel stupid trying to discuss films in the courtyard amongst the cool kids smoking cigarettes. I find a certain succour in disappearing behind the blinking recording buttons and experiencing the world through my headphones. It takes on a mystical quality, a private moment I only share with myself and a way to tune out the world. It is my shtick. And by now I know everybody in school has some sort of shtick, a mould they fall into so that others can understand them better, without the troubling differences and nuances that come with having thirty kids from Scandinavian, Latin and Arab countries congregate in a villa with Czech professors.

The professor clears her throat, waiting for my response.

'Look at it from the back of your head.'

She has an entire theory about how, with the cloud of conditioning weighing us down, we've lost our ability to see clearly. We often indulge in something called 'otherisation', she says. 'The zoo effect,' she once triumphantly exclaimed in a bid to show exactly why Steve McCurry's work sucked. I don't understand much of what she says. She talks herself into a frenzy and often whips her fingers swiftly on top of the heads of the students to get them to use their 'mind's eye'. I know she isn't an especially successful photographer, so she teaches in a small community college in Prague, a far cry from Parisian gallery halls. I don't know how to tell her that bearing witness often also means keeping your mouth shut. That speaking up can elicit ridicule and, worse still—indifference.

An eager Puerto Rican girl answers on my behalf. My mind wanders to David. The way he speaks without blinking for several minutes.

Mostly, he strolls about our cramped school property, always dressed in a black bomber jacket. David is neither particularly attractive nor ugly. He looks like what I imagine an AI-generated image of the average Caucasian man would be. Tight-cropped dusty blonde hair, cool blue eyes and hands that do most of the talking. He attends every class and participates enthusiastically. He doesn't even hide behind his mobile phone or laptop screen. He just stands there and looks like he's never really listening to you. He can't be found at any after-class drinking affair or smoking cigarettes with the gaggle of film kids in the courtyard. There are some rumours about how his father is in a Swedish prison, but it's hard to verify any of this. Besides, who could verify it?

Making friends is harder than I thought. It doesn't matter what you look like, what you wear or how often you party; all that matters are your ideas, the films you're inspired by, the number of hours you spend on your edit and what cinema you can reference during lessons. It almost feels like a deliberate attempt at some sort of esotericism that eludes me.

Three years in Delhi, spent at a desk job scripting reality TV, binge drinking, barely making rent and spending unfettered time with Medha, enabling each other's questionable decisions, have left me ill prepared. The newfound freedom—both heady and suffocating—that had come with moving to Delhi right after college, along with pay-checks that felt fat at the time, and the general lack of inhibition, made things seem easy. But here, I am cocooned in a confined space with a multitude of ideas, thoughts, ways of being, speaking, eating, fucking, breathing, filming; it feels like language acts more as a barrier than a way to connect or understand. Still, I can always find solace in the singular task of recording sound. A footstep on dead leaves is a sign of autumn. If the steps are slow and empty, it could mean danger. If there are children laughing in the background, it means warmth. The click of a lighter, the slow inhale of the first puff, the sharp exhale of breath on a cold winter morning, the faraway sound of the television, the static between radio channels, the crackle of wood splinters as fire licks them up. Sounds that feel at once comforting and non-intrusive, like an old school friend you rub shoulders with on long walks, but don't have to speak to.

David doesn't have a social media presence, just an account on Instagram with a bio that reads: *Invertebrates for Life*. He has pictures of phasmids, mantids, whip spiders, roaches, beetles. Each photo has a detailed caption about their origin, species and lifespan. He only ever posts his face if there is an insect perched on the bridge of his nose. Hundreds and hundreds of insects, one after the other. I once saw a post about a pair of dead cockroaches he'd buried in a miniature coffin carved from mahogany or oakwood. They lay beside one another, their spiky legs in the air, their antennas still, their bodies bloated with death. The caption talked about how one had died from grief over the other's untimely end. A video accompanied the photo, where David lit a candle and closed the casket while a hymn played in the background.

The night David approaches me, I hurry home from school to research what mixing kits would be the best for his set-up and lose track of dinner or the sound of the church bells.

The next day, on my way to class, I spot David on a bench in the courtyard, seated beside a young girl. She wears a bright red quilted jacket and a gold septum ring. She is gaunt with a sort of heroin chic look about her. Her face is impassive as she listens to him. I don't think I've seen her on campus before. As I come out after class, I see them walk out of the main entrance, her arm looped into his, and suddenly, they look much older.

For the next few days, I see them together everywhere. Walking in step on cobblestone roads, eating soup across from one another at the nearby *restaurace*, huddled on the couch at the school café. Through fragments of conversations, I learn that she is an exchange student from a liberal arts school in America, that she briefly worked for Cirque du Soleil in Chicago and is now studying acting in Prague. Her Instagram handle is @thesweatiestwomanintheworld and has videos of her pirouetting through the air, her legs wrapped around colourful silk binds cascading from the ceiling; photos of her in shiny purple leotards holding headstands; time lapses of intricate yoga poses and circus acrobatics. Our eyes meet in the school cafeteria. Her face breaks into a shy smile, and I feel like I should introduce myself, but she collects her cup of coffee and walks away.

I don't think I am particularly lonely, but on some mornings, I wake up and look at the church steeple outside my attic window and feel a sudden emptiness crawl through my stomach and settle into my throat. I try to keep it at bay by running errands, smoking cigarettes on street corners while politely nodding at strangers in fleece jackets. I frantically re-check my schedule; there's got to be a class, some class I could attend. I could go to the park, but the grass is cold and the horizon dipped in mist. Sheets of ice cover the walkways, so I settle inside my warm room and put my field recordings together, creating loops and loops of aural journeys, strange radio shows, picking up random dialogues from various movies and stitching new narratives out of them. The disparate sounds keep me company, and every time I take a break, the silence begins to creep in again. I let the hourly sound of the church bells lull me to sleep.

Today, I'm rudely awoken by my phone vibrating on my pillow. It's 4 a.m. and Medha's calling. I answer with groggy uncertainty; nothing good's ever come from an early morning call from Medha. She immediately launches into a panicked tirade about how the exhibition is going to bomb, how she doesn't really know what she's doing, how they might replace her with another artist whose dad has connects with the South Delhi gallery. I listen, half-asleep and disinterested, as she tells me she's coping with her anxiety by doing a deep clean of her studio, about how she wants to save up to buy a Dyson to take out the dust bunnies from the corners because a white girl on Instagram told her but nothing, absolutely nothing, can help with the chemical smell of turpentine. I don't remember dozing off, but when I wake up, I'm late for class.

The night before the shoot, I realise I haven't asked David for the script. I stay awake as the alarm goes off. It's 5 a.m. on a new moon night, and I feel nauseous. I feel like I am stepping into my first-ever performance, a nervous debutante against whom the odds are stacked—perhaps due to the colour of my skin, or just my lack of talent. I book an Uber and swear to myself I'll take the tram more often. The cabbie regards me with an aggressive indifference, glancing at me occasionally in the rear-view mirror as I take in the empty streets.

I remember drives at this hour in Delhi, where most people I knew from school and other South Delhi parties had never moved out of the city, lived in their parent's palatial homes with chauffeur-driven Pajeros and access to swanky farm-houses, didn't need to get real jobs on account of their sizeable inheritances and had a lot of time to spare. It was easy to get swept up in the unrelenting attention of fairly attractive men and women; being young, hot and hip in the capital felt like an endless dream, a joyride without a destination.

On set, the lighting set-up is halfway finished. A single 650W HMI beams a pool of yellow light onto the carpeted floor. I set up my Fostex kit, securing the shooting perimeter with wires that I neatly tuck out of sight. I test the room tone, pad the walls with acoustic membrane, check the levels to cut noise. Soon after, I stand in a corner and admire my handiwork. Alexandria, who's booming, nods at me and cracks a few jokes at David's expense that I smile along to.

David enters with the girl, and the energy of the room changes. He doesn't introduce her to us, but I hear him address her quietly. Elizabeth.

'Have you read the script?' Alex turns to me.

David explains the scene to Elizabeth in a hushed tone in a shadowy corner and I see her cross her arms protectively. I click record as the clapper takes his position in front of the camera.

'Scene one, take one.'

The soft whir of the recording begins; I have my left index finger and thumb holding the volume button and the right one on the knob that controls gain. I feel the strain in my muscles melt away and I fuse with the Fostex kit. Sound of a door unlocking, footsteps across the carpeted floor. I adjust the gain as the footsteps come closer. A hand clasping another hand. The sharp inhale of nervous breath. The scratch of a fingernail on nylon. I adjust the levels. I close my eyes and the yellow fades into black. Sharp clang of a belt unbuckling. Creak of a couch. Fabric shifting, adjusting to accommodate somebody else. More creaks of the couch that reverberate in the studio. Mental note to dial down the reverb later. Heavy heaving and the rhythmic thrusting of a body. David's breath is slow and heavy until it picks up pace. Elizabeth makes no sound except a soft moan that is soon muffled. A harder thrust and a whimper. Breathing that picks up pace and turns into pulsing grunts. A loud moan that trembles in its timbre and breaks in its pitch. Metallic belt fastening and a zipper zipping up. Zipping up sounds most different from unzipping.

'What the fuck, man?'

Alex's thick Malmo drawl breaks the illusion. I look up at the scene. Elizabeth sits with her legs tucked beneath her on the couch, her stockings askew, her glittery dress ridden up her thighs. David gets off her. Everybody is staring. I feel like retching.

'What the fuck was that?'

Alex squares up against David. She looks like she might push him right in the chest. I think I see a moment of terror on his face before he excuses himself. The cinematographer clears his throat and the sound rings across the room and clips on my headphones.

*Ouch!* I snap them off and suddenly, everyone gets busy again.

The camera is wrapped, and the HMI switches off. The studio is momentarily doused in darkness until white tungsten light fills up the room. Alex drops the mic stand and mutters to herself as I spot the red of the recording button and switch it off. Elizabeth is frozen on the couch like a timestamp. I hear the water running from a tap in the bathroom next door. I know I have to check the kit to see if the recordings are in order. For a brief moment, I think of Azhar for the first time in almost two years. His hands around my neck and the sharpness of his bones against my muscle. I finally look at Elizabeth.

'Are you okay?'

Elizabeth straightens her dress without looking at me, gets up and walks down the stairs, disappearing from view.

I ask for a moment of silence before I take the room tone. The electric sound of the radiator that all European rooms have embedded in their structural DNA courses through the recording kit. Everybody leaves without a word. I'm aching to return to the familiar warmth of my attic room. Alex grabs my shoulder and asks me to accompany her to the Dean's office.

'What did you see exactly?'

'David, during a scene, masturbated on the actor.'

'That is quite an accusation.'

Dean Thomas was busy packing up for the day, placing piles of folders and papers into a briefcase, switching off the gilded lamps in his luxurious office, when Alex barged in, with me meekly following behind.

'More serious than what he did?' she says, her voice hard.

Thomas blinks a few times; to dispel his growing despair at being delayed, I think. His blonde hair is greasy; it's swept to a side on his balding head and he looks sinister in the falling light.

He looks at me. 'Do you corroborate Alex's account?'

'Why are you cross-examining us when you really should be expelling David right this minute!'

'Alex, please. I cannot assume he's guilty just because you insist he is. I would naturally need Elizabeth to come forward.'

He's beginning to bumble like an idiot.

'Sophia, tell him.' Alex looks at him defiantly, her arms crossed against her grey sweater, a booted foot tapping impatiently on the carpeted floor.

The right thing to do would be to confirm Alex's claim. But, the fact is that I didn't *actually* see anything. What's also a fact is that David entrusted me with the sound for his thesis film; his degree is contingent on it, and if I attest to something I haven't really seen, would that be honest? Or would I be jeopardising his degree on a partial truth? Degrees are imperative. To get that coveted job, the nice apartment, the girl with warm hugs, the live-in domestic help to give me timely chai as I sit on my recordings. David needs the degree.

Also, why would the Dean believe Alex? Our intimacy coach taught us several classes on navigating scenes like these. I'd seen David there, rapt with attention, often interrupting with questions that were somehow drowning in depth and redundancy at the same time, eliciting annoyed groans from fellow classmates and tiring the professor. David always tried hard to win the intimacy coach's favour but only managed to evoke thinly veiled contempt. The only real crime David could be accused of was having an inflated sense of self and going on tangential conspiracy theories about Josef Sudek and the Nazis.

'Wasn't his film about Me Too?'

Dean Thomas clapped his hands with a dramatic finality.

'Well, that settles it then. We'll wait for Elizabeth to come forward. You girls are coming out of a long shoot. Go home, get some rest.'

On our way out, Alex brushes right past me, furiously texting on her phone. I call out to her to grab some dinner, but she pretends she doesn't hear me over the call of the wind and turns the corner.

The next morning, I collect my coffee when the barista speaks to me for the first time in nine months. She tells me they have a committee hearing at six today. Her plastic-rimmed glasses sit at the edge of her nose like she's ready to judge me. Does she harbour a certain apathy for the strong, bitter smell of coffee beans roasting, as I often do when I walk along the abandoned tram tracks with my Fostex kit in tow, ears perked for sounds of insects or an underground rumble, picking up nothing but the sharp howl of the wind?

'You were on David's set?'

I reach into my pocket for forty-five crowns.

'Why would they keep a committee meeting at 6 p.m. on a Friday?'

She looks at me like I'm crazy. I heard she fell in love with an Indian boy who wouldn't have sex with her unless they got married. They broke up three months later, and she's been residing in gruff anger ever since, her arms working methodically at the Nespresso machine and frothing milk with an uncanny focus on the hundred cappuccinos she served each day.

The bell above the café door *tings* and David enters. I slip a fifty into the barista's hand, nod at him politely and slip out. As I light a cigarette outside, I see him skip his order, turn around and stride towards me with purpose. The kids in the courtyard take a break from their smoky flirting and watch him in silence. I stub the cigarette and walk towards class. He falls into step with me.

'How's it sounding?'

'Good, pretty good. Clean audio.' I speed up.

'Want to go over the audio after school today? Maybe at yours?'

'What about the committee hearing?'

'What committee hearing?'

Before I can respond, he disappears into a classroom.

Alex leans over, halfway through a scene from *Mulholland Drive.*

'What you did yesterday was fucked up.' I ignore her.

'The girl is sixteen!'

'She's sixteen?'

Alex looks at me like I'm scum. Who's she to judge? Alex doesn't even pay her own tuition; her government takes care of it while I make a million rounds to the immigration office in the hope of a visa extension, only to get a meagre month, post graduation, to hunt for a job. I sit in the corner of the remarkably Soviet-looking office, sinking further into the tattered chairs where an overweight Czech man, smelling of beer, smoke and sweat, breathes down on me before venomously whispering, *indická děvka*, which loosely translates to 'Indian whore'. I'd taken a four-week course on spoken Czech, and it's helped me navigate taxis on drunk nights, the subway system and racist immigration officers. I highly doubt it will help me get a job.

'You better come to the committee hearing.'

At 6 p.m., I stand alone at the tram stop. I am hungry, but I glimpse a bunch of students, including Alex, hanging at the panini place near school, deep in discussion. I walk right past, a scarf covering half my face. I'm sure I can scrape together a soup or a sandwich from the leftovers in my fridge. I scroll through Instagram and realise that Elizabeth's profile has been deactivated.

In Delhi, my attraction to men was always underscored with a baseline revulsion.

It's as if I knew exactly what they were capable of. My friends were often assaulted with comments on how short their dresses were, how much leg or cleavage they showed, the colour of their lipstick, how attention-seeking they were; every day, they carried such accusations within themselves. The ones who eventually escaped it look back at that time with an equal measure of detachment and horror. The ones who stayed annihilate themselves with doubt every day.

I remember when Nayna, a distant friend, vaguely called a 'party girl', accused a DJ of sexual assault. While the details have become foggy, I do recall the comments section of her post on Instagram, littered with people who didn't believe her, who ridiculed her for her short dresses, and blamed her for leading men on for free drinks and drawing too much attention to herself. I remember some women being outraged at the prospect of a predator in their social circles and others defending him and, consequently, themselves.

Before long, Nayna's accusations were lost in a din of comments, likes and shares, as her assault became a topic of debate. Her sizeable following on Instagram fell by a few thousand. I spotted the guy a few months later, surrounded by friends, gyrating at another party in Delhi. Nayna moved to Madrid with her boyfriend, cut her hair short and started a zine on women in music. She owns a cat now.

At the tram stop, a chilly wind blows around David and me. I can feel passers-by watching us, confused by the racial overtones of a shifty white man and a nervous brown girl. I take a step backwards to increase the distance between us, but David comes in closer and speaks about his edit. My eyes move to the yellow, crusty tartar between his front teeth, the cold blue of his eyes, his hands waving frantically through the air, his pitch rising with excitement. I only come around to the present when he mentions Elizabeth.

'Elizabeth's acting left a lot to be desired but I don't blame her, she's only sixteen. I thought I'd prepped her sufficiently but clearly not.'

He looks away and kicks a pebble that's come loose.

A few hours have passed since we've been cocooned in my apartment. The sun has dipped beyond the horizon. An empty box of take-out pizza lies discarded on the bed alongside several empty coffee cups. I'm experiencing some sense of disassociation, like I am watching myself listen to the sounds I've recorded from a corner of the room.

'It's excellent. Probably the best sound anybody's done this year. Don't be surprised if you win.'

I feel my muscles relax as relief cascades down my spine. It's been a miserable nine months. I've not really made any friends, the weather is relentless, I run out of money every month and the man at the café where I eat lunch every Sunday never smiles at me. The pointlessness of wanting a job in the Czech Republic, breaking down on the subway occasionally, being stalked to my apartment in the middle of the night, getting my ass smacked by a man with a scar at a club, having a pen-knife wielded at me by a teenage boy on the subway and sleeping with a guy I met off Tinder who wouldn't pull out when I asked him to—all that seems to fade away briefly.

In the basement of an extravagant Sainik Farms villa, turned into a cocaine den for some grotty party—replete with average DJs, men with coin-sized pupils, the faint smell of warm beer mixed with sweat and unabashed staring—I caught sight of a man on the dance floor as I stood swaying in front of the enormous speakers, techno thumping through the sound-proofed room. He wore thin-rimmed glasses, a scruffy beard and a blue ikat kurta. He rocked from foot to foot, moving to the music with a kind of nervous energy. I wanted to chat but didn't know how. So, I resorted to staring at him, hoping he'd catch my eye and walk over. Outside, the Delhi cold was particularly biting. Gulmohar trees for as far as the eye could see. Flashes of headlights as Beemers and Range Rovers whizzed past me.

He spoke to me at the kebab stall. I don't remember the conversation too clearly now, but I remember being taken by his voice, his hair, his smile. He worked as an investigative journalist and was doing a story on Delhi's biggest slum. I spoke to him about the odd jobs I did to make rent. He told me about his dying cat and his favourite female authors. I spoke about my estrangement from my parents since their unannounced separation. He tutted in sympathy while his orb-like eyes rested on me. I remember feeling warm at being seen, a strange sense of detachment from the rest of the party crowd; this connection was special, and I was lucky to have found it most serendipitously.

On the bus ride to a chalet David's uncle owns, I look at the vast swathe of snow that covers the landscape. The sharp spikes of the linden trees stand tall, devoid of any leaves or warmth. No birds swarm the sky and no animals emerge from their burrows. I've never been invited to spend a weekend somewhere by a man without the idea of sex being implied. But the country has its own charms and I'm sick of the stifling perfection of the city centre. I've agreed, though I don't know how to explain my sudden kinship with David to Alex and the rest on campus or to myself. Maybe, if we down enough Becherovka, I can get David to talk about what actually happened on set. I feel like I am betraying my crew members, especially Elizabeth.

We turn up at the edge of the chalet, embedded in a deep, snow-covered forest. The setting sun casts an ungodly shadow over the looming structure. Peeling paint exposes red brick, several rooms lead to a hall-like area filled with antiquated objects. Soon, I am called to chop blocks of wooden logs piled outside. It is numbingly cold, and the wind is an icy blade across my exposed cheeks. I labour through the chopping, inviting a corny laugh from David's uncle, Marcel.

Marcel is a robust man with deep-set eyes, fine wrinkles and a stern look that dissipates with a wide grin. He is absolutely delighted to meet David's exotic friend. It's only after much convincing on our part does he stop referring to me as David's *přítelkyni*, or girlfriend. He asks me if Indians play football and whether we have plumbing systems in our homes. Later, I check Instagram on the weak WiFi connection; Elizabeth's profile is still deactivated.

David skins the fresh carp as we sit in the kitchen, the orange fire licking the insides of the soot-lined chimney. Marcel tells me about working his way up from being a bouncer to the owner of one of the first few clubs in Prague. He talks about the legality of hard drugs and the meth problem most people in the country seem to have. He swigs from a pungent plum liqueur as he talks about the rising rape cases. My eyes feel heavy with the wood and cigarette smoke. I lay my head back and survey the chalet, which evokes a strange, contrasting image—one entrenched in the brutalism and sparseness of the Soviet era, another drenched in the excess of the Christian period. David soaks the fish in butter, garlic and some Indonesian herbs Marcel picked up on his travels. My mind wanders with an old Gypsy tune, and my eyes close gently.

---

After a shared kebab roll, the man offered to drop me back home on that cold Delhi night. I sat beside him in the car, conscious of our sudden closeness, as he rolled a joint beside me. The bluetooth played Mehdi Hassan and the warm air from the heater wafted through the car. His car smelt of citrus and whisky. Did I smell of sweat? We shared the joint in a kind of weighted silence. I told him where I needed to be dropped off, and as the car glided on the main road, I took in Delhi's expansive vista. Clear, wide streets, stray dogs guarding metro stations, yellow lights collecting in pools. Everything was accentuated in my mind—the party, the crispness of the night air, our connection. He leaned in without much warning, and his lips grazed my neck. We began to kiss as the driver looked straight ahead, trained not to remind us of his existence. Kissing turned into heavy petting, and his hand slipped under my shirt. I stopped him and tried to come up for some air. I was feeling dizzy when his hand snaked under my skirt. I felt the edge of his fingertips across my crotch. I sprung backwards—*too soon.* He seemed to have not heard me. He continued kissing my neck and caressing my thigh. Maybe I said it too quietly. His grip got stronger on my upper thigh, fingers pressing in. *Stop.* I barely hissed the word. His nails dug into my muscle.

From the corner of my eye, I saw that we were crossing Medha's street. On a sudden impulse, I opened the door, jumped out of the moving car and hurtled onto the sidewalk. I bruised my elbows and lost an earring as I broke into a half-sprint to her main gate, and the car stopped a few metres ahead. I rang the doorbell thrice as he poked his head out of the car, yelled, 'Cocktease!' and slammed the door shut.

The car disappeared around the corner as Medha opened the door.

Half-asleep, she fixed me some chamomile tea. Yoko and Ono, her neighbour's Shih-Tzus that she was dog-sitting, curled up like furry balls around her feet. I clasped the mug and felt its warmth radiating into my body.

'So?' she asked as she settled on her bed.

I blinked at her.

She looked at me with sleepy eyes—I knew I didn't paint a wholesome picture with my smudged mascara, cracked lipstick and boozy breath.

I told her about the party, about how I lost my friends in the crowd, how dated the music was, how average the kebabs were, that I didn't tell her before, but I got into film school, that I would dearly miss her even though I'm mad at her, that Yoko was almost human and could sense that I was sad, that I forgot my apartment keys and had to barge in on her like this. She noticed the hickey on my neck and the pressure marks on my thigh. Then she threw me a blanket, turned her back to the wall and went to sleep, her gentle snores melting into the sky as it broke into a pinkish dawn.

I come around to David at the stove. He's engrossed in the fish as I book myself a cab. From the kitchen window, I see Marcel on a phone call. The taxi turns the corner and floods us with a Biblical yellow light. On my way out, I give a confused Marcel a quick hug, tell him how long the fish needs to be steamed and slip into the cab. As the taxi drives out on the icy path, I watch my jagged breath fog up the window. We turn the corner, and the chalet is swallowed by the night sky.

From the cab, I imagine what talking to Medha would be like. It's 4 a.m. in Delhi. She'll pick up after two rings. We'll be the only two people awake in the world. I'll speak to her about how I miss painting in her studio together, how I finally tried tofu, about waiting on her bathroom pot as she bathed for too long, flitting about gallery openings and jazz nights, about how difficult it's been to make any real friends here, about what really happened that night I turned up at her doorstep.

# 4

# CHENNAI

THE AIRPLANE FEELS STUFFY, TOO HOT, THE seats too cramped, the aisles reek of pickle and mustard oil, the air hostesses' make-up isn't blended right. Everything feels overdone, stereotypical and wrong. I can't put my finger on why. The vowels of a foreign tongue grate on my nerves; foreign, yet from within my own country. My tired brain jumps to hateful clichés when I hear a man sitting behind me on a phone call. I want to ask him to shut up; the flight is about to take off.

Exceptionally irritable, I've felt little of the snugness that a childhood friend's wedding should bring. Instead, I feel anxieties and fears—familiar and new—sitting at the base of my navel, sitting as tightness in my chest. Inhale, exhale, repeat the steps, go through the motions until I can manufacture some of the happiness I'm supposed to be feeling. I suspect that the discontent stems from me.

When I first received the 'Save The Date' as a WhatsApp forward from my best friend from ninth grade, I thought it was a joke. Who gets married at twenty-six? But then, I got a video call from a sunny-faced Sonia, who beamed while bathing in the diffused light of the posh one-bedroom apartment she shared with her fiancé and gave me an ultimatum; there was no way I could miss her wedding. She was the first in my inner circle, which had a rotating tribe of people I met through my life across various cities, to be getting married. I wouldn't say I was particularly attached to anybody beyond the casual FaceTime twice a year on our respective birthdays, but I blamed my disillusionment on forced virtual conversations more than on the natural drifting apart. I knew I had an accurate reputation for being a flake, and while I could barely feign the enthusiasm I imagined she expected me to feel, I was also looking for a reason to get out of Bombay.

I hadn't entirely adjusted to being back. My attempts at getting a job in Prague had turned out to be futile, so I did what most Indian kids who study film abroad do—move to Bombay with egg on my face. My father barely concealed his disappointment in the hurried ultimatums for me to make money, to find a nice house in a nice part of town and stay with nice girls, to grow my hair out, quit smoking, read my Friday namaaz. They were delivered with their usual acerbity, punctuated with colourful abuses in Hindi, not hurled at anybody in particular, and phrases of resignation in Urdu. I nodded along; I needed the money.

Ten days before I'd had to leave Prague, presumably for good, I moved into the studio apartment of the boy I was briefly seeing. The house was fifteen minutes from school, a few minutes from the underground bar I'd grown to love, and the Kino. I'd spent many Friday nights watching movies dubbed in Czech, the scent of fresh beer and pickled sausages in the air.

We were thrown into early-day domesticity, spending hours naked on the double bed with windows opening out into the main corridor, playing loud music so the neighbours couldn't hear us. I watched him take showers in the tiny bathroom that jutted into the kitchenette while I chopped onions. Every day, we fucked like it was our last day on Earth, content in the knowledge of something we knew didn't need to last.

Bombay has none of the romance and all of the drama. I shifted in July when the rains had the streets heaving. Every morning, I wake up in my tiny room on the first floor to loud horns, street hawkers yelling, men barking into cellphones, and my heart pounds uncomfortably. Every day seems like the same trip around the seventh circle of Hell, the same rock I'm destined to keep rolling up the hill. Every day, I wait for the final tipping point—rainwater dripping from the ceiling onto my laptop, rotting food in the fridge that my flatmate leaves behind, getting laughed at during interviews, Bollywood parties at Soho House where a director assumes I'm the girl a producer is fucking, breaking down in the car ride back home, but it never really arrives.

I land in Chennai on a muggy day. At the wedding venue, I take in the balmy weather, the air that smells of a pungent, tired sea, knock-off designer perfume and cocktails made with cheap alcohol. This over-the-top bourgeois wedding, nestled in the posh quarters of a boutique hotel by the beach, summons my inner critic. I'm not sure if it's because of the expensive, rather gauche bar where a mediocre negroni costs a grand, or the attractive sommelier's disapproving brows that disappear into his hairline when I choose the least expensive wine on the menu. It could be the oblivious American working-class hero from Wisconsin with his steady diet of greasy cheeseburgers and Coke, or his second-generation Asian-American girlfriend, with a Chinese father and Vietnamese mother (the right degree of exotic?), who steers every conversation towards herself and her modern-day immigrant inconveniences.

At Radio Room, the bar where everybody congregates for an informal 'meet and greet', I finally see Sonia, my childhood friend, who's been sending me increasingly excited voice notes in the weeks leading up to this. Despite warm greetings and liquor trying its best to smooth every social interaction, I am out of place amidst the throng of guests making small talk. I miss my former friend, even though she is right there. She was my first real friend at a ridiculous time of unshaved legs, abundant acne and crushes on boys with dull personalities. At fourteen, she had chucked my first packet of cigarettes out of the window of my eighth-story home and in retaliation, I had thrown her phone to the floor. She is everything I am not. Charming, warm, open, loving. I am everything she isn't. Aloof, snarky, weird. We had taken to each other without judgement, Indian schoolgirls in Dubai, and fallen into our own groove of friendship. We eyed attractive Arab boys in libraries, walked by the beach in a strange land where we didn't know the language but couldn't get enough of the exotic sights, sounds and social hierarchies. Together we understood what it meant to be an uncool immigrant, to live in a particular pin code, to allow ourselves to be sexualised as teenagers. We went through our first heartbreaks and first major bouts of depression together even as we slowly grew apart while pursuing degrees on different continents.

I move from event to event, cocktail dress to Indian attire, with a lingering sense of nostalgia and a marked blankness. I am here for Sonia, but I don't feel the need to be charming or friendly or approachable or distant or sexy. I don't feel the need for anything.

Decades ago, my parents had their whirlwind romance that spanned continents and religions. I know how that turned out. Once I believed that I, too, would meet the right person at eighteen and marry them and live out the various boring but ultimately safe rituals of a high school romance turned life-long partnership. Now, the idea of a wedding, of a marriage, of a life shared with one person looks like some other girl's dream.

At a bar called The Library, its name legitimised by a wall lined with first edition hardcovers locked behind a glass panel, their dusty sadness proving they've never been opened, I sit across from the American couple. 'Do you meditate?' Wisconsin boy asks me. I catch myself before an audible groan can slip out. He briefly tells me about his brush with drugs, how he's debating selling his DJ-ing gear since he's been unemployed for four months, and how that's taking a toll on his Brooklyn life. We discuss his siblings, growing up Catholic and their desire to move to New Orleans. The Asian girl wants to get married at Monterey Bay Aquarium and tells me stories of working as the only Asian copywriter in a largely white agency. I marvel at their easy, almost simplistic relationship, the blind spots that come with growing up with an American passport, the myopia that comes with believing the country you're born in is the only world you'll ever need to inhabit. The girl whips out her phone and shows me her family in LA. Her regal grandmother, grandfather with an oxygen tank, a muscular pit bull, the buff younger cousin, the 'work hard, play hard' second cousin, the matching Christmas sweaters. Her ease with her dissonant identities and her doting boyfriend make me slightly jealous. We smile widely, take sips from each other's drinks, exchange antique silver and gold-plated neckpieces for an event later and hug goodbye. Away from the wedding bedlam, I feel a grudging affection for her.

The sangeet begins with all the aplomb one would expect at a fancy Indian wedding. Copious amounts of liquor, a lavish buffet, a DJ spinning house remixes of Bollywood classics from the nineties and generations brought together by the blend of tradition and intoxication.

I haven't had much of an appetite since I returned to the country, which meant I couldn't keep up with the drinking. It could be depression, but I'm not too sure. I tried looking for a therapist in Bombay, but soon realised there's no way I could afford one.

In the soft lighting of the basement where the sangeet is taking place, I tug at the hem of my black cocktail dress, bought at a popular fast fashion chain outlet, and thank the lord that I've lost weight since my move to Bombay. I survey the crowd decked in expensive suits, silk saris and twinkling diamonds. Is my outfit too slutty for this decidedly Indian affair? Sonia's eighteen-year-old brother grabs me by the wrist and pulls me towards the bar. A pale, lavender liquid in a shot glass materialises, and I clutch it with desperation. The brother's eyes are glazed over with a post-charas haze. He bounces on his toes as a group of people—including his parents—form a circle and clink shot glasses. I slip away, handing the shot glass to the bartender. *Hide it.* Sonia finds me through the crowd and makes her way to me.

'Are you not going to dance to shitty Bollywood songs at my wedding?' she says as she drags me towards a throng of people moving to some loud filmy music.

I shake my head vigorously, accompanying her to the dance floor despite my inability to climb out of my head and be present for her.

Sonia's family are diamond merchants from Gujarat who immigrated to Dubai—the land of opportunity, abundance and no taxes. Her father accumulated enough wealth to raise three kids in a palatial beachfront home, send them to one of the better international schools and finance their move abroad. The shots are a celebratory indulgence, an attempt to impress overlaid onto their endearing Gujarati simplicity. The husband's family is from Tamil Nadu and Punjab. His father is the CEO of an Indian airline fading fast into obscurity, and his mother the good wife. Despite their obvious wealth and privilege, I sense a veiled judgement towards the girl's family's lack of sophistication.

Sonia's cousin walks towards me across the carpeted dance floor, his face dappled with disco lights. A flash of a house party in Zizkov, a suburb of Prague dotted with functionalist architecture, on last New Year's Eve. Neon lights, gangly bodies snaking across a makeshift dance floor, the guy I was briefly seeing, behind the decks, me whispering into his ear, giggling, shining with the glow of some sort of infatuation. The news of David leaving school and going back to Sweden or Ukraine. Whispers about Elizabeth pressing charges. The feeling that the ground beneath me had caved in and not knowing whether it was the drugs or the rumours.

Life's displacements are like tectonic plates shifting beneath me, the heart and mind struggling to create and conquer old meanings in new contexts.

The boy goes by Nemo and compliments my hair and my moves. I give him a sincere smile and excuse myself. My initial response to compliments is to accept them and then look away. This isn't a tactical move nor a sly manoeuvre to seem mysterious. Maybe it is shades of discomfort, that slight consciousness of having been on display and yet the pleasure of being noticed. Either way, I really just don't know what to say.

Outside the ballroom, I light a cigarette and observe the flames across the expanse of water, flanked by Grecian columns on either side. I lie down on the cold marble, lehenga askew, hoping to see some stars in the sky. I take a selfie where I pout sadly. I don't quite like my face when I smile; my teeth seem yellow against the coat of wedding make-up, and my cheeks stretch out. The smile never seems to reach my eyes. I send it to Medha, who texts me promptly: *you look very sad.* I'm too tired to tell her that weddings make me sad, making me feel selfish, which compounds the sadness. The theatrics, the promise of forever love, families coming together to bless the couple with a radiant future, cherub-cheeked grandkids in tow, only make me think of my failed affairs, my lack of desire or capacity to make it work.

Somehow, the idea of a breakup or separation doesn't seem too dramatic on paper. It seems manageable, feminist almost, but in real life, with each heartbreak, I feel closer to spinning totally out of control. I read in an article that anxiety was a manifestation of pain suppressed, but that felt too simplistic an explanation for the emptiness I felt. I don't feel like texting Medha all this for fear of sounding like a whiny idiot, and instead, ask her how her collection is coming along.

A whiff of Versace. I chuckle inwardly at the contours of my hyper-capitalist upbringing as a slender boy in a sharply cut three-piece suit slides up next to me.

'Nice suit.'

'A good suit to cry in.'

I immediately like him.

'I cried this morning after three years. It was so beautiful,' he continues in a distinctive drawl, his diction chiselled with expensive schooling. He sits up and begins to roll a joint.

'Crying is cathartic.'

'Yeah, antidepressants don't ever allow that sort of release.'

He passes the joint to me. I'm unsure how we've slipped into such an intimate conversation so easily. I look at him, eyes narrowed. I am drawn to his pale skin, freckles and eyes with schisms of empathy and impenetrability. We pass the joint between us, discussing the merits of male contraceptives, the current political climate in the country, raising puppies. I withdraw slightly as he showcases a certain type of martyr complex, placing himself at the centre of the nation's political turmoil. He pulls me back by telling me about his mother's internalised patriarchy and how hollow victories feel when they're against your parents. Our effortless conversation is interrupted by a gentleman who's down a few drinks, staggering up to where we are seated, slurring as he shakes our hands, his eyes lingering over my neckline. I feel a familiar flicker of irritation despite the pleasant pot-induced haze and excuse myself again.

Back inside, there's some commotion about some perceived insult by the groom's father. Why does institutionalised marriage even exist anymore? Why is the bride's father's identity inexorably tied up with the grandeur of his oldest daughter's wedding? Despite coming from a relatively regressive North Indian family, my father only ever mentions marriage as an afterthought, a private joke shared between the two of us on a phone call late at night. The thought only really occurs to him in passing when I say I want to shift jobs or cities or continents. After my parents decided they wanted different things and, more importantly, didn't want them with each other, we all developed an almost sinister sense of humour to deal with the separation. All talk of marriage faded into sardonic jokes about how they should have expiry dates, feeding into my fatalistic assertion that being alone is the only constant.

I am sharing a room with Sonia's other friend from school, whom I've avoided through the wedding functions despite recognising her. When I return to the room's amber-lit darkness, I cannot focus. The girl is snoring like a truck while I try not to breathe too loud. Later, she helps me tie my sari as I take my place beside her in front of the bathroom mirror. We both press our faces with powder in silence, me conscious of the music playing from my laptop. She wants to borrow my eye shadow palette; I apologise for only having nude colours. She laments the weight she's put on through her adult years in Bangalore, working through late nights, often forgetting to eat. I glance at her sideways.

'You're beautiful.'

'Thank you, you're kind.'

'I'm not being kind, I'm being honest.'

She meets my eyes and smiles—a genuine warmth filling up her eyes. That's all it takes. One sincere lie after years of avoiding each other, and suddenly, I feel the warm rush of winning somebody's favour when you least expect it.

Over the next couple of days, when I find myself slinking out of parties early or hiding behind marble columns to smoke, I often receive texts from her, checking in. I reply in monosyllables but don't go to her.

After a hazy sequence of ceremonies and rituals, the wedding's finally over. Still, there is a drunken brunch and some sort of reception to follow. I go for a swim, savouring the solitude of the cool water until my thoughts are interrupted by the arrival of Maria—a Greek friend of Sonia's, with no understanding of personal boundaries and a propensity for flattery, who I'd vaguely glimpsed through the wedding. She tries to make conversation as I continue my swim.

Maria wants to talk to me about the guy she hooked up with last night. I notice the tension between them as he comes out to the sun-beds. What does sex look like when Maria has it? How conscious is she about her body? She says she thinks I'm the most beautiful girl at the wedding, after the bride. I'm flattered but later bemused by the off-hand comment, as though beauty superseded everything I might have to offer, as though such a compliment was anything but definitive and entirely suffocating.

Later that morning, I observe Sonia's friends flock around her; air kisses and goodbyes. She glides through the hugs and the pleasantries with the ease and charm of a politician. Finally alone, we nurse our hangovers with juice and I feel the pressure to say something. But what can I say that will not be weighed down by shared histories or stories? Should I ask whether she has already thought of the time when she might not want to be with Vivek anymore? Does she know what the moment was when we drifted apart, inexplicably but surely from being attached at the hip to living such different lives? Does she remember?

Instead, I ask if she still plans on pursuing her PhD, my eyes brighter than usual with the wine. I falter when she wants to know about my love life, my mind turning over the various threads of romance resistant to definition, paling in comparison to the weighty, resounding certainty of marriage. I lay my head on her shoulder, and we take a few selfies—ephemeral moments to be captured and shared. Moments that make sure that once I recede into the comfort of my solitude, I can still reach out and indulge in a past that no longer exists.

I make a concerted effort to dress up for brunch. Something about being away from Bombay makes me want to pretend to be someone else, hoping that this physical transformation will enable an emotional one. But, instead, as I record bitchy voice notes to Ma, who asks me to be thankful for a fully-paid trip and a five-star hotel stay, I'm overheard by Sonia and Vivek.

'You're just a pretentious filmmaker who's entirely self-involved.' Vivek's face cracks into a silly, self-satisfied smile.

'You'd be right, except to be a filmmaker, I'd actually have to make a film.'

Sonia breaks out of her post-wedding haze, the unremitting lull of satisfaction only some of us can afford, to defend me. 'Sophia has a tendency to agree with anything negative said about her, even if it isn't true.'

Why am I here, why did I miss the memo and turn up overdressed for this event, why are my facades so brittle; why was I expecting to feel less lonely around this loud, stylish crowd?

---

On my last night in the city, I slip away to meet Michael—a journalist who once advised me on a script that never went anywhere. After a forty-minute rickshaw ride, I find myself at a rundown rooftop bar overlooking a beach, barely visible under the night sky.

Michael is a good listener, unafraid to wear his limitations on his sleeve, leading a wilder life than his slender frame and kind eyes suggest. We last met years ago at a swanky Gurgaon bar, and today, I worry about the unsaid discomfort of knowing each other through Azhar—the longest relationship of my life so far that feels almost imagined at this point.

Yet, I find myself relaxing in this presence, the tension in my shoulders and back receding as my tongue loosens with the wine. The conversation goes from film to collective anxieties—the lack of money in attempting to pursue an artistic life in a developing country, the possibilities for art in a nation on the brink of fascism, the absurdity of legal contracts and gold bands meant to bind people together. It feels fitting that I'd feel comfortable talking about the things really bothering me with someone I barely know.

Old friends tend to pull me in directions they remember me from, into patterns they once constructed with me. I have a habit of wanting to give before somebody can ask, even when it isn't something I desire, so my relationships can often exist in the limbo between truth and avoidance. Often, I debate telling people what I really feel, what I really want from them, but then stay quiet.

Childhood friendships are now defined by how much of an effort one is willing to make to turn up at each other's engagements, weddings, baby showers and anniversaries—the gradual, inevitable shift into 'acceptable' constructs. Theoretically, I understand this, but seeing Ma shift between friendships, slippery like an eel, was difficult to understand and process as a child. Every time I grew attached to one of her friends, she got into some sort of unexplained fight with them a few months later, and we never saw or spoke to them again. Many such incidents gave me the impression that I'd imagined these people. Ma assured me I didn't have imaginary friends as a child, but I couldn't understand how she could cut out people she'd known her entire adult life with such clinical precision. I remember her being a blubbering mess of emotion when I was a child, and now all I see is a pointed indifference, evident in her ritualistic phone calls.

I find comfort in Michael's uncertainty, in the humility that comes from not pretending to know all the answers, in the shared identity of being an outsider.

We finish our drinks and walk through empty Chennai roads towards the main highway, dodging stray dogs, lazy bulls, parked cars and buses. As he calls me a taxi, we chat absent-mindedly about the incoming rise of right-wing supporters in Tamil Nadu. I argue that the state's political mechanics would never agree to a largely north Indian political party gaining and exerting majority control; he's doubtful—the fast deteriorating state of the nation relegated to an intermediary chat before the taxi arrives.

Inside, I feel a pang of longing for the private jokes Sonia and I used to share, how easily my dumbest comments made her laugh, and how widely I'd grin when she was impressed by my most transparent ploys; the pockets of ease in our childhood, now almost painful to recall. I remember how often, in social settings, she rolled her eyes at me after running out of patience or charm, how often I called her up as a teenager, beset with tears, hiding in my room, fruitlessly attempting to drown my parent's rising voices with some vapid pop album, how she defended me against senior boys when I refused to grant them the respect they felt entitled to. I suppose this is why it's hard to let go of old friendships even when they distinctly seem to have run their course.

I remember, vividly, a moment from two nights ago when all the girls—the loud ones from New York, the shy ones from Dubai, the pretty ones from Chennai, the rich Gujarati aunties with large hips and larger jewels—congregated in the bride's suite, attempting to help each other with the folds of our unravelling saris.

Sonia, decked head to toe in a bejewelled lehenga that weighed over ten kilos, her skirt unnaturally starched, standing across me, against the setting sun, a complete silhouette, asked me how she looked. Her hair was perfectly coiffed, swathes of make-up across her elegant face, her expression as vulnerable as the text messages I hid behind. At that moment, she was all of fourteen years old again, and I couldn't help but smile.

# 5

# BOMBAY

I SIT ACROSS THE OTHER FELLOWS AS THE grant head, Suchitra, a woman in her late fifties with a mop of curly, grey hair, her sunburnt neck swathed in a wrinkled cotton sari, beams at us. I scan the room, and everyone looks visibly nervous; we're an obviously eclectic crew, even if our 'otherness' is what ties us together. I'm pulled to make a comment or pass a joke to slice through the tension, but I refrain. Something tells me it may not go down well—this isn't the crowd that Medha and I have run into in the past, while gatecrashing parties in rooftop bars or the embassies of Nehruvian Delhi.

'Mirza Rehman: spoken word poet and classically trained singer, Muslim, trans-woman. I'm writing a one-woman play narrated through songs exploring gender, the marginalised voice and my journey of coming to terms with being at home in my body.'

Simultaneous snapping of fingers and nods of appreciation.

'Maham Islam. I'm a writer and dancer from Shillong with an interpretive dance project that I perform in my bedroom as I navigate spaces, my body and memories through movement.'

'Aabid Khan, filmmaker. My film is about two women from rural Bengal whose dreams intersect as they fight against patriarchal forces in their small village.'

'Naaz Farooqi from Delhi. I'm creating a miniature collection of Muslim women from history and depicting them more as subjects with agency and authority and less as objects of desire.'

It's my turn. I talk about the premise of my script, but I jumble all my words, and my voice feels like it doesn't belong to me. A Muslim girl and a Hindu boy fall in love against the backdrop of increasing hate crimes in India. That was it. That was all I had. Without an arsenal of important words and essential degrees, I'm unsure of how to define my work.

'We are living in an unprecedented time. We all hoped it wouldn't come to this, but it has. And, it's brought us to an unpleasant but unavoidable crossroads where we have the chance to make history. Belonging to the minority in the line of fire has its uses. It is our privilege and duty to tell the stories that are being erased, to embody the voices that are being silenced. The fight is long and difficult, but you have me and, more importantly, each other. Until then, we hope to support your work like we would support our own and insha'allah, we'll have some brilliant, young voices as the symbols of protest as this fellowship concludes. Salaams,' Suchitra finishes with a flourish, a practised smile etched across her face, and everybody snaps their fingers like we are at the world's worst poetry slam.

I'm not sure if her speech is meant to be motivating. It's tiring to be defined by my last name, and my privilege has made sure that I've been cushioned against most of what Muslims are going through. I can't rent a house in some parts of Delhi or Bombay, and often I feel panic crawl up my chest every time a cop stops me at a naka or when I stand before an immigration officer scrutinising my passport. The guy I was briefly seeing in Prague became distant with time when he realised I'm Muslim, despite my earnest insistence that I wasn't practising; experiences that didn't amount to much except a painful consciousness of my last name. Even though I grew up in Dubai, where being Muslim was the norm, and had a Maulvi come home to teach me the Qur'an in Arabic, I mostly suffered through it, partly due to teenage rebellion, and partly because of a vague suspicion of being asked to blindly believe in something. Islamic studies—moral studies disguised as religious teachings—were mandatory in school until the ninth grade; *the price of dishonesty is self-destruction, love your friends, help a man in need, respect your elders, there is no God except Allah.* As I looked at Suchitra, I was reminded of these lessons. Is it bigoted to cherry-pick five Muslims from different parts of the country and put them in the same room to talk about their struggles as a minority? Is it cultural appropriation when a woman named Suchitra Iyer uses 'insha'allah' and 'salaam'? Perhaps it's not appropriation, perhaps I am being harsh, but it certainly is off-putting since it reminds me of the one day a week my Dad decides to be a good Muslim.

Right after the Friday namaaz, he abandons his routine persona, made up of gallows humour and a bitter indictment of everything around him—his secretary, his boss, the guy serving him coffee, the coffee, the car that cuts ahead of him, the client who demands too much of his time—and turns into the most gracious Muslim in the country. The morning namaaz is followed by Tarawih and several catch-up calls with his siblings in Lucknow, where they discuss the volatile political on-goings of their state. Post these calls, gripped by an inexplicable fatherly urge, he speaks to me with a distant kindness about the good that's promised to us if we just follow the ayat, alternating between reward and fear.

Suchitra's desperation to be an ally reminds me of my father's sporadic evenings spent memorising the Qur'an, driven by a desire to ensure safety post-death, haunted by the abstraction of jahannum. In the off chance that there is the possibility of heaven or an afterlife, he turned to the janamaz, much as Suchitra turned to the validation that yes, she would be the one to save us.

For Ma, the idea of hell is not so concrete, despite her fleeting return to her Arya Samaji beliefs, spurred by the death of her parents. For her, true hell is the abstract suffering of others; she's more concerned with the neighbour who beats his wife, or their oldest son who needs a job. I have trouble believing her altruism, perhaps because of how loud it can sometimes be. But I suspect it's mostly because she doesn't end up being much of a mother—a reality I've long since accepted.

Whatever my feelings for Suchitra may be, I am thrilled to receive funding for my original script well before it's actually written. I had the bare bones of an idea, so I sent them a proposal on a whim. The happiness I felt upon receiving the acceptance email was immediately marred by my experience on the ad film set where I was working then.

Since moving to Bombay, I'd been working as a director's assistant. My job involved helping the designer source costumes, making call sheets for each shoot day, making sure the actors were on time and keeping track of a steady supply of gourmet coffee to fuel their performance. It was an ad starring the captain of the Indian cricket team, and I was asked to stand next to the camera so I could be in his eyeline while the cinematographer shot him seated on a conveyor belt, cradling leather suitcases and duffel bags like he was dangerously attracted to them. For about an hour, we were locked in a staring contest. That's the closest I've come to intimacy in Bombay.

Sometimes, the banality of it all made me want to gouge my eyes out, especially when I considered how demeaning it was to be a postgraduate in filmmaking from probably one of the best schools in Europe and still be treated like dog shit on set. But it paid the bills, and I was too tired to enjoy the luxury of self-doubts and questions like if anybody was taking a twenty-seven-year-old seriously, or if the work was supporting my real ambitions.

This was at least better than the other film set where a production manager stood disturbingly close to me every chance he got, touching and rubbing up against my thigh, butt, back, tit. I debated bringing it up with the director and ultimately refrained, realising the set needed him more than they needed me. For another film shoot outdoors, I couldn't pee for several hours, leading to a UTI that felt like I was pissing shards of glass. I could rarely discern whether I'd gotten a gig based on my talent or if somebody in the production crew was just trying to get me into bed.

But the lowest point in this dodgy trajectory was signing to co-write a film with Manu. Manu was strange—good-looking, but less since he knew it. A filmmaker in his late twenties, close to my age which was refreshing. But the charm only lasted that long; he was ultimately a Delhi boy with money, arrogance and neuroses. He had made a few films already. One about a domestic help who spies on his employer's wife cheating on him and masturbates to it, and another an indie feature about a cricketer fading into obscurity, as he tries to stay relevant through sex addiction, driving expensive sports cars and learning how to play the piano. His themes intrigued me but his narcissism masquerading as critical self-awareness annoyed me. He believed himself to be an auteur.

A producer I met on set took pity on me as I shopped my ideas around to anybody who'd listen, and put us in touch. Manu confirmed me as the co-writer for a pathetic sum of money. A didactic Virgo, he met me at a café that became our haunt for over six months of brainstorms while we cooked up the story for his next feature. I think we also became friends, but it's hard to say. Manu hardly ever revealed anything about his personal life that wasn't in service of the script. In response to his aloofness, I divulged more and more about my life, my experiences, dreams, ambitions and anecdotes, excavating from deep within my psyche to impress him and justify my credit as the co-writer.

Sometimes, we went to gigs together in bright bars in the abandoned mills of Bombay, listening to a band whose sound was between gypsy jazz and ballroom gospel, while drunk girls as young as sixteen flirted with him and asked if we were together. At times, I played out what a potential romance with him would be like and realised I wasn't attracted to him in any way except theoretically. Besides, I was just painfully lonely. I hadn't really been with anybody since Prague, or even believed I could fall in love again. Azhar felt like a distant memory, although sometimes, I checked his Instagram to see photos of him and his young daughter, now five years old, whom he seemed to be obsessed with.

Her in socks branded with the Arsenal logo in red, her in oversized sunglasses, her fiddling with a radio station, her against a poster of Biggie, her with a mohawk. I thought about whether I found the kid cute but knew I didn't; she had her mother's flat nose and Azhar's straggly hair, always a bit grimy, plastered to her temples. Maybe her sibling, if they decided to have one, could have a better shot.

I should have sensed something was amiss when Manu began printing the drafts I emailed him and marking mistakes in bright red ink, like a frustrated school teacher. But things really went south the night we ended up at a party and did a few lines together, after which he asked me to consider doing something other than writing. I don't remember reacting, but my delusions about our closeness were apparent to me. A week later, when I sent him the final draft, glad that the project was finally coming to a close, I received an unfriendly email asking me to hand over all the files because I'd been fired. It was signed 'all for the benefit of the film'. I felt rotten and humiliated and emailed him all the files without asking for my final payment, a decision I would regret as next month's rent rolled around.

That was my last attempt at writing before I received the grant.

It's been a few weeks, and the script's off to a good start. Although not significant, the initial sum of money has ensured that I can blissfully reject all advertising gigs coming my way and focus on my writing. Although, it would be much easier to do without my new flatmate—Ekam, a sitar player in training from Jalandhar.

I had initially agreed to give him the other room when my original flatmate—a quiet, unassuming girl from Shillong working in fashion—said she was moving in with her boyfriend, because I believed waking up to the sounds of sitar would be the least disruption I could get in a city like Bombay.

Ekam was tall and burly, so I assumed getting anything done around the house—throwing tarpaulin across the roof during monsoons, fixing bulbs, haggling with the pest control guy—would be easier. He could take care of domestic banalities while I prioritised my work.

I was astoundingly wrong. Ekam, despite his crisp kurtas and pensive manner, was a red-blooded, hot-headed Punjabi. He attended one class at the music school over several weeks and never graduated beyond the linear scales. I couldn't play music out loud since it interfered with his practice, and he pestered me to drink whisky with him every night. I refused, citing deadlines, but one night, after several days of being holed up in my room with nobody for company but a lone lizard, I finally caved and joined him in his room.

I'm learning a lot about Ekam tonight. He's thirty-six years old and dropped out of college since he got mixed up in local gang wars. I'd always imagined him to be younger. There was also the matter of a girl who broke his heart and drugs, he admits, his eyes glistening. His sudden vulnerability makes me extremely uncomfortable. I hope he doesn't believe we're friends because I agreed to drink with him one night.

'I had a dangerous spell with drugs too.'

He's bewildered at my admission; he assumed I was a nerdy girl with glasses and an anti-social disposition. It's not the first time I've heard such an assessment of my personality, so I don't do much to dispel this notion. Ekam gets over his initial shock and launches into a monologue. He tells me how his parents send him a lakh every month to help him sustain his lifestyle, since a musician needs to hobnob with the right people. He wants me to believe he needs to dine at expensive restaurants and attend after-parties dressed in impeccable suits. He tells me the cost of maintaining his look, which is necessary to be taken seriously as a sitarist, is upwards of fifty grand a month—his bespoke kurta-pyjamas made from Tussar silk don't come cheap.

He slurs as he refills his glass and my eyes dart to the clock on the wall in his room—it's well past midnight, and my plan is to wake up with the first light to give a final push to the draft, but I'm unsure of how to interject his ongoing soliloquy.

He tells me about how he's the oldest person in his class and feels his teacher, a Russian woman in her late thirties, is attracted to him, but he isn't keen to get caught up in any such whirlwind affairs. That he's met a young Punjabi girl who works as a medical intern at a government college and wants to make it work with her because she gets him; her mellow temperament gives him space to express himself freely. I'm not sure if he's even aware that I've been fidgeting incessantly, trying to inch my way to the door. His voice cracks mid-narrative, and for one dreaded second, I feel like he's going to cry.

'I know I'm not living the life I imagined for myself when I was younger or even what my parents wanted for me. My brother shifted to Canada years ago and is married to a real doctor who's pregnant with a boy. My parents have gone mad with pride. Back home, people look at me and think I'm this typical Punjabi man, but I definitely don't have the mentality for it. I like nicely stitched clothes and manicures. I believe in self-care Sundays.'

He studies the flaky skin on my legs and continues.

'And so should you. I'm good-looking, so I have easier access to most things, but it's not like I really belong. In this city, I'm nobody. The other musicians don't invite me to gigs. They make fun of my muscles; I know you laugh at my English too. But it doesn't matter. I have a dream of making a life worth living, and I will one day.'

Without warning he picks up his sitar and begins to play; the lone, melancholic tone bounces off the bare, white walls and mixes with the sounds of the horns and mewling cats. From the balcony, I watch the moon, the loudness of my embarrassment drowning in the new raga he plays. After a while, I leave his room and close the door behind me; he doesn't turn and keeps plucking at the strings, and I know, somewhere in my heart, that we're quite alike.

Next morning I wake up and try to write, but ordinary domesticities have me on edge. First, the coconut wallah drops in with fresh coconut juice for Ekam that I have to collect because he's passed out cold in his room from his night of indulgence. Refilling the water pump. Entertaining a teenage boy asking for donations for the local temple. The morning carries odd voices to my bedroom—intermittent drilling from upstairs, my neighbour, with whom I share a wall, gargling loudly, a lady chatting on the phone about her bikini wax gone wrong. My deadline's in a few hours, and nervous energy radiates through me.

I'd pictured a mad creative streak, unbroken by reels of teenage girls' twelve-step skincare routine, carousel posts on ten signs of intense chemistry, ads for skin patches meant to ease menstrual cramps but instead, I check Twitter and Instagram every ten minutes. The more I think about the deadline, the worse the self-doubt becomes. I obsessively reconsider every line, at the precipice of sinking into full-blown despair.

The tiniest movement in the house grates on my nerves, from Ekam putting the kettle on to his smoker's cough that's worst in the mornings. I feel my skin crawl with a thousand tiny insects, and I want to throw my laptop against the wall, draw the curtains and slide into bed, only to emerge in an alternate reality where I have nobody to impress.

I call Medha who disconnects after a few rings. I consider for a moment before I call her again. She picks it up in one go this time.

'I haven't showered in a month,' she chews her nails until a bit breaks off and spits it out with ferocity.

In the video, she looks manic, her eyes bulging and distorting from excessive caffeine and lack of sleep, I assume.

She's sheared her long and curly black hair to a buzz cut, a few inches left on top of her shiny skull, and coloured it blond. The curtains are drawn in her studio, blocking natural light. Instead, she's installed fluorescent lighting, so the room is bathed in a sickly glow like in a hospital ward. Her nails are chewed down to stubs. She paces the room, her pixelated face bobbing on the video.

I ask her if I can see some of the new work, and she lets me peek before she throws a sheet over the canvas.

Splashes of pink, orange, green and beige in a self-portrait with her blonde hair styled into a mohawk, holding a phone up like she's posing for a selfie. There's a curiously sad expression on her face; the piece is titled 'Non-Fungible Token'. I tell her it's fucking good and immediately regret it as she shrieks and asks me to stop lying to her. She asks me to check the exhibition brochure she's forwarded to my phone.

I flip through it—a French-Maharashtrian artist working with silk and acrylics exploring nature, simplicity and birth; a muralist from Baroda exploring tradition and domesticity and a Delhi artist working with oil and enamel on spirituality and organised chaos. On the last page, tucked away in a corner, is a small write-up on Medha and her collection of self-portraits through the changing seasons. I spot three typos and see they've used a low-resolution photo. I want to bring it to her notice but refrain when she waxes poetic about the Delhi artist's amorphous forms and how she's being too literal by bringing definition and figures to her work. How aspiring to Rembrandt's colours and style is too lofty an ambition.

'They could've given you more space in the brochure.'

'Sometimes, I just need your support, not your opinion.' She lights a joint and studies me, her expression unreadable.

'Okay, sorry.'

'Anyway, I have to go.'

'Wait, are you still mad—' She hangs up before I can finish. I stare at the phone and consider calling back. But, instead, fearing an argument or fight that would kill the quiet of the remaining few hours, I go back to the script as Ekam begins his sitar practice in the next room.

It's 8 p.m., and I'm twenty pages from the finishing line. I should charge ahead, power on as they say, but the walls of my room seem to be closing in on me. My stomach hurts in pangs, and I remember the article I'd read about a bad gut not just being a symptom of anxiety, but the root cause of it.

From my window, I can hear the faint sounds of distant karaoke and the muted thumping of club music mixing with televisions playing cricket. The city seems too much, too alive, and the words of my script burn into my eyes. I know I'll feel guilty if I go out for a drink, but I also know anything I write now will be garbage.

I check my Instagram and find a German-Algerian producer playing micro house at a bar. Bandra is really living up to its reputation of being the hipster neighbourhood of Bombay. I'm not sure who I can ask to come with me, but I can't imagine spending another evening listening to Ekam drone on about his ambitions, dreams and fears. So I take a quick shower, dash on some lipstick, jeans and a pair of sneakers and head out alone.

At the bar, I down vodka sodas out of plastic cups, the edges of which cut into my lips. I stand there alone like a loser, as shiny, attractive people mingle with one another. A few scatter around the DJ console and speakers and move methodically to the repetitive beats. I watch the producer mix, and then a group of young girls wave their hands in his face, squealing with excitement. Another guy, perhaps his manager or agent, gently guides them back to the dance floor, where they jerk their limbs like they're possessed. The DJ is easily in his mid-forties, balding with a dad-bod, complete with a slight paunch, and I don't understand the appeal outside of an obvious daddy kink. The music is great though.

Outside, I light a cigarette and run into a random acquaintance who's appalled I'm at a gig alone. He wonders if I'm doing okay and promises to give me company after he gets himself a drink. I thank him for his kindness, but am secretly irritated by his patronising concern, when a bony guy in glasses walks over and offers me a joint. We exchange names and share the joint as I watch a drunk couple across us engage in a hushed, furious fight. He asks me about what I do for a living. Then, with a sheepish smile, he introduces himself as Kunal. He's joined by his flatmate Mateo, a Spanish guy with a mop of brown curls, who is good-looking in an obvious manner and leans heavily into flirting with me. He's a film professor teaching at a local university.

Mateo talks about various things—his love for small batch coffee he sources from an estate in Pondicherry, a cross-country biking trip to Ladakh on his Royal Enfield, and how he studied filmmaking at a Parisian university but is deeply moved by Satyajit Ray. Judging by the look on Kunal's face, this seems to be Mateo's routine. I briefly entertain the idea of going to bed with him but can't muster the energy or attraction for it.

I leave the bar to flag an auto when Kunal stops me and asks me for my Instagram handle. I slip him my phone number instead.

In the auto ride back home, the exhaustion of the last few days washes over me, and I begin to cry. The auto-wallah peers at me through his rear-view mirror but then directs his eyes to the road. I'm thankful for his respectful discretion.

I wake up to a cryptic email from Suchitra that says we need to get on a call. I'm surprised she's read the script this soon but also flattered. I drink too much coffee and follow deep-breathing exercises on YouTube. Ekam's shrill alarm clock rings, and I'm amazed at the arrogance of somebody setting the alarm for 11 a.m. I briefly browse through one-bedroom apartments, studios, anything that'll give me the cherished space and time I need to work on my writing, only to be reminded that absolutely nothing could fit my budget in this city. I try to read a book of horror stories and think of how impossible it is for me to frighten myself in a place where I can never physically be alone while my limbs ache from a kind of permanent loneliness.

On the video call, Suchitra calls out my script for entertaining clichés, having a heteronormative lens, putting men on a pedestal and most importantly, not being Muslim enough. Where are the hijabi women whose husbands have been killed in hate crimes? Why do I insist on employing the male gaze while writing my female character? She iterates that I need to investigate my hatred for women and write something that truly makes the liberals shake with fear in their boots, that my script has to act like a manifesto for the country to wake up! Her eyes gleam with disappointment, and once again, I'm sidelined as the bad Muslim, a misfit, the opposite of a model minority, cancelled by the Right and now probably cancelled by the Left. I ask her why she gave me the grant to begin with, and she says she likes my style and the themes I touch upon, but she's expecting minority struggle at the heart of it. I'm unsure what to make of that, but I nod and agree with every accusation, convinced of my absolute and stunning lack of talent.

'I'm with you, and I'm sure you can do better, Sophia. Just remember—the struggles of those silenced should not be in vain. Salaams.'

When I wake up, a single stream of drool has hardened into a crusty white on my grey bedsheet, and the calm of the early morning sky is disturbed by LED street lamps and the occasional mewl. My head teems with a thousand thoughts; the grief from last night, briefly alleviated by sleep, comes back in full force.

What is the role of the artist I'm meant to play here? Grants are as reliant on market forces as any other corporate job. Did I con myself into believing that being in India and working on my art made more sense than being an outsider overseas? Is my feminism broken? I don't have access to guaranteed trust funds with quarterly payouts, like some of my friends working on their books or films. My foreign degree alienates me from my peers here, with their FTII education and salt-of-the-earth films. I'm not quite hip or immigrant enough for the diaspora either. I have no other skills except putting pen to paper and being ironically detached from everything, which is probably less of a sexy artistic disposition and more a symptom of low-grade depression. There are no answers to be found anywhere; not in cinema or literature or meditation or YouTube astrology videos, and now I have the agonising task of rewriting the script in a way that could appeal to the sensibilities of a woman called Suchitra Iyer, who thinks saying 'salaams' at the end of every sentence is what makes her truly liberal.

The sun begins to creep in through my bedroom window with a gentle pink. On the sidewalk below, I notice a silver-haired lady arranging fresh bombil in zig-zag patterns on a blue plastic sheet while a cat sniffs around her with a keen nose. Behind her is a gutter filled with discarded packets of chips, medicines, trash, rotten fruit and leaves. I feel dizzy, so I lie down again—no romance or accolades can pull me out of this despair, thick and sticky like honey that hurts my teeth and makes me wish I'd learnt how to pray as a kid.

I dream of my tenth-grade history teacher, with her immaculate saris and thick plaits, slashing large chunks of my essay in bold red with remarks like, *indecipherable handwriting, appalling explanation, if you carry on like this, you'll be condemned to mediocrity for the rest of your life.* In the dream, I walk around a dark maze with thick, prickly shrubs that seem to be breathing and tall trees that block my view of the sky. I try to find my way out, but when I reach the exit, it's another dead end. A shadow appears in front of me, and I begin to sprint, convinced I'm being followed. I run across the ground, which first turns muddy, then slushy, and I slip and fall face down. I know crying would make me feel better, but there seem to be splinters lodged in my throat and the darkness of the night fades into the brightness of my bedroom, when I open my eyes and place a hand on my head, checking for fever. My body is warm, and my pulse is erratic. I turn to the bedside table to grab a glass of water, but an invisible weight seems to be compressing my movements. I check my phone, and there's a message from Kunal. He wants to know if I'd like to meet sometime.

*I'm really sick. Unable to get out of bed. Come over? Bring coffee.*

I wait for his reply with my eyes half-closed, not expecting much. I need to hydrate and eat. I'm not sure when I fall asleep again.

I wake up to the harsh sound of the doorbell, feeling disoriented. For a moment, I wonder if I'm back in my childhood home. I can hear the familiar sounds of Dad shaving and Ma setting the breakfast table in the distance—the bustle and warmth of a family home I haven't experienced in a decade feels within reach but is an illusion. I drag myself to the front door, my body drenched in sweat, now that the fever has momentarily broken. I get a whiff of a faint scent of sleep and sickness from me. Kunal leans against the wall, his bright eyes hidden behind glasses, holding a cup of coffee and a brown paper bag. I leave the door ajar and return to bed while he comes in, takes his place at my desk and breaks the sandwich into bite-sized pieces.

---

The fever lasts for ten days. Kunal insists I go to the doctor, but I don't have the energy or the inclination to pump my body with antibiotics. I know how my body responds to rejection, and it's just a matter of time before the experience will wash over me and become a memory I no longer have to cling to. But until then, he visits me for a few hours every day, supplying me with Crocin, sandwiches, fruits, fresh juices, multivitamins. On the eleventh day, I can sit up again, so I immediately go back to the script, and with a loose grip on reality, rewrite it top to bottom. I tell myself these are the changes I want and need to make, and it's nothing to do with Suchitra's feedback. I take apart the characters, the structure and try and infuse some diversity and experiences which aren't from a privileged lens. I read newspaper articles of hate crimes, lynchings, Muslim men hacked up and dismembered for simply falling in love with Hindu women, elderly men beaten up on the mere suspicion of transporting beef, young girls stalked and threatened. While I write, Kunal becomes an inseparable part of my space and routine.

At night, my chest feels tight; my mind and body are torn between constantly wanting to be alone and being around Kunal. I try to learn how to not take my moods and emotions so seriously. I understand how deceptive their nature can be. I am acutely aware of man's self-serving nature as I witness my own self-serving nature. I am acutely aware of my hunger for love, for its declaration as some sort of a contract, for somebody to tell me they'll stay, except somebody did promise and didn't. Stories seem to serve no purpose.

Everything seems excessive and bloodless. I want to burn my to-do lists. What have my to-do lists achieved except for a heightened state of anxiety? I want to nap, go for a run, drink coffee, switch to Diet Coke and cuddle and hold Kunal's hands in quiet alleyways.

I wake up early mornings, my limbs still burning from a fever that refuses to dissipate. The usually busy streets of Bandra are quiet during these hours; I can hear the sweep of a broom and the loud cawing of inky black crows. The sky has never been bluer or clearer; the trees are like furious strokes of green against the sky, and a bright sun filters down the empty roads and into my bedroom. In moments of fever-fuelled panic, I reach out to Azhar, searching for answers to existential questions but secretly yearning for answers about our relationship. He entertains and accommodates me, and there's a resurgence of that old feeling that perhaps I'm not over him.

I hate my instinct to seek comfort wherever, anywhere.

Medha finally calls me and apologises for not being in touch. I want to tell her about the script, Suchitra's disappointment, the fever, how I think I'm falling in love with Kunal, but suspect it's undying gratitude for his relaxed presence and wry jokes. But I stay quiet. A part of me wants to punish her for being absent, and another part of me misses her and the ease of our hangs.

She tells me about Julia, the girl she started seeing a few weeks ago and yet it feels like they've known each other for longer. How Julia is nothing like the girls she's dated before and understands the abstractions of her art, despite working with the Embassy. She tells me how Julia cares about climate justice, has real friends whom she meets for dinner parties in cosy living rooms, instead of stumbling her way blind-drunk into some South Delhi party while downplaying her queerness to make others feel comfortable. How refreshing it is to be with somebody who is a real adult, who goes to bed and wakes up at the same time every day, who dabbles in the stock market. Plus, the sex is gorgeous.

'So, you're drowning yourself in basic comforts?'

Medha is so giddy with love that she doesn't even perceive this as an insult. She tells me how her exhibition finally has a title—*The Self, Undone*—and Julia loves it. I stifle a mean laugh. I don't know why I act this way. She tells me I should watch the live stream of her exhibition on YouTube.

'And you have got to stop dating straight women thinking you can love them into being gay.'

'That's the most offensive thing you've ever said to me. Actually, no, second most offensive. The most offensive thing you've said to me is how you wish you were gay like it's a hot TikTok trend.'

I'm not sure if she's joking because surely, I've said worse things to her, but she hangs up soon after, asking me to not take it out on her if I'm having a bad day.

It seemed like everyone was capable of love except me. Or that the love was there to be had but as hard as I tried, I couldn't feel it; much like I was standing under a waterfall wearing a wetsuit. I'm furious at myself for wanting her attention but partly pleased that she is, now, at least half as rattled as I am.

Does this need to provoke stem from Ma? To pinch at insecurities to elicit a reaction. To withdraw because the attention felt solicited and not unconditional. I have vague memories of her silent treatment, sticky and palpable like sweat on a sweltering hot day, permeating through the house when my father stayed out late, entertaining sketchy clients or maybe meeting other women. Who knows at this point? On these particularly leaden days, the rotis she made were burnt, the dal tasteless and the sabzi lacked any salt. I had worries of my own and would waste hours on MSN chat, on the newly acquired computer in my room, sulking over how I'd not been invited to any of the bowling sessions the other kids in school were getting together every weekend for. The heaviness of Ma's breath, floating in from the room next door, poisoned the air but what could I do? I had no idea how to help her. I still don't.

I finish the last scene of the script and go for an early morning run, passing my neighbourhood chemist uncle with his cheery smile, a litter of tiny puppies growing bigger by the day, the toothless woman begging at the main intersection, a shop that sells fresh flowers not yet open for business, a skinny dog sniffing around a restaurant, the shutters of which are up halfway. My calves ache as I pick up the pace. Sweat runs down my spine. I pause to let a wailing ambulance cross and collapse at the entrance of a small park hidden behind some dilapidated buildings.

Inside the park, an older woman, dressed in a yellow paisley dress, kneels in front of a makeshift altar at the mouth of a small chapel. Her hands are clasped together, and her head is bowed in intense prayer.

Back home, I throw pasta together in the cramped kitchen, the fumes from the sauce settling into my hair and make it frizz. I'd open the window, but a pesky rat wreaking havoc in the building found its way inside once. As I slather the pasta with extra butter I've earned after my run, I think of how, after the abortion, I was acutely depressed for the first time in my life. I'm not quite sure how it came about so suddenly, so surely. I couldn't get out of bed for days; I spent my time under the covers, face turned away from the window, any inkling of the sun irritating me and sleep sitting on my eyes like stones. Back then, Nihal introduced me to a Hungarian neuroscientist on YouTube who broke down depression scientifically—in a way that was easy for my sluggish brain to digest.

In a post-industrial society, environmental stressors range from being honked at to a colleague's passive-aggressive email to spending too much time on screens. The body goes into fight or flight mode and produces excessive cortisol. The same response it had historically to genuine threats like blood-hungry predators when we operated as hunters and gatherers. Years and years of functioning in a hyper-capitalist society, trying to make a living out of being some kind of artist in the twenty-first century and the almost comical delusion of that endeavour, the glass ceilings, heartbreaks, religious divides, cultural differences and immigrant woes—I can feel all the cortisol in my body.

As the tomatoes stew, I wait for Sonia, who's shifted to a small town in Tuscany with her husband, to take my call. I could make friends in Bombay, but everybody here irritates me to varying degrees. My options are the posh Bandra crowd who still live with their parents to avoid paying Bombay rents, attend techno gigs on weekends, speak solely about summers in London like it was a taxi ride away and show up at parties with an 'expat of the month' on their arm. Or, the film crowd—deep, dark circles under their eyes that scream hustle culture, the neurosis from a combination of sleep deprivation and cocaine. FaceTime calls offer some version of intimacy, especially when getting a drink with someone in silence, without the pressure of performance, remains a distant reality.

Sonia's been selling handicraft dreamcatchers, jewellery with precious and semi-precious stones from India and yoga mats with designs commissioned from Adivasi artists in local stores around Prato and online. I scroll through her work as I eat and notice how uninspired the crafts are while she tells me they sell for seventy euros a piece. She tells me about how she and her husband got robbed a few weeks after they moved into their new home in Prato. She thinks it was a crime of vindication since she found her expensive lingerie cut up and in tatters. She reminds me that she doesn't set too much store by material things, but they're starting their life with meagre means, and her plans for the future seem to have turned on their head. Unsure of what that means or what I can say to it, I stay silent. I can always blame it on the internet lag if she asks. She says she loves how happy I am and that my eyes are shining. I wonder if the familiarity is manufactured or if she does know me well.

In an auto-rickshaw ride, I feel a deepening silence between Kunal and me and the suggestion of an imminent kiss. It makes perfect sense, but instead, I point to the full moon, so clear and throbbing with a dull, orange glow. Instead of holding each other, we stop at a fast-food joint and pick up fried chicken. We never really talk about officially dating but choose to navigate the various accoutrements of the new relationship with mellow ease and distinct demarcations between 'his' and 'mine'.

I'm often amazed by how much he cares. An upper caste Hindu boy born into the one per cent of wealthy Indians with unrestricted access to various continents, jobs, visas and opportunities; why should he particularly care about my retrograde career, fuelled by an insane need to prove something? Even my dysfunctions are getting less cute with age.

The email arrives with cold-blooded indifference in my inbox.

*After much deliberation, we've come to the difficult but necessary conclusion that we would not be able to proceed with the project (feature length script) 'End Times' as part of the Grant anymore. We respect the time and effort you've invested in the project but unfortunately the decision to discontinue this partnership is in the best interest of the larger focus and mission of the Grant. Please refer to clause 4.1 as per the contract attached.*

*Ravi (marked on this mail) will be able to help you with formalities.*

*Wishing you the best,*
*Suchitra*

I break into a cold sweat, feeling increasingly uneasy. I pick at a stubborn cuticle until fresh blood springs from the side of my nail. I have a manic urge to smash everything in the room, but I sit still and take five. I see my chewed up nails, the overdue electricity bill on the corner of my desk, the email glowing on the laptop screen. I wipe my sweaty palms on my thighs, feel the shape of my hip-bones against the cold wood of the chair, look at the pen-stand that was a gift from Kunal and briefly picture his clavicle where I rest my head often. I hear the neighbour frying something in the adjacent house, the call of the scrap dealer and my phone vibrating.

It's Dad. He asks me if I need money. I remember the time in college, when I mentioned my wisdom tooth removal to him. Against instinct and habit, I told him I was scared, and he asked me if I needed money. On the one hand, I despise his neoliberal need to believe that money can fix any problem, plug any unpleasant emotion that wells up like sediment from a blocked kitchen pipe. But, on the other hand, I understand why he's unable to tell me that he loves me, that I'll be okay and that it's okay to be scared. It's because he's unable to tell himself these things too.

He tells me he doesn't like my Instagram selfie and says I look sad. What does he know about being sad when he hasn't had his heart broken for several years, lives in a well-lit apartment with its own terrace garden and a heated community pool and eats grilled salmon for lunch?

'Only a boomer can be happy in the year of #metoo and that fake godman being elected chief minister of the state you grew up in.' I'm venomous about his Deepak-Chopra-like positivity.

'Beta, you're so grim. You sure you don't need money?'

I tell him I have to get on a work call and go for a run. When I can't spot the litter of puppies at the end of the road, I'm racked by an overwhelming grief.

Kunal's put me through to one of his childhood friends, a lawyer who once advised a famous screenwriter for an intellectual property altercation. The lawyer cuts my call and asks me to send him all my correspondence with Suchitra and the grant contract.

*by when do you think you can get back to me? kind of freaking out.*

My text hangs in a silent limbo, and I don't feel like talking to anybody, including Kunal. I Google local tarot card readers in my neighbourhood. Medha went to one when she deliberated coming out to her parents, and the tarot reader predicted an auspicious time for it. I didn't think it was necessary; even though Medha had helicopter parents, I couldn't imagine them balking at the idea of a gay daughter. If anything, they'd embrace the fact with open arms, if for nothing other than to prove how progressive they were.

I find a tarot reader—my neighbourhood has more spiritualists and self-styled shamans than general physicians—and hail an auto to get to hers. In the auto, I fruitlessly attempt to block the waves of nausea washing over me, which I assume are either tears or bile fighting its way to the surface.

The tarot reader, an ordinary-looking woman with greying hair and greyer eyes in a blue denim shirt, wearing bracelets fitted with topaz stones, tells me my Saturn return is beginning soon, and I can expect to relive traumas, both from this and the past life, during this cycle. She says I'm set to learn unforgettable lessons through this period that will carry me through the toughest times, eliminate the toxic and make space for the new. She sees the desperation in my eyes and how I hang on to her every word. She asks me to work on my relationship with my father and not judge my mother. I'm not sure how to tell her that my conversations with them are limited to superficialities of *did you have lunch? How's your sugar? How's the weather?* When what I really mean to say is *I miss you. I wish you could understand me better. I wish I could stop blaming you for everything that's gone wrong.* She looks at me, her eyes brimming with pity, and I study the various figurines of gods behind her: Mother Mary with a halo made of golden wire, her eyes wide open, an expression of peace and pain co-existing on her face, Buddha in patchy green stone—onyx or perhaps jade?—sitting in meditative repose, Lakshmi Devi in brass and a golden Arowana fish, its little mouth agape. She tells me I need to tap into my femininity and let the principles of adaptability, intuition and positivity guide me. Then she asks me to pay her three thousand rupees.

I walk out of her sandalwood-scented office and stand by the side of the road where a young child, his feet bare and dusty, springs to me with his hands outstretched and taps my thigh, indicating that I give him money or food. We look into each other's eyes, and for a moment, I think of the crushing futility of everything.

'Why would you sign this contract?'

The lawyer finally calls me and speaks hurriedly, like this is a major inconvenience in his day full of pending deals where he could be making millions. It probably is.

'It's not a grant contract; it's a commercial one. It clearly says the work belongs to them once the assignment period begins. I'm not sure what you want to do about it. You could go to court, but do you really have the money? Chalk this up to a teachable moment and move on.'

I haven't moved from my bed in about eight hours. Kunal sends me a series of texts—*what did the lawyer say? you okay?* A meme from the account @mememasturbation. *plans tonight?* To cry myself to sleep. Smoke abundant hash. Dodge everybody's calls. Sink further into this self-imposed exile. Try and find ethical porn I could masturbate to, only to realise I have to pay for it and then end up logging on to Pornhub, despite knowing their dubious history in publishing revenge porn without consent. *probably staying in,* I text blankly. *its new year's eve,* his message says and before I can reply he's calling me. I slide further into my blanket, away from the phone that vibrates threateningly in a corner, its glow illuminating my dry skin and the hollows under my eyes. He sends me a sad selfie, and his quirks that usually make me laugh only succeed in annoying me today. I roll a joint and smoke it supine.

Ekam knocks on the door, says he's heading out to some expat party and asks if I want to join him. I'm in the mood for something strange and fucked up, so I agree, wear all black like I'm heading to a funeral, and leave with him.

The neighbourhood is still dressed in Christmas lights, and there's a maddening crowd on the roads. Men in tropical shirts and expensive sneakers, probably Yeezys or Adidas, with gelled hair and eyes bright with early evening drugs, accompanied by women in short, sequinned dresses and high heels, totter on the potholed roads.

Young men, migrants from Himachal, Bihar, UP, Assam, stand outside bars in ironed shirts and trousers branded with logos of restaurants or bars, and hand out pamphlets: *Free drinks for ladies, Buy 1, get 1 one free. Special 31st dinner menu complete with starters and dessert.*

There's manic energy in the air with people desperate and determined to have fun, to purge the previous year's mistakes and other bullshit by drowning themselves in substances designed to help them forget.

We leave the main street and walk down a darker, narrower road. A large water tanker stands obscuring a men's loo. On the other side of the road, a young boy, about sixteen or seventeen, in a kurta and jeans, straddles a scooter. As I cross the tanker, I glimpse a man getting head by a woman on her knees while he grips her by her hair. I immediately look away, excited at having witnessed it and ashamed about encroaching on something private. I quicken my steps. I wonder if it's some sort of exhibitionism, but nothing about the scene feels sexy; I know the young boy is next in line.

We finally arrive at the house, a run-down Portuguese villa worn down by time and rain, with untamed foliage enveloping it. I don't know what party Ekam plans to attend in this property that looks abandoned, but as we climb up the tapering staircase, getting smaller with each step, I can hear faint music ensuing from a floor I don't see yet.

The staircase opens to a terrace with a smattering of white people, their smiling faces and glasses of wine illuminated with twinkling fairy lights and the bright glow of the full moon. Ekam squeezes my arm, gives me a wink and blends into the crowd. A tall, bald guy with pupils like coins, clutching a bottle of beer, nods at me. I make a beeline for the bar and ask for neat vodka with ice. The dissonance of being one of the few brown people in the room takes me back to the memory of underground clubs in Prague where everyone looked vaguely threatening. I feel like I could disappear from the face of the Earth, and nobody would notice. There is nothing else to do except get blind drunk.

I make some forgettable conversation with a rotating tribe of people about social impact, the business of precious stones in Jaipur, music festivals in Belgrade, the ease with which we can get imported cheese in the neighbourhood, restoration projects in Orissa, listening rooms in Costa Rica, beverage bars in Bali and other various things. I talk a lot of shit, content in the knowledge that I'll never have to meet these people again, while getting increasingly wasted. A girl offers me cocaine from a vial around her neck, and I hesitate before I refuse. Mischa, a young Russian entrepreneur, is the host of this transatlantic party that feels like it could happen anywhere in the world but in a quaint neighbourhood of Bombay. Through a smattering of chats, I learn that she runs her own fitness studio for Bollywood celebrities and the uber-rich, where she teaches pilates, animal flow and something called 'inclusive fitness'.

It's difficult to talk about inclusivity in a room full of tall, thin, white people, who're mostly straight and blonde, so I sneak to a corner, hidden from view, to smoke a cigarette, where I run into the bald guy from before who tells me they're about to begin the ceremony. The music changes from ambient techno to gongs, what sounds like whales and chanting. Most people sit on jute mats around Mischa, who pours hot water into a ceramic gaiwan. Ekam breathes deeply, his eyes closed, while wisps of steam emerge from the teacups as she pours boiling water into them. Ayahuasca ceremony? In the middle of Bombay?

The guy tugs at my hand, and I sit beside him. The cup passes to me, and I sneak a peek. There's a little brown mushroom with a tender, white stem at the bottom. I've never done psychedelics before, but a blanket of calm seems to have descended upon the crowd and under the cloudless night with the thick, polluted air and about five minutes away from midnight, hankering to conclude this dumpster fire of a year, I take the first sip of the tea.

In about twenty minutes, the lights begin to twinkle as the crowd disintegrates to different corners of the terrace. To one side, Mischa and Ekam snuggle under a blanket. The bald guy squeezes my hand as if to say, *you're good.* And, I am good. I feel great. For the first time, I make an effort, I smile for no reason. The railings of the terrace seem to be melting into the ground. I have an urge to look over, and as I do, I feel a wave of nausea, so I crumple, clutching my stomach. My companion strokes my back, and I'm thankful for his kind, reassuring presence. My face is twisted in agony but what I really feel is an intense pleasure that seems to be devouring my senses. The music distorts and becomes clearer, like I'm at a live orchestra underwater, with musicians playing solely for me and beautiful humpback whales gliding through turquoise water, their complex pulsed calls travelling through the ocean in varying symphonies. The sound carries me to the surface with a pink sunset. The sky breaks into a rainbow of colours, and I lean into a fern next to me; I can see its leaves opening and closing, like deep breaths, like it's communicating with me in a language only I'm meant to understand. I lie on my side, bring my knees to my chest and close my eyes. Stars dance in front of them, and I feel exalted in their presence. Consumed by their brilliance. Marked and defined by their lightness.

I walk back alone from the party, the roads are empty save some men huddled together on pavements around a small fire burning. Time has stretched and distorted. The Bombay air has an unusually sharp chill, and I can walk easily with fewer cars on the road. The coconut trees sway in the distance with the coastal air, and the scent of temple incense sticks mixes with the smell of overripe fruits and a flowering tree. For a moment, it's all painfully beautiful. As I come up, the street lights warp and form geometric patterns; a woman in the corner, setting out her newspaper and blanket to sleep on, turns into a corpse with a glittering tiara, and I blink my eyes furiously to dispel the image. I cross a children's park with a seesaw painted bright yellow, and monkey bars painted the red of a pomegranate. I have the sudden urge to climb them, but I resist and continue walking home.

I don't remember passing out but when I wake up, Kunal's at the door.

'You texted me.' He doesn't wait for my answer and heads to the kitchen. I stare at the ceiling where the peeling paint makes amorphous patterns.

He comes in with a glass of orange juice and a plate with soft eggs on toast. As the drug wears off, I feel like a young child, full of wonder and innocence, like nothing terrible has happened to me yet, and it's easy for me to cave into his arms. My instincts seem to have boiled down to primal ones—cleaning myself, cutting my nails, prepping lunch. Sex has taken on a new dimension, as has language. Language has been reduced to its crudest, or perhaps most effective, proportions. Soft kisses, moans meant to attract attention and warmth, my truest disposition coming to its fore. Hand holding, languid lovemaking, nothing over the top, nothing flashy, just basic, utilitarian and somehow, entirely complete. I feel no desire to mull or wallow in my own despair. I'm just holding on to things that carry any meaning at all. I don't particularly care about tomorrow.

'I've met a lot of artists, but nobody as dedicated as you. You make things happen. It's okay to be sad.' Kunal's eyes hold me with a steady stare, like a helpless baby or a needy kitten.

We're in the first flush of love so I understand why he puts me on a pedestal. I'm not sure how to tell him that the drive he sees—setting goals, making to-do lists, downloading apps for productivity, earning cash, spending it, buying things, rejecting the culture of buying things, wasting hours on social media, setting time limits on my phone apps—is just a farce. A way to not sink into the darkness. That, since the abortion, everything's shifted. I feel too much, and yet I am consistently disconnected. It's easy to say it can be traced back to my family. The harder truth to accept is the trauma of unfulfilled relationships, weeks of unhappiness, years of performance and pandering. That when good things happen, I'm pulled to the darkness. That I am essentially boring. If I'm left to my devices for long enough, I will languish, wallow and then self-destruct.

Kunal leaves after a few days. I notice his toothbrush with frayed bristles in my washroom. I step into Ekam's balcony for a cigarette. I haven't seen him since the night of the party. I check his door to find it unlocked. I walk in, only slightly ashamed, and find the room in complete disarray. The King Koil mattress is without a bedsheet, tufts of foam poking out in places where the cloth has frayed and torn and polythene and paper bags lie scattered across the floor. I flip the light switch, but he's taken the bulbs. I walk around the room, kicking the plastic bags to one corner; they come flying right back. I find an empty baggie, presumably for cocaine, near the foot of the bed and a used condom, which I drop in horror. The cupboard is bare, and his luggage is gone.

I pick up the phone to call him, change my mind and go back to the balcony to finish my cigarette. I'm hesitant to call Medha, but my inhibitions are lower after the trip. As she picks up, I realise I haven't asked about her exhibition nor watched its live stream. I infuse my voice with cheeriness, and she cuts me short.

'Stop pretending like you care. The exhibit bombed. Everyone hated it. They all thought it was too self-involved.'

'But your work is about narcissism.'

'No, it isn't. You'd know if you'd been listening.'

'I do listen—' I argue, half-interested.

'No, you don't.' Her voice gets really small and quiet, like she's speaking to me from another planet. 'You never listen. In fact, you've been a pretty shit friend for a while now. You even missed the live stream. What's the excuse this time? Another boy? A bender? Some shit at work? I have a life too, you know. I've got my own problems. You using me as your punching bag is the last thing I need right now. I've got things I want to do; my first exhibition was a total wreck to the point where I'm probably a pariah in this self-congratulatory South Delhi circle jerk, I've got bills to pay—'

'No, you don't. You live in your grandfather's house.' I hate myself as I say it, but I can't stop.

Stone cold silence on the other end of the line, followed by muffled sobs and then frantic scratching, like she was trying to rub the day off her face. A moment after, the line goes blank, leaving a dead silence behind it. At least, telephones had the courtesy of beeping to drive the point home, unlike cellphones: *You've been hung up on. Reduced to a mass of humiliation.*

'I'm sorry about missing your exhibition,' I say, to nobody in particular.

# 6

# SPITI

NEITHER OF US PAYS MUCH ATTENTION when the jeep first jerks to a stop. The high desert mountains tower in the glaring sun, brighter than the flash of torchlight in a dark forest, brighter than anything I've seen in my life. Sparse vegetation dots their surface, and orange sea buckthorn peeks from behind rocky formations. The dirt road undulates before us, gravel crunching under the wheel, dust settling on the jeep's windshield.

Medha and I've been taking turns driving the Jeep her uncle had left for us at the Shimla airport. but she didn't trust me to drive after the two beers I had for lunch at a café on our way to Kaza. So after a brief argument about whose playlist was going to play on the road, we fall into a surly silence, her brows furrowed behind rectangular sunglasses that accentuate her sharp jawline, her blonde cropped hair a glittering halo. Not that I need my music to play, but I have nothing to do for long periods except look at rocks and hills untouched by civilisation, enclosed by a steel grey river snaking through the ravine, so guttural and loud that only the engine's roar can block it out.

The car itself, a dinged-up Jeep, groans as it makes its way through the steep curves of the uneven, barely-there dirt road. We stopped using the air conditioning once we crossed Mandi, a low-lying district in Himachal, mostly because the toxins cleared from the air, leaving nothing but dust particles. The air is cold, sharp and precise, like a tall glass of beer after a long day. Several taxis cross us, helmed by skinny men in sunglasses, rudraksha bracelets hanging from their wrists. Their sinewy muscles twist and flex as they race through the highway before it peters out into the single dirt lane that makes overtaking impossible. She drives with one hand and smokes a joint with the other.

The trip, although peppered with unnecessary bickering and stubborn silences, takes on an easy quality as some drum and bass plays on the stereo, taking us back to our days in college. We relax. She jokes about getting older, about getting accustomed to how life never stops spewing shit at you. At least we have each other to be grateful for, we laugh. We bitch about Ekam and how he hasn't returned the apartment keys or collected the car he left parked in my building's driveway. How he hasn't been responding to my texts, and I have no idea what I should do next. She tells me about her recent fights with her dad. How his ugly ego reared when she talked about her future as an artist, how a bombed exhibition didn't mean no gallery would want her, how she was young and there was hope.

Is there really hope, or are we just destined to have our labour exploited while making others money? Our entire generation is dealing with a rapidly disorienting loss of identity and self-belief through the fast-evolving features of social media. Mental breakdowns are now being referred to as 'mentie bs' on Instagram. It's commonplace to share trauma and make jokes about it. 2017 has been India's sixth hottest year on record. Since there is a time and place for everything, I don't express any of my accelerating concerns. Instead, I am happy to take whatever moments of peace we can muster.

Netting covers the massive cliffs to keep the soil, debris and loose rocks from rolling downwards and crashing into cars, causing inevitable, horrible accidents. When the Jeep jerks to a stop, angry rap with a heavy baseline emanates from our car. Although the song has now stopped, I imagine the lyrics about death, life in Queens, chest-thumping about money and fast cars, wafting in through the windows of the few houses that freckle the landscape.

We look around, trying to gauge where we are. We haven't crossed a single village for a few kilometres. While I'm sure we've missed the turn to the village we're meant to spend the night in, Medha is in a kind of spiky denial.

'We should've stayed back at Tabo.'

'How does *that* help anybody?'

'I'm just saying. You have to stop being so defensive about everything I say.' I light a cigarette.

'You're making it sound like it's my fault.'

Well, I wasn't *making* it sound like that. I'd been happy to stay another night in Tabo, but she had an itinerary planned down to the tiniest, most insignificant detail, and any deviation from the plan was a crime akin to murder. I've always sensed a certain obsessive need for control in her. When we used to stay over at each other's, she'd remake my bed every morning after I'd made it, tucking the bedsheet under the mattress and smoothening out any final kinks on the taut bedspread. When I travelled, she would insist on packing my suitcase, dividing my clothes, socks, underwear and make-up brushes into precise piles and encasing them in the identical travel bags she bought on Amazon. She would then place the bags into the suitcase with the focus and dexterity of someone playing Jenga; my things trapped in neat gridlocks. The packing was neat, almost sacred. Quite often, she took it too far. Once, I remember, we were lying on her bed in a lazy haze of pot. The lit end of my joint burnt the edge of her bedsheet before I could realise. She locked herself in the bathroom and burst into tears, calling me out for not respecting her things, wailing about how her ex-girlfriend had bought it for her from Zara Home and how India didn't even have Zara Home. I had to stifle my laughter, but luckily, her door was shut, so she couldn't see me.

'It's okay if we don't make it to every village we mapped out.' I know nothing about the Jeep, so I'm not sure how I can be of any help to her, but the least I can do is ease her anxiety. But apparently I have said the wrong thing.

'I don't think we'll make it to *any* villages now, so you can be happy.'

'Why would I be happy about that?' I ask, incredulous.

She ignores me and grumpily pulls out a map tucked into the back pocket of her jeans. I'm not sure why she thinks she's Lara Croft, but something about her 'let's get down and dirty' attitude softens the simmering resentment I've been feeling towards her since the car broke down. She pops the hood open and checks the reservoir before pouring some coolant.

'That was our last bottle of water,' I grab the bottle from her.

'Somebody will come soon.'

'How many cars have crossed us in the last hour?'

She pretends to not hear me and walks back to the driver's seat. She starts the ignition, and it snarls for a second before dying down with a whine. I walk to the edge of the road, barely hemmed in by a broken divider painted yellow, and watch the river gush below. For a moment, I imagine what it would feel like to dive headlong, where the current might take me, whether the river is deep or fast and how many rocks are dotting its bed. When I look up, the mouth of a cavernous mountain gapes at me. I look around; nothing for miles except an endless stretch of dirt road glittering like a tiara in the harsh mountain light. I know there's no point checking my phone, it died a while ago, but when I look at the sun, I know we have about two hours left before dusk. Driving through these roads once the light goes out is nothing less than a suicide mission; I haven't seen a single street light since we entered the valley. A gritty wind collects around us, and Medha lifts her t-shirt to wipe her eyes.

As I walk back to the jeep, I notice drops of dark liquid staining the path, tiny droplets leading like breadcrumbs to the belly of the car. I'm not excited about dirtying my pants, since I'm not too sure when I'll get to have my next shower, but I squat nonetheless and slide under.

Long, metallic pipes, beige from the dirt, stare back at me and an overwhelming stench of fuel wafts up my nostrils and clings to my throat. I cover my nose with the thick shawl that was once Ma's and poke around until I find the crack in the fuel tank. I slide back out and see Medha's face, her eyes narrowed in suspicion and disbelief that irritates me more than being stuck at the edge of the Earth.

'I think the fuel tank's bust.'

Medha lets out a muffled scream that sounds like it's coming from a distant, ancient land and kicks the tyre hard with the toe of her dirty hiking boots. Groaning, she hobbles to the boot of the car and emerges with a packet of chips. Ripping it open with ferocity, she stuffs some in her mouth, chewing methodically, her eyes looking out into the distance. She hands me the packet, rolls up her jeans and walks away from the car, down the road soon obscured by the next hill.

'What the fuck?' I yell.

'I'm walking to Kaza.'

'It's at least another twenty-five kilometres. You want me to stay here alone?'

'You have a better plan?'

I safely assume that to be a rhetorical question. I try to recall at what point in the road trip matters began to go south. Things were strained between us, to say the least, especially since we hadn't really addressed our last few skirmishes. But I guess I refused to pay much attention to the unsaid things since we didn't really get to see each other that often.

Defeated, Medha perches on a rock and scans the empty road. I settle back into the car. Medha had created a detailed visual mood board of the trip, including the itinerary planned down to the last minute and a Google map legend with the several marked pitstops. She had purchased new hiking shoes, packed a medicine bag containing antibacterial gel, a strip of ibuprofen, lozenges, anti-nausea medication, a tin of Altoids, several tampons and a fat bud. The bitterness between us had dulled like a faded stain as we planned this trip, exchanging frantic plans in voice notes leading up to the day we left Delhi. I got a series of texts from her on what woollens to pack, where to buy cheap thermals, how many pairs of underwear to carry, what hiking books to purchase and how barefoot hiking boots are superior to mountaineering ones. I had only brought the one trusted pair of Nikes I owned, leaving the rest to Fate.

I'm pretty sure I have some rolling papers lying around; what else was there to do except get high? We were probably going to die out here, either from starvation, dehydration or an unexpected landslide, crushing the jeep and us in the process. Finally, sweet salvation from the utter futility of being alive, at last one with the Earth again. I don't think either of us could've imagined this was how things would end, but the warning signs had been flashing for a while now.

I should have read the writing on the wall at the second homestay we'd checked into. It was in an isolated village, and the rooms didn't have hot running water or heating. April in the valley was still harsh, hovering between five to ten degrees and plunging into the negatives at night. After we ate hot rotis with watery gruel, we'd made our way through several glasses of whisky to keep us warm through the night, concentrating hard on making sure our bodies weren't touching as we lay beside one another on the hard bed, a strong gush of wind surging through the gaps in the roof, halving the leaden silence into two. Every creak of the wood board signalled a primeval spirit or an earthquake; either way, we were frozen, our bodies hardening and the cold seeping into our limbs, turning them into the tundra aching for a warm touch of the sun.

As I smoke the joint, I think of how Medha's penchant for novelty often obscured her ability to see things through. She was the kind of person who believed owning the right gear was half the battle won when attempting something for the first time. For a successful meeting, she had to wear a fancy watch and crisply ironed clothes; it was imperative to smell nice. She'd wear gobs of highlighter across her high cheekbones to gain entry into some club. She'd look as perfect as one of those Kardashian filters on Instagram, which evens out all the texture from your skin and elongates your nose while sharpening your jawline. She was a magician with make-up brushes, and while I envied her skills, I also wondered how healthy her self-image was. While she did operate based on a stringent set of rules, adapting to crisis wasn't her strong suit.

A beat-up Maruti van turns the corner and makes its way to us, jolting and bouncing off the gravel. Its engine emits a steady, terrifying hiss and a man in a white wifebeater with a grey bandana wrapped around his head stares at us with hazel eyes as he crosses us and then rolls to a stop ahead.

The backseat of his car is loaded with numerous unmarked cardboard boxes held together with sticky brown tape. He gives us the universal look of *do you need help.* Medha signals that he carry on but I notice the deepening shadows across the rocks. I explain the situation to him in my average Hindi and ignore his eyes darting to my chest every few seconds. He tells me there's a mechanic in the nearest village a few kilometres away, and he can drive one of us there.

'I'll go, you wait here,' I say, turning to Medha.

'No, *you* wait. I'll go.'

'Let me go, you know more about the car; you should stay with it.'

'Exactly why I should be the one to talk to the mechanic.'

She grabs the shawl off my neck, wraps it around her, concealing her bare midriff from his probing eyes, and slips into the passenger seat. She faces ahead but I can picture the look of determination behind her sunglasses, and for a moment, I'm stricken with panic.

'What's in these boxes?'

He gives me a lopsided smile, revealing tight-set teeth, stained with nicotine, and starts the ignition, kicking a pool of dust in my face. I watch the car before it turns the bend and disappears from view. Gripped with a sudden terror, I hurry back to the jeep, uncorking the last bottle of beer with the end of a lighter. The liquid that's turned warm in the afternoon sun glides down my throat with little effort. I crush bits of hash and sprinkle tobacco on top. After the first few puffs, I begin to ease into the evening.

This trip was supposed to be a way to get away from *it all,* a break from the anxiety of not being able to write again, of having to go through the painful process of finding a suitable flatmate for the room Ekam had abandoned in the middle of the night. I had blocked Suchitra and her cronies on Instagram since their posts calling for writers to complete my script was too much to bear, even for someone as desensitised to the horrors of the film industry as me. Dad had begun enquiring about the extra money he'd sent across before film school, but I was living pay cheque to pay cheque and even the slightest deviation from routine life, such as this holiday, was enough to put a gaping strain on my spending capacity.

Things with Kunal had also taken on a peculiar shade. We'd fallen into a comfortable pattern, initially. He'd come over after his editing gig, dressed in his standard beige pants and black t-shirt with indecipherable lettering in Kanji. We'd smoke a joint, watch an indie film and kiss at the halfway mark. I rewatched several films I'd already seen in school—

Bergman's *Persona*, Varda's *Cléo from 5 to 7*, Jafar Panahi's *The White Balloon*—but watching the same films with a new lover is a different experience. I studied the expressions on his face, the wonder in his eyes as he focused on films from decades ago, prescient and more relevant today than ever before. As the movie concluded, his warm hands would travel across my sweaty body before we descended on the bed. I developed a habit of brushing my teeth, tapping a light sprinkle of water under my armpits and between my thighs, and swishing mouthwash at the back of my throat, trying to rid myself of the itchy, velvety taste before I could settle back into bed and discuss the films. This unexpectedly charming routine lasted a while before my libido took a nosedive. I lost interest in sex around the same time I lost interest in the films. The films that had compelled me to think soon gave way to Netflix binges of bad plot lines, regurgitated through trite actors, a steady hum to drown out my cavernous anxiety, a certain restlessness at being unsure of whether I'd ever write, or really love, again.

Soon, I learnt that the steel rod placed in Ma's right foot, when she was diagnosed with polio at nine, was dissolving. After several rounds of doctors and a series of expensive tests, one inexplicably including an MRI, the conclusion was that her body wouldn't be able to handle another such surgery at her age. She was advised to take steroid gel injections, which the doctor claimed would help ease the pain for about a year and keep the inflammation down for longer.

Along with the injections was an endless list of prescriptions; strong antibiotics, anti-inflammatories, and rounds of physical therapy culminating into shock-wave treatment that stuns the nerves to stop the pain. I was used to seeing Ma in some degree of emotional pain for the better part of my life, but seeing her disintegrate physically was too much to bear. I knew I couldn't afford this trip, and perhaps, it wasn't behaviour befitting a twenty-eight-year-old, but the need to escape was too strong, too familiar not to honour.

And so, here I am, supine in the back seat of a malfunctioning jeep, in the middle of a desolate mountain valley, waiting for Medha to return—*if* she returns, though I'm too terrified to even consider the alternative—from the nearest village with help, as the hulking peaks reflect the fast-fading light. Through my half-open eyes, I see two crows take flight into the evening sky, a baby squirrel hanging from the beak of one. The squirrel's furry tail thrashes wildly in the air, giving the crow a hard time before it perches on a branch and smashes the squirrel against its rough bark. The squirrel twitches once before all life seeps out of it.

I'm almost dozing when Medha returns riding passenger in a car more derelict than her uncle's Jeep. The mechanic, a Tibetan man with a weather-beaten face, the apples of his cheeks reddened by the harsh mountain sun, I soon learn, is mute. He slides under the belly of the car, and when he emerges, he walks back down the road we came from. He looks for the missing piece of the fuel tank that's allowed the petrol to trickle out. With the valley wind swelling, I can see goosebumps on Medha's arms.

'How are they going to get the car out of here?'

She shrugs, disinterested in anything I have to say. I'm not sure why she's angry with me or when her tendency to poison the atmosphere with her bad mood will go away. The mechanic returns and gestures to Medha that looking for the missing part may take long, and it's best if we accompany him to the nearest village. I'm not sure what Medha plans on telling her uncle. Will he expect her to reimburse him? I know that neither of us is in the financial position to be able to do that, but I don't see what else we could do. While I am sure the valley is too high, cold and barren to have predators lurking in its sparse forests, the idea of being here after sunset, guarding an inanimate object against unknown forces, seemed ridiculous. So I follow the mechanic back to his car and slide into the front seat. Perhaps Medha could get a few minutes of sleep in the backseat, and much as I knew she liked to be in charge, I could be the one to stay awake and take in the sulphur-blue darkness of the evening.

'What do you think you're doing?' She stands with her arms crossed, a silhouette against the setting sun. 'We can't just leave it here.'

'We have no water or food. What if it rains? What if there's a landslide? Or a snow leopard? The car's on its last legs. I'm not going down with it.'

I can see her brain whirring in real time, naturally assessing the most clever, devastating way to attack me. Coming up with nothing, she slips into the back seat and slams the door so loudly that the sound echoes for several seconds.

I'm famished when we drop our bags into the stuffy guest house room, the door of which won't shut. The village hasn't had any electricity for three days and has sunk into darkness, which my eyes are just getting accustomed to, along with the flickering amber lights of lanterns fashioned out of tree resin and deer skin. The usually golden lichen, growing in sprays across the rocks, take on an eerie glow, illuminating our path as we hunt for dinner. The roads are empty but for the occasional small bonfire at the corner of the street, a huddle of men in chequered beanies and mufflers around it, a bottle of unmarked muddy liquid placed beside them. The suffocating scent of moonshine clings to the cold air, while a metallic hospital smell hangs about the men. Walking down a particularly steep hill, I lose my balance and Medha grabs my elbow to steady me. We both break into simultaneous giggles. The atmosphere, stiff and unforgiving, opens a crack, and for a moment, it's easier to breathe.

We arrive at the village's centre, where a lone liquor shop stands, mobbed by an army of waifish men, bags under their eyes, their skinny elbows jutting out of their puffer jackets.

Next to the shop is a dhaba with sickly yellow light emanating from a single bulb, casting angled shadows on the face of a young boy spinning rotis on a large pan sizzling with oil. We take our place on the rickety plastic stools outside the kitchen, and Medha rolls a cigarette. I signal to the young boy for two cups of tea.

'In therapy, we learnt a technique where we role-play and pretend to be the person we have grief with,' Medha says, wrapping her jacket tighter around her.

'But why?' I take a sip of the sugary liquid, letting its warmth soothe my chafed throat.

'Let's just try it.'

The boy places two plastic bowls of hot, clear soup on the table between us. She slurps a large mouthful and some runs down her chin.

'I read this piece in *The New Yorker* about how therapy-speak is damaging our generation. It talks about how using such words robs people of actual trauma, when the language of pain itself is so thin.' I fish out a small bottle of local rum from my jacket's pocket and pour both of us some, splashing it with Coke, and take a big gulp. I know what I'm doing. Medha looks pained.

'I'll be you, and you can be me.' She pushes an entire dumpling into her mouth and chews it with speed like somebody may snatch the plate away from her. I get the feeling, sure as the changing of ocean tides, that this isn't going to end well.

'I'll start,' she says a bit too brightly. 'The last few years have been insane, a lot has come to pass, and I have begun mistaking my trauma for my identity. There's a lot I refuse to process and instead project on to the people who dare to get close to me.' She picks up the bowl of soup and gulps it down.

The nerve. As the rum makes its way into my bloodstream, I feel the anger I've tried to keep at bay rush right back.

As a kid, I'd vaguely heard my teachers and parents refer to my 'anger issues', but hadn't ever paid much attention to it. I remember a few stray incidents—being angry at another girl in sixth grade who mocked me for failing the Arabic exam and throwing her pencil box at the wall; another incident with my father, who had the maddening habit of tickling me. I threw a fat book at him from across the room, and it made contact with the corner of his eye. I remember being beaten afterwards, with chappals and a belt, while Ma tried to tear me away from him in vain. She wasn't exactly my hero, though she may not have hit me; her steady, cold indifference was punishment enough on most days.

I had stood up for Medha during her worst times, chosen her over my other friends, and put up with her mood swings. Yet here I was, in a village that even God seemed to have given up on, listening to her misguided indictment.

'I have self-aggrandised notions about my art and weaponise my queerness to make others feel lesser. I'm blind to my privilege, and I like to blame external things for my lack of success when it's my own laziness and indulgent self-doubt.'

'I love playing the victim,' she says, her voice rising an octave.

'I'm incapable of maintaining relationships since I am demanding and withhold affection.' The rum has settled in my limbs, bringing with it a sense of bravado.

'I'm in a relationship, mind you. What about you ignoring Kunal's calls since you've been on this trip?'

I see that she's broken character. Typical.

'What about the fact that when I'm going through a tough time, you're nowhere to be seen?'

'When are you *not* going through a tough time? It's only bad days with you. I'm your friend, not your therapist.'

'Yes, you're right. It's my fault for coming from a broken home and having it tough. Forgive me for not having the privilege of parents who give a shit and rich uncles who want to support a deluded career in the arts.'

'Every time I decide to do my own thing or take my space, you act like I'm punishing you. Everything isn't about you, Sophia. The world doesn't revolve around you, although I know you love to believe that. I struggle as much as you do, if not more. Try dating girls in Delhi at our age and tell me how that goes. All you have to cry about is how pathetic men—whom you consciously seek out to compound the hate you feel for yourself—treat you, just like I predicted they would. It's not cute or funny anymore. It's pathetic and needy. Grow up!'

I know I've entered the abyss, that sunken space of rage where I'm capable of saying anything, doing anything, where conceding defeat isn't an option, and where I will not rest or stop until I hurt the other person as much as I'm hurting.

'You want to talk about pathetic? What have you done since college? You don't pay rent, your art is unoriginal and derivative, and when you don't get the exposure you feel entitled to, you blame it on nepotism while indirectly benefiting from it. You're so quick to place yourself on a pedestal. Being queer doesn't automatically absolve you of all moral dilemmas. You still have to function in this world as an entire person, just like I do! But at least I have the grace to admit I can be a total shit sometimes. I can't remember the last time you admitted to anything. Must be nice, coasting through life in a state of perpetual denial.'

I'm heaving and can feel entire oceans of anger boiling and swirling within me. I feel possessed by a foreign spirit, yet I know it lives within me, and I feel ready to destroy everything to build from scratch again.

When I sense Medha is too shocked to retort, I fall quiet, the adrenaline suppressing any waves of shame or guilt that rise like bile to the surface.

'Right,' Medha whispers and I want to shake her until a cry—in defence or anger—falls out of her like coins from a trouser pocket, but she sits still as stone.

The mountains coalesce into a formless mass of black in the sooty night; all the places touched by the sun, grit and wind, invisible to the naked eye. A half-moon hangs in a sky peppered with so many stars that it forms a smear of light in the darkness. Being a cavewoman must be so much easier. Just foraging for berries and playing with domesticated wolves before dying at the ripe age of thirty when the village would dance around with my naked body before throwing it into a deep gorge. What an easy way to live, instead of a thousand inevitable ends that carry the ghost of a beginning with them. Medha, too, looks far into the distance. It seems like she might be watching the men clear out from the liquor store or the mangy dog sniffing around the dhaba dump for scraps of food, or perhaps she studies the road running into the belly of the village, calculating the walk back home, the silence between us intensified by the loam-like darkness and words we can never take back.

The heavy quiet between us is interrupted by what seems like a fight erupting outside the liquor store. A man in a thick sweater, blind drunk, lunges and takes swings at another man, one with a slighter build, who grabs the drunk man's arms and attempts to placate him. The drunken man's eyes bulge out of his sockets, and he slurs—a series of garbled, incomprehensible words, the meaning of which is impossible to grasp. His fist makes contact with his friend's face, and his glasses fall to the ground. The young boy from the dhaba jumps in, fishes the glasses out from amidst this absurd show of masculinity, friendship and inebriation, and hands them to their rightful owner. The drunk man, content that he's defeated his friend, swigs from the bottle and is walking away from the scene when his friend sneaks up behind him, grabs the bottle from his hand and smashes it to the floor. The honey liquid, the colour of overripe peaches, disappears into the cracks in the asphalt. Pieces of jagged glass glitter like diamonds, reflecting and refracting light on their shocked faces. The drunk man teeters and falls, slumping down the side of the road, at the edge of a Border Roads Organisation sign, asking the tiny village's three thousand strong residents to be mindful of drinking and driving, and cradles his head in his hands. I hear muffled sobs, but it's hard to tell from this distance. His friend walks up to him with purpose, casually side-stepping the glass, grabs him by one side, tucks his shoulder under the other armpit—you'd think he's taking him into a side-hug—hoists him up and begins to walk. The drunk man's head hangs low while his friend assures him in calming whispers. We watch them hobble down the road while a thick, shapeless fog travels across the village and blankets it in silence.

The morning comes in bright and sunny, like the promise of a new beginning, like we hadn't completely lost ourselves in the bloody guts of the previous night. The sky's clear and blue, and soft clouds, like the fleshy bits of a cat's paw, float with ease. The snow-capped peaks have never looked clearer, green shrubs beam in the diaphanous light, deep mouths of pink and purple flowers open and close rhythmically with the valley wind. A light drizzle from the previous night has wiped most houses, painted in bright greens and blues, clean; front gates shining with pride. Electricity's finally back after three days, so the village is preoccupied with a flurry of activities.

Across the homestay, an older woman deftly weaves white and yellow yarn against a wide wooden comb, a pile of woollen rugs with diamond-shaped patterns placed behind her. A few feet away, a man knocks a hammer on the head of a sharp nail to carve letters in the Tibetan script. The metrical sound stops as he dips the nail into a pot of cherry red ink and brings it back to the polished pebble with a sense of renewed purpose.

Medha emerges from the shower and slips into her jeans and a thick sweater. I light the stove, scoop out finely ground coffee from its packet and ladle it into the mocha pot. She screws the metallic top and places it on the open fire, blue-orange flames engulfing its base. We sit beside one another on the chairs with frayed armrests covered in old leatherette, bits of cotton poking in places where the tear is, and watch the village come to life. I think of the man and his friend from last night, and wonder if they too are sitting together in some unknown room, waiting for their coffee to finish brewing.

# 7

# FARIDABAD

AT HOME, IT SEEMS LIKE EVERYTHING'S changed. The living room is overflowing with plants; a snake plant next to the sofa, bonsais by the window, spider plants trailing the windowsill. Ma's showing off the coriander and basil she's growing in the vegetable garden. Her Carvaan radio plays old Hindi movie songs that aggravate me, and when I turn the volume down and retreat to my room, Ma turns it up again, louder this time. I wonder if this is what having a younger sibling might feel like. She walks into my room without knocking and displays the new fabrics she picked up at last month's cottage emporium sale, followed by her jewellery collection, inquiring if I'd be needing her diamond ring anytime soon. I ignore the insinuation and, instead, tell her to avoid stepping out in the city's putrid air. The January fog has enveloped the city in its chokehold, disrupting flights and halting traffic, and the sky makes me feel like I am in a war zone. Briefly, I am reminded of Beirut's grey skies and the distant sound of drones buzzing a few miles from the seaside hotel.

'It feels like the end of the world, might as well look good, darling,' she counters.

Her cheeriness is terrifying. Ma's been on some crazy bid to lose weight—works out twice a day to Jane Fonda workout videos in the middle of the living room and refuses to eat together. Every time I start a chat over a meal, she remembers she has to digest and paces the entire house, her arms swinging wildly by her side. I ask her if her thyroid or blood pressure is okay, but she tells me that she just wants to look hot. I notice how the skin on her face sags and the pigmentation around her mouth. At some point, she asks me if I'm seeing anybody, and I stay quiet. I stopped telling her about my relationships since she referred to my time with Azhar as an 'episode'.

'Do you want to die alone? Beta, you have to adjust. It's not like being around you is a walk in the park. I will go soon, who will you have to call yours then?'

I'm stabbed by anger and suddenly, my period arrives. I curl up on the bed, clutching my stomach in pain. Ma brings me a hot water bottle. Bleary-eyed, I tell her about the botched grant but she dismisses it with a flick of a wrist.

'Something better will turn up.'

'What can be better than receiving a grant for my original idea?'

'Soph, they didn't even pay you anything after the first instalment.'

She leaves the room, already distracted by the doorbell or fragrances from the kitchen.

When Ma called, I could tell she was upset because when I asked about her leg, she ignored the question and spoke about how her fruit guy hasn't been sending the right lychees. She said she missed her sister, who she hadn't spoken to after a silly spat with over a game of Scrabble two months ago. She coughed a lot, and when I asked her if she'd been using her nebuliser, she ignored the question and instead irritated me with platitudes about whether I'm eating or sleeping well. I wanted to tell her to drop the act, the routine mechanics of being a mother only when it suited her, but then she told me she's lonely and asked me to come home.

I'd been sharing my flat with Sucharna, an account planner, since Ekam left. It was a strange experience. She had a temper and labelled everything that was hers in the fridge, pantry cupboard, bathroom and living room, in bold black letters. Despite my insistence that I'm allergic to cats, she fed stray ones at the front door. The times I tried to initiate a conversation, her eyes darted with nervous energy and she checked her phone often, as if willing it to ring and offer her an escape.

Since Spiti, some months passed doing odd jobs to pay the bills. I tried not to get lost in Kunal's life, but it was difficult since I didn't have much going on in mine. When he asked why I hadn't kept in touch during the trip, I blamed it on bad network. He seemed satisfied with my lie.

I'd slipped into a leisurely yet unfamiliar routine with Kunal. I attended parties at his friends' sea-facing apartments, discussing their various artistic practices—experimental theatre, heritage restoration, foreign education consulting. I ate dinner with his parents at fine-dining restaurants that made me distinctly uncomfortable, answering questions about my career goals, why my parents lived apart, why my mother wouldn't leave NCR, where the combination of patriarchy and pollution was particularly toxic. His parents seemed to have a certain chip on their shoulders, but their weekly family dinners, of which I was now an understood part, followed by a few glasses of wine, became an inescapable part of Kunal and my relationship. They'd share stories of their global travels, Kunal's genius knack for the piano, perusing photo albums of the few years they lived in Singapore and Zurich, listening to old Hindi songs from their record collection. Sometimes, I'd stay the night and wake up to a plate of fresh fruits and a frothy cup of coffee made by Kunal and would spend the day listening to records, napping, reading and looking out at the Bombay skyline, which was particularly striking from his thirty-fifth story home. I had the distinct feeling that I was inhabiting a life I did not belong to, but the warmth of his family home, and the ability for us to be in each others' company in silence, connected by our shared love of obscure films, retro disco records from Tokyo, Beirut, Tehran, our political ideas, we falsely believed were radical, often based on opinions picked up from *The New York Times* and *The Atlantic*, and his gastronomic love for the most extravagant food in town and the concept cocktail bars, thrust me into a life I'd only previously encircled with trepidation.

My friends in the city had dwindled to nothing. The more I retreated indoors and into my phone, it seemed like everybody on Instagram seemed to be making big moves with little transparency around how. People were launching boutique perfume brands, artists were collaborating with homegrown Indian labels to sell clothes—posts about their craft and work routine, carousel posts of the Italian coast and quaint European towns, ending with the classic shot of painted nails glistening against a pistachio gelato. If I was left alone too long with my thoughts, a particular poison seeped into my mind. The chasm between the modest life I lived in my two-bedroom apartment with meagre natural light and the various middle-class trappings I tried so hard to disassociate from, and the quiet wealth of Kunal's family, was beginning to catch up.

I knew I should feel something when I saw the setting sun, the palm trees swaying in the monsoon wind, a busy badminton court on top of the posh twenty-story building across mine, but instead I was gripped by a quiet blankness.

So, when Kunal went on a family holiday to London, I grew resentful of everything he had that I didn't: an intact family, a childhood bedroom to go back to, a safe space to keep his vinyl, old notebooks with scribbles of his feelings and emotional storms, stacks of *Financial Times* and old issues of *The New Yorker*. His clothes stayed in neat piles in one place, one home, and this sense of ultimate rootedness lent him mobility, fluidity and the ability to move between cities, people, lovers and passions with ease, knowing there was a ground zero to return to. I was unable to take any such risks. My sense of threat was far too heightened. Accumulating even a little—a relatively stable relationship, a place I could call home in passing, a best friend I wasn't currently speaking to—made me anxious. I've always been unsure of slipping off the edge, into a pit I can't climb back up from, of being forgotten, of being erased, of having to confirm that I'm alive only when somebody else does.

I knew the stifling and dusty old house Ma moved into when she separated from Dad, where the relentless sun beat down on all corners, wasn't the answer. Still, I felt like I needed space from Bombay.

I texted Medha, informing her that I'd be coming home for a bit. There was no reply. I checked her Instagram and saw that she'd shared a reel where a girl with a septum ring and blue hair talks about how loving a straight girl was forcing her back into the closet.

I call Kunal, who launches into a sullen monologue about how vacationing with his parents and staying at the Taj in London is not exactly his idea of fun. He tells me how his bags were held up at Heathrow and how his mother, angry with the entire family for not paying attention to her, shut herself in the hotel room with her laptop. He tells me how she spends too many hours on her cell phone in a day, and wonders if all mothers are crazy.

'That's really sexist, actually,' I tell him coolly.

'She thinks I don't prioritise her because I didn't accompany her to her root-canal surgery. It's just a root canal, not a gall bladder surgery.'

'Root canal today, gall bladder tomorrow, cancer day after.' I light my joint and take a lazy inhale.

'Are you stoned? It's 2 p.m.'

'I'm unemployed, Kunal. Calm down.'

Kunal says he's late for lunch and disconnects the call. Later, while I help Ma de-weed, by plucking out taproots from her bed of carrots, caked in mud and sweating buckets, she asks if I have a healthy sex life. I don't dignify her question with a response. She presses on about how important it is and how that led to her eventual separation from Dad.

In college, Ma found a bag of weed in my room when she came to visit me in my PG in Pune. I pretended I was carrying it for a friend, horrifying her further. She confiscated the bag, and later, I discovered she smoked it with her friend. She came back home stoned out of her mind, and I had to make her peanut butter and jelly sandwiches, which upset her stomach.

'Ma, it's best if I don't take relationship advice from you.'

'According to you, everything's our fault. Not because of your drug days or poor decision-making.'

With a hurtful pang, I think of the stubborn silence Medha and I have pulled on each other since Spiti.

'You know what they say—like mother, like daughter.'

I pluck out a particularly stubborn taproot and semi-dry mud sprays on the floor.

---

I skip lunch to go for a run. I can't put up with Ma's sulking as she prepares dinner or the incessant banging of pots and pans. It's only been a week, and I'm already counting the days to when I will return to the emptiness of my home. She's horrified at me running when the AQI has crossed 405, but I need to sweat the anger out. I cross several dogs flopped on the tarmac, and finally collapse under the shade of a gulmohar tree, out of breath, and pull out my phone. A flurry of texts between Kunal and me.

*my mother is driving me mad*

*be kind to her*

*stop patronising me*

*why are you always out to attack everybody? first your mom, now me.*

I come back home to find that Bhavna aunty, Ma's friend, has come to visit. I exchange pointless pleasantries with her. She updates me on what's been happening in her life—about a clueless client who presumed her to be the secretary at a meeting, about her daughter wanting to transition medically, about her adopting a new puppy in order to persuade her otherwise.

'But Aunty, it's ultimately Rosh's choice,' I say, indignant.

'Not if I'm paying for the surgery, the hormones, the therapy.' The colourful glass bangles on her dainty wrist tinkle as she waves her hands in agitation. Ma shoots me a familiar warning look.

'There's enough research to show that sex-reassignment surgeries improve quality of relationships and overall well-being. They also prove that kids who experience gender-affirmation have better mental health and depend lesser on substances.'

'But we still live in India, beta, what is everybody going to say?'

'So, send her abroad. God knows you can afford it,' I say, surveying the fridge for snacks, my eyes roving over a bunch of green grapes, fresh paneer, a bottle of milk and a small katori of mint chutney.

'She told me she goes by Rohan now,' Bhavna aunty turns to Ma, hoping to find a more sympathetic ear.

I'm about to launch into my argument when Ma switches the radio on, and the voice of Runa Laila travels through the house, cutting our conversation short. I'm glad. Everything about Bhavna aunty irritates me. How can somebody as cool as her, someone with an elite education and a chamber in the Supreme Court, who sat the bar exam in two countries and now settles disputes for multi-billion dollar companies, be worried about how people will react to Rosh wanting to be called Rohan?

I slip into the shower, letting the hot water ease my sore calf muscles. I study Ma's expensive tub of cream, reading down the list of anti-ageing ingredients, from retinoids to vitamin C to grapeseed extracts to niacinamide. I scoop a finger full and apply it in broad strokes across my cheeks, jawbone and forehead. *Self-care.* The word has taken on a particularly devious meaning in the recent past, and the anxiety of living in a hyper-vigilant world heightened by constantly being perceived online.

In Bombay, I often watched a series of cleaning or restocking ASMR videos that helped quell my late-night anxiety. In order to be desirable or worthy of attention, Instagram taught me I had to follow a five-step showering routine. I Googled products I'd never heard of and added them to my cart, hoping to sustain the momentary flash of happiness that dissipated before another video on a hygiene routine popped up; naturally, I'd missed adding lip scrub. Why wasn't there more conversation about the price tag attached to the idea of self-care? *Self-care Sundays.* Why was self-care about indiscriminately cutting off anybody who didn't live their life by the same values as yours?

When did somebody disagreeing with you become tantamount to gaslighting? I moisturise my legs with a vanilla-scented lotion I find on her dresser. It isn't enough to write a book or compose a song or make a painting these days. One has to make the painting, record the process on an iPhone time-lapse, write a pithy caption for it with the relevant hashtags and post it on Instagram at the time of the day where it gets the most traction; between four to six in the evening if you're in India. The family unit has collapsed, and yet we are expected to display naked, capitalistic ambition so we can consume more to dull our senses.

I hear Bhavna aunty and Ma giggling like schoolgirls, singing and teasing each other. I know Bhavna aunty's ex-husband shifted to Bangalore to be with a much younger woman, running an aerial yoga studio. She recently got the keratin hair smoothening treatment, began wearing bolder lipsticks and lost weight.

Later at night, I start a job search after dinner by poring over listings on LinkedIn and various Facebook groups and blast-emailing companies with my updated résumé. I switch to Twitter—eleven suspicious suicides in New Delhi, a Muslim boy beaten up for drinking water from a temple's tap, a lake in Bangalore catches fire and burns for thirty hours, a lawsuit against a news channel for portraying the Uttar Pradesh police in bad light, cat memes, dystopian jokes. From the next room, I can hear the faint rumbling of Republic TV or Times Now and my mother blithely chatting on a phone call. She speaks in the voice she's adopted from her time in the HR department at a telecom company—a pleasant, low-pitched tone that's impossible to get angry with. I tiptoe to the other room to catch a glimpse of her draped on the bed, legs atop the bolster, twirling her hair with one finger. She looks like a sixteen-year-old.

I enter her room without knocking—she falls silent. *The family albums*, I mouth, my eyes probing her expression. She points to the bottom-most drawer of a wooden chest, and I pull it open, collecting the numerous small and large albums in my arms. I return to my room, closing the door behind, but leaving it open just a crack so the voice can filter through. I try to listen closely but can only hear a low, steady stream of indecipherable sound.

I sit on my bed and flip through the photographs—several dedicated to my first, sixth, seventh, eighth and ninth birthdays with me in colourful dresses in satin and velvet fabrics from the newly opened Giny & Jony in our neighbourhood in Delhi. I remember the black and silver polka-dotted velvet bow that wouldn't stay put in my baby hair. Photos of Ma and Dad holidaying in Rajasthan, atop sand dunes and around trees, holding hands and a packet of chips and grinning ear to ear. Photos of my first trip to Europe with my grandparents—my parents couldn't afford to come—snacking on ice creams and chocolate chip muffins at various tourist spots.

Ma's made notes at the back of each photograph. *Soph's eighth birthday, 1998. Aadil drank too much and gave Soph a sip of his beer. She cried for a long time,* at the back of a photo of me beaming at my birthday cake. *Udaipur, 1994. Soph ran a high fever. Aadil and I found a doctor in a small village,* at the back of a photo of me atop a camel, making a face as twisted as a dry raisin, ready to bawl, while my Dad squinted against the desert sun. *Aadil and I in our first apartment, 1990.* Ma and Dad lounging on cane chairs in a balcony with creepers along its edges. *Soph and Aadil gardening, 1996.* Dad de-weeding and me hanging around him with a bowl-like haircut. I devour the photos like they're a prisoner's last meal. I know the photographs don't capture the yelling matches, broken furniture, excessive drinking or me waiting alone at home for them to return from work or a party.

I put them all back neatly, encased in the thin, silvery plastic of the sheaths.

Ma watches a documentary in the morning about how Siberian tigers are hunted for their body parts. I put the moka pot on the burner and as I wait for the coffee to bubble up, I spot her phone lying on the slab. I play around with the password before I crack it—my birth date. I go straight to her WhatsApp and after going through some inane chats on Whatsapp groups, I come upon pages and pages of chats with somebody named Tahar Rahim, an Arab man who claims to work as a heart surgeon at the Spire Liverpool Hospital. He texts her every morning with a saccharine 'good morning beautiful' and before she sleeps with 'thinking of you tonight'. I'm afraid to check the photos folder, but I do it anyway and find pictures of his two daughters—blond and with their backs turned to the camera, so their faces aren't visible. The next photo is his selfie with a surgeon's mask draped on his chin. A few selfies of Ma with bright lipstick and her hair surrounding her face like a halo. Her angles are all wrong, and the light hits her face poorly. There are chats about his life and hers. The surgeon says he's divorced, and with a pang, I see that Ma says she is too.

I deep dive through Tahar Rahim's Facebook. Why would a man twenty years her junior, in another part of the world, take such a searing interest in Ma? The profile has photos of Tahar in scrubs, leaning over surgery tables and inside operation theatres. His back is always to the camera, and his face is turned away from the light. Over the years, Ma has come into some money. She is fond of precious jewellery and has been collecting it over a lifetime; the Delhi house is also in her name. I log into her net banking and see that a sum of twenty-thousand rupees has been transferred to an international bank account. I Google the hospital's number and call their reception. I ask to speak with Dr Tahar Rahim, but no man of that name works there; the receptionist informs me in a distinctly Scouse accent. I disconnect the call and wonder, for Ma's sake, if he's moved on to another hospital but instinctively know that's improbable.

The omelette is tasteless, the coffee too milky, and my cramps feel like a baby's kicking my lower abdomen in rage. I feel miserable. My mother is cheery, asking me if I'd like to eat spinach stew for lunch as she switches off the documentary at the point where they show Russian poachers grinding the bones of the Siberian tigers to powder to be shipped in women's handbags to China. Her skin is taut on her arms, and her face shines in the morning light. I've definitely not inherited her naturally luminescent skin, although age has cemented its mark around her eyes and mouth. Her eyes glimmer with some unidentifiable happiness.

My mother, now fifty-three years old, with a Master's in economics and an MBA, hasn't worked a day in the last two decades. The move to Dubai, so the family could be together, derailed her career. Though her father has set her up with a good inheritance, when I look into her beautiful hazel eyes greying with age, I understand her resentment, her disillusionment with her life and her inability to talk about her depression. I see how pandering to please her father, husband and the rest of society has worn her down, palpable in the sadness she carries wherever she goes.

Sometimes, I see myself in her; when she politely nods at somebody talking, but I know she's drifted in her head, how she replies in witty quips when she feels vulnerable in a conversation, how her humour can be cruel and how frustrated she feels with a world that doesn't see her anymore. When did she go through menopause? Is she lonely? I don't really know anything about her; I don't know my mother at all. And now, I may have lost her to a man lying to her and taking advantage of her.

I call her sister, who gloats about her son's engagement and her husband's promotion. I listen with little interest and when she is finally done, I swear her to secrecy and tell her about the fraud, Tahar Rahim.

She doesn't seem concerned. 'Didi's always been this way. Obsessed with her beauty and the attention of men. I didn't tell you this before but even when she was with your dad, she had a friend whom she met often.'

I feel my ears turning red hot from anger and embarrassment. I thank her for her time and honesty and hang up, my head buzzing with the information.

Am I destined to end up like my parents? I'm already well on the path. I seem to embody their worst bits. I can't hold on to a relationship for longer than a year; I lose interest in sex after the first few months of being with someone. Even with Kunal, I always wait for the other shoe to drop. I don't have a steady income, and my career as a sound recordist or a writer has failed before it could start. My bitterness, disdain for most things, oscillating simultaneously between the feeling of abandonment and the feeling of suffocation, makes me impossible to be around. Was Medha right about all that she said about me in Spiti? Despite age and time, Ma's still distantly orbiting her own life, prey to some soulless bastard on the other side of the globe, manipulating her for her money, now that her body is no longer a consideration.

I note his number and take screenshots of his shared images. A Google Images search takes me to the staff page of a Lufthansa flight. The photos are of a flight steward. I find his Facebook; his name's Alexie, and he's from a small town, northwest of Greece, called Kastoria. He's engaged to an animal veterinarian and flies with Aeroflot. He likes to sail, barbecue and visit museums in various cities. I type Tahar's phone number in a caller-ID app, and it takes me to an anti-scam page on Facebook created by the Thai police. I try translating the message from Siamese to English. Google does a pretty shoddy job, but I get the general gist.

I message Tahar's number, abusing him, threatening to report him to the police, and ask him to leave Ma alone. He replies in broken English. *call your police. police can't touch me.* I ask him what he wants and he responds. *everything.* Panic courses through my body, and I call Medha, who, to my surprise, picks up. I explain the situation to her but jumble up everything because I'm halfway between screaming and choking with tears.

'You should've chatted with him, pretending to be into him and gotten more details. Soph, do you ever pause to think?'

Before I can respond, she tells me Julia broke up with her. She had said she needed to be alone with her thoughts, that being in India had reminded her of growing up in Ystad and the sense of oppression that came with it. Medha implored her with memories that seemed to only carry significance for her; the time they got drunk at the dive bar with their favourite chilli chicken while they lamented the stale beer. When she kissed her in the middle of the road and told her that she loved her. Julia said she loved her, but she loved herself more. Medha had asked her if it was about the money and assured her that she would pay her back the minute she found a job. After her exhibition had bombed, Medha hadn't been able to find a job, despite me repeatedly texting her about opportunities I came across on Instagram or LinkedIn, dismissing graphic design as beneath her artistic sensibilities.

Julia told her that it wasn't about the money; she just needed to be by herself, maybe return to Stockholm. Medha tried to reason with Julia, who asked her to stop flogging a dead horse.

'I can't believe Julia compared our relationship to a dead horse.'

'I just told you my mom's getting catfished and you're moaning about a girl who's too chicken-shit to be with you?'

I hang up, seething, and storm into Ma's room, holding my laptop under her nose, images from the YouTube explainer videos on romance scams, the anti-scam police page and Alexie's Facebook profile beaming in her face.

Ma gently keeps her book of crosswords away. I can tell she's livid.

'So what? Let them take advantage of me. Why can't I enjoy some attention?'

I stare at her like she's crazy. I am angry that some prick like Tahar Rahim feels entitled to Ma's attention and affection when I barely get that privilege.

'I just can't believe you would go through my phone like that.'

'I did it for your own good!'

'I did not raise you to be this way.'

Tears are running down her cheeks. I remind her of the time she intercepted my email when I was eighteen, found half-naked photos I'd sent to Azhar and grounded me for a month.

'You were barely of legal age. And dating a man ten years older than you!'

I tell her it's not any different from her texting a man twenty years her junior.

'I don't question your promiscuity, who are you to question mine?'

A flash of the last time I'd met Azhar. I was still entirely obsessed, even though he barely called. We didn't have much to say to one another, so whenever we did meet, it quickly devolved into hateful sex, but ever since his wife got pregnant, I'd stopped taking his calls. At the club, I drank too much, and we stumbled into one of the quieter back-alleys—hands and mouths all over each other.

I wanted to tell his wife over a plate of greasy hangover breakfast and juice. Now that he has a daughter, it felt wrong, but a part of me wanted to punish him and make him suffer half as much as I had. He pleaded with me to not say anything, that his wife only pretended to be progressive. Eventually, she was persuaded by fairly strict morals and would find the transgression unforgivable. That he loved her, and she was his entire world. I didn't react then, but I know he knew, with that, he'd wounded me forever.

As Ma cries softly, she asks me why I judge her. I assert that I'm her daughter and would never judge her. But I suspect she might be right.

At night, I can't sleep and recall one of our last few family holidays together. We stayed in a stone cottage at the edge of a forest, back when tigers still roamed the jungles and rampant deforestation hadn't forced them to find higher grounds or turn up in people's backyards. I must've been about eight or nine years old, but even as a young child, I never really cried or threw tantrums or asked my parents for much. I consistently got good grades, unsettling competitiveness underscoring everything I did. I always felt like I had something to prove. I was a fat child—'baby fat' is how my Dad referred to it—wore glasses and felt a consistent sense of separation from my friends evident by the times I wasn't wanted at the park where kids played tag or at the birthday parties with expensive pencil boxes as return gifts. I tried winning friends over by throwing live performances of puppet shows and plays. Still, most kids believed I was either vying too hard to be the teacher's pet or trying to be a smart-aleck in class, so they only included me out of a vague sense of obligation.

Ma and I were walking back to the cottage from dinner, me skipping behind as Ma walked ahead with her signature limp. I spotted two lanky boys, about fourteen or fifteen years of age, awkwardly hanging out in the property's garden, sharing cigarettes and bouncing on the swings made for little children. The boys crossed us on the path, sniggering. *Move out of the way, bitch.* The words fell out of their mouths like rough stones, sounding both foreign and offensive. I, of course, didn't understand the weight of its history, but the unoriginality of the slur didn't lessen its heft. Ma didn't react. She just wrapped her shawl tighter around her and continued walking. I remember feeling a hot anger surge through me, and I wanted to break their faces with my bare hands. I hardly slept that night, turning in bed with recurring images of brawling with the boys.

The following day, I found them lounging on the swings again. They glanced at me like one might regard a trivial insect. I picked up smooth, round pebbles from the ground and launched them without hesitation. One, two, three, four, five stones. Most just collided with their jackets and plopped back on the ground, but one of the pebbles hit the shorter one on his ear, and another made an impact with the taller one's arm. They both howled in pain and looked at me, but I'd already started running away to the cottage. I leaped inside, locked the door behind me, and collapsed, heaving, my pulse racing. My parents stared at me over their morning cup of tea, bewildered. I laughed and laughed, high on adrenaline, until my stomach hurt. Later, Ma had to apologise to the boys' parents, who looked as arrogant and unbearable as the kids themselves, but they left the same day and I felt victorious.

That night, Medha FaceTimes to tell me she's under my building. Baffled, I go downstairs, averting my eyes from the guard on night duty. She's come to pick me up in her old WagonR, the colour of an eggplant. I sit beside her as she swerves dangerously on the empty roads of Faridabad. She keeps the window down, and the icy January air numbs my cheeks. She stops at the entrance of a small mela about half an hour from my house and steps off. I follow her into the crowd, passing men and women gathered around a bonfire to our right. They drink hot milk sweetened with jaggery and raisins. We pass carousel rides painted in bright yellows and reds, kids licking ice-creams and people shooting air guns at water-filled baloons. The discordant noises jolt me out of my head, and I follow her to a flamingo pink ride, a Ferris wheel lit with fluorescent white lights, that comes to a clanging halt before us. We both climb in, and I sit next to her, inhaling her signature scent of peppermint and freesia. As the Ferris wheel starts and the pod jerks, I scream sharply and promptly quiet down as Medha laughs at me. We stay silent as the pod ascends through the air. The stalls on the ground, people chatting, the buildings, everything becomes smaller and smaller until they lose shape.

'So, what happened?'

'I was going through her Insta, a bit obsessively I should add, and it all kind of came to me. How manipulative she's been. How she pushed me into being with her exclusively. I was sure I didn't want to date anybody like that; you know how attached I get and how long it takes me to get over things. The moment I told her I loved her, she withdrew and started sleeping with a colleague. She didn't even have the nerve to do it in person!' Medha wrinkles her nose like she does when she's about to cry.

'She broke up with you on text?'

'She used her work as an excuse to only see me on her time, she judged me for having friends who aren't as rich as hers. White supremacists, all of them. She took me to her office parties and flirted with everybody. Like I had any other choice except getting drunk.'

'She sounds like any other rich white girl.' It's better than saying, *I told you so.*

'She's a bitch.'

'I don't think she's half as interesting as you paint her to be. I think *you* are what made her interesting, until it got too real so she bounced.'

The Ferris wheel seems to fly into the air. We both see beyond the nearby apartment houses, with people encased comfortably in their apartments, to the barren farmlands and wastelands, factories that spew toxins into the morning air, shut for the night. The moment is beautiful and full of pathos.

'I think you may have been right about some of the things you said about me in Spiti.' My eyes sting from the warm tears pooling in them.

'No, I wasn't. I was just being vicious.'

'No, you were being honest. It's okay, I know I'm a shit sometimes.'

'Yes, you are.'

'God, we are so cringe,' I lean back and survey the emptiness around me, avoiding looking at how far the ground is.

'Your mom will be fine. She's too stubborn to let anybody fuck with her.' She smiles and squeezes my hand. I nod as I laugh, because I know she's right.

'She's got to make her own mistakes. *She's* your mother. Not the other way around.'

'Damn, they teach you that in therapy?'

'I think you should move out of that shared apartment, by the way. Get your own place. We're thirty years old. It'll be a game changer, trust me.'

'What did you think you'd be doing at thirty when you were young?'

'It's silly.'

'Go on, tell me.'

'I thought I'd have my own gallery in Delhi and would be exhibiting in Berlin, Paris, London. I'd be famous and to preserve my mental health, which even back then I sensed would be trash at thirty, I'd retire to a tiny Balkan island and live out the rest of my days off social media, fall in love with a small-town European, maybe travel the coast in the RV we buy together, make our own candles . . . you get the idea.'

'Why specifically Balkan?'

'How is *that* the detail you want to focus on?' She laughs and I'm immediately gratified.

'Well, in an alternative life, I'm thirty with two kids. One's really good at piano, the other plays football. We live in a clean, walkable city where time doesn't stand still and the weather changes, so our moods can too. I shoot quaint, independent films about the things I care about and, somehow, make money doing that. And the only things that go wrong are paper cuts or injuries from sanding down a boat—I guess we own a boat—and adding too much salt to the pasta. Nothing big ever happens.'

'You like it when things happen,' she says as the pod approaches the ground and stops with a jerk. A young girl drags her mother by the hand and waits for us to vacate impatiently. Her mother looks scared so the girl assures her in an adult tone unsuited to her tiny body.

'Mummy, we can do it if the birds do it.'

In the twilight zone before sleeping, I think of Ma and me on a pristine beach with white sand, a bale of turtles ambling to the ocean. The ocean is ferocious near the shore. It tosses and turns me, and the salt water gets into my nose and hair. A new mother lets her day-old puppies suckle, and a few metres away are endless starfish that have come in with the low tide. They appear dead, but they're just resting—they'll recede with the high tide and go back home. The wind blows through Ma's hair, and she laughs as she takes my hand and we stroll along the shore; I chase sandpipers, their white bellies glistening in the daisy-yellow sun, and they spring away from me, skipping until they take flight.

In the morning, the sky is extraordinarily blue and the trees glimmer in the sun. There's a knock on my door and Ma enters. She slips into the bedcovers next to me.

'I've blocked him.'

She lays her hand across my forehead. I cave into her like a newborn and sleep some more.

# 8

# BANDRA

I'M FALLING OUT OF LOVE WITH KUNAL.

The change begins very imperceptibly; I slip out of his arms in the middle of the night while stray horns blare outside the bedroom window. Shrill, unforgiving, louder in the dead of the night. The inexplicable pang of irritation sits hot in my belly when I make tea for us every morning. I try to remember the last orgasm and see only the comfortable routine our bodies have fallen into. We fall on top of each other haphazardly, without too much care or heed, like marbles rolling across the floor—careless, jumbled. Him on top, me on top, him on top again, edging me to the brink of orgasm; I moan, then he moans, and we collapse in each other's arms. I keep my eyes open as I come.

I read online that steady eye contact during sex cements the emotional and spiritual bond between partners, so I try meeting his eyes one time, while he's on top, and he holds my gaze with an expression I can't read. It isn't the kind of rapture I imagine all men might feel they thrust into me, but a wavering sense of control, an almost nervousness to impress, an embarrassment at being seen. A moment later, he moves away and buries his face into my neck. I know decorum dictates that we cuddle, but I slip away and sit on the pot, inhaling the scent of sex and feeling a kind of numbness.

Sometimes, I position my head to exaggerate my moans in his ear, similar to how I've seen in porn, but he never reacts. I like to believe it turns him on. I spend a lot of time on porn websites, often leading me to rabbit holes. Most times, masturbating is much more efficient but leaves me with little to no desire for him. I buy an expensive candle, some massage oils, and an aloe vera lube, but they sit on my bedside table, collecting dust. I'm not sure at what point I arrived at this intensely dislocated relationship with sex, but here I am, thirty years old, and my libido is dead. I consider therapy, but I'm not sure if I can afford it between rent and the other expenses my scant income supports. I sometimes wonder if the dysfunction is genetically coded in me, lasting unhappiness in romantic relationships even when nothing seems to be wrong, a complete lack of desire or ability to confront and the crippling dependency on others to feel good.

Sometimes when I see my parents, I see myself. I'm desperate to not confront the inevitable. I treat them harshly, like they're disposable; I indict them for not understanding me even though I offer them nothing real about my life. Nobody in my family knows how to be there for each other.

Blaming family is perhaps too simplistic. I can instead blame technology, screen-time that has pervaded every waking hour except when I shower or run. Endocrine disruptors in candles, plastic, incense sticks, non-stick pans, GMO foods—

watermelons larger than a human head, oranges sweeter than synthetic candy. I could blame astrology and my birth chart, the particularly odd alignment of Mars, the planet of sex drive and aggression, with Venus, the planet of fertility and love. The state of political affairs. The recession. The burgeoning industry of sexual wellness that includes vetiver massage oils, bullet vibrators made with medical-grade silicon and updated editions of the Kama Sutra, suited to the modern lifestyle and the stiff modern body. My need to equate violent fucking with attraction. *Being constantly attracted to somebody seems super draining,* Medha texts me.

On days I feel particularly lazy, I blame my father. My father doesn't understand why I had to fall in love with a Marathi Brahmin, as if love was something I had any semblance of control over. I'd successfully managed to hide the relationship from him by constructing a moat of solitude around me, fortified by emotional distance. We relegated our relationship to phone calls filled with platitudes that irritated both of us. I'd inherited his immediate impatience with anything that didn't conform to his way of being.

When I did finally tell him, already on the defensive—like I was revealing a debilitating addiction, I could feel the paws of shame clawing at my stomach. He was silent at first, withdrawn and formal for the next few days. Finally, he accused me of deceiving and disobeying him. He seemed especially hurt by the disobedience, as if the only true mark of love was obedience. My father, in a stunning display of contradiction, asked me for Kunal's birth date, time and place of birth to run it by a maulvi in Bangalore, who claimed clairvoyance and had been helping him out with the business and personal affairs for several years. The irony of consulting a man to know the future, while claiming to uphold the tenets of a faith that forbade fortune telling wasn't lost on me, but I've long learnt not to say much. My father's fits of anger—hurling mobile phones, remotes at the TV set, flinging his glasses to the ground between yelling matches with Ma, led me to the confusion that came from loving but being afraid of him.

I remember coming back home after six months away on a school exchange trip. Six months that felt like an entire lifetime. My father picked me up from the glitzy Dubai airport and I looped my arm into his and then we rode down a highway, the yellow orbs of street lamps and an arid desert stretching out to both sides. Dubai always wore a forlorn look. A strong whiff of pungent *itr* enveloped my senses as I stepped out. Notes of nettle wafting from the desert. I'd always feel a bit out of place, conscious of my awkward gait and bespectacled face, a womanly body but none of the attendant grace and charm. Hugs with my father were always also a peculiar shade of awkward. I would be intensely torn between wanting to howl as I hugged him from the pure frenzy of having missed him or sleekly avoiding his embrace to immediately launch into an equal parts hysterical and sincere fit. We'd carry out the Friday evening ritual of driving to Aroos Damascus, the local Syrian restaurant for their fresh fare of seafood platters and heady mixed juice mocktails topped with Sulaimani tea. I'd talk endlessly—regaling him with my six months at this exchange trip, nestled at the foot of the Himalayas with six hundred other girls and all the various niggles of daily life. I was going to be sixteen in about a week and had spent the last six months cooped up in a school, following a regimented diet and fitness routine but still made fun for my bony frame, too long a chin, wispy hair, beady eyes—pubescent girls can be unceasingly cruel. I'd furtively watch the tall Syrian waiters with aquiline noses and light eyes with their thick Arabic accents and stoic demeanours. I hadn't kissed a boy yet. I felt conscious of such thoughts in front of my father who dug into the food with gusto, with wild abandon even, and I remember being slightly put off by his provincial mannerisms. I studied my father and his heavy jowls, sharp, almost arrogant eyes, his slightly protruding belly digging into his jeans, shapely, almost feminine legs that I've inherited, the aquiline nose, the lingering pull of his youth and attractiveness. I thought of how far he's come from the dusty byroads of Kanpur. My father picked up one half of a large, yellow lemon and squeezed it onto the grilled lobster. He tore apart the two thumbs before cracking the middle open. With a shiny fork wiped clean on the table mat, he made his way into the lobster's meat. I watched him eat, happy, eyes shining, feeling comforted and whole in his presence. My steamed fish was brought out with its tiny bones intact and before I could make my way through it, he grabbed it and decimated it into pieces, painstakingly taking the bones out and lining them in a corner of my plate so I could eat my fish with a complete lack of fear. Later, we got into his car, an SUV in a muted colour and drove around the brightly lit roads of Dubai, deserts on one side, neon-coloured malls advertising Chanel on the other side as I played music. He turned the music down often to receive phone calls and spoke in dulcet tones of whispered *asalam waleikums* and furtive business deals I never really bothered listening to. From the inflections in his tone, I could tell how important the person on the other side of the phone was. Over the years, my father had flirted with several small-medium sized retail businesses, from textiles to electrical fittings to nightclubs to rice—flitting from one business to the next when not immediately presented with results. He had a particular way with people that inured them to his volatile fits of temper and slightly condescending attitude. His hands-on approach to life stood in stark contrast to my insecurities and sensitivity. Other memories of him at home; busy doing his finances on reams of paper, bleaching his many white shirts and wife-beaters, cooking mutton on Sundays, although this ritual became less frequent with time. Ma did the heavy lifting; making sure I got my meals on time, supervising my fractions every evening, counselling the Pakistani neighbour next door through her marriage, even though my father engaged with them hesitantly since they were Shia'as. I navigated his various strongly held, often contradictory, beliefs, acutely susceptible to the changing nature of his moods.

I wish I could say it was something as simple as Kunal being emotionally manipulative or being a narcissistic or a creep with a roving eye. But he is everything I imagine a good partner to be—talented, tender, funny, stable. There's nothing visibly wrong, but I know we are both feeling it. He's stuck at a desk job, editing for fourteen-plus hours a day while I scrape by doing odd freelance gigs, starting and abandoning my script with startling impulsiveness.

Spring is here, and I'm bloated, distracted and anxious. We haven't had sex in several months. Yesterday, at the neighbourhood bar Kunal and I usually frequent, I got unusually high, and things started looping. I saw a woman sizing Kunal up while she flipped her hair with sexy abandon and gave him 'fuck me' eyes. I couldn't stop watching. I giggled uncontrollably, felt an inexplicable loss of control but also at ease with everything around me. Kunal's friend recently described a girl who he went on a date with as 'looks good in a swimsuit'. I need to watch what I eat and swim until I'm out of breath.

Kunal is reluctant about marriage. I'm not sure how I feel about it either, so I don't demand answers or even a serious conversation. Ma drops hints about us settling down, claiming that at least it would give me something to anticipate. I dismiss marriage as heteronormative, but I think I'm just scared. What if I marry the wrong person? When's the right time for marriage? Is it possible to be a feminist and a wife? Life would be easier if I could just hold a job, clear my bills, pay my taxes, eat my meals on time and settle into the guiltless pleasure of not thinking too hard. Instead, I accumulate stubborn belly fat and growing resentment.

Sonia, who is pregnant, calls me. She tells me life has a way of making way for everything that happens in it, but I haven't quite figured it out the way she has. She did her Master's overseas, married her second boyfriend in a lavish wedding in Chennai and secured a promotion at the job she bagged right out of college. She is the woman who gets it all. I am done with wanting to stay in touch or confiding in her about my secrets and misgivings, like we once did, sitting in the school music room, vibrating with unbridled love for one another, defined by possessiveness, not yet marred by the fashionable cynicism of our adult years.

Medha, too, gets over the failure of her first exhibition and takes up a desk job at a design studio where her colleagues grow their own tobacco, call each other by nicknames they assign and nap during office hours. Everybody seems to be growing, moving in exciting new directions, while Kunal and I struggle with our careers and our drab sex life.

I exile myself, so I can finish the script I abandoned after the grant fell through. In a haze of scenes, characters, cigarettes and a distorted circadian rhythm, I find myself drifting, dreaming of other men, other lives. We both simmer separately with a slow-burn detachment. Kunal says he'll finally get down to editing his film, but he begins spending one too many evenings at the local bar. We douse each other with mechanical *I love yous* scattered across our days, drinking our respective coffees in sullen silence. Sometimes, we fight—about him working overtime, a stray comment that I latch on to—and unleash a vicious cycle of mean truths about one another. Most evenings, as I sit by the window watching the clock turn hands, steady anger rises within me.

I get a text from him telling me that he'll eat at work, and I grab something fatty and disgusting, touch myself and nod off to a fidgety sleep. I don't realise when he comes in and slips into bed, and I often wake up with his back to me. Sometimes, I hold him. Sometimes, I slip out and watch him sleep. Watching him from a distance brings me to tears on most days, and I enjoy the lack of articulation.

I can't bring myself to tell Medha. To her, I have everything that can make me happy. A beautiful two-bedroom house complete with stainless steel rain showers, instant hot water, an ironing board, a double-wall oven, a four-burner gas with a sleek chimney, a built-in wardrobe, an L-shaped couch upholstered in velvet—a gift from Kunal's mother—a 52-inch smart TV, a reading corner stocked with smart titles, tall snake plants, and a small balcony converted into a terrace garden that his mother's gardener tends. A gilded cage. I try growing mushrooms amongst the flowering plants that bear no fruits, but it gives Kunal a runny nose, puffy eyes and a persistent headache, so I abandon the project.

I tell myself I have no time to write, but the truth is, I have no desire to. No, that's a half-lie too. I have nothing to say. So, I spend my time buying things online. Things we don't and will never need. I buy overpriced solar-powered garden lights, and now they pulsate feebly on top of plants I don't take care of, even though I've always wanted a garden.

In the summer, I throw a party. I wear a too-tight top, tits out, and put my black jeans on, knowing I'll never look more beautiful than at this moment. I plan everything down to the last detail—the wine, the hashish, the lights changing colour to the music, the sound system that was a gift from his parents, the snake plant that seems like the only marker of time passing and the right balance of intoxicated men and women. He says he wants to wear the shirt with the tropical pattern; I wrinkle my nose in disdain.

'You don't like the way I dress.'

'That's not true at all.'

'I'm wearing a patterned shirt with shorts.'

'Not the shorts.'

'Okay, but the shirt stays.'

The shirt doesn't stay. He stands by the edge of the door as people trickle in. He has a nervous disposition: twitchy fingers, a smile that lights his face up, cheek to cheek. Veiny arms and bony hugs. Everybody seems to be helplessly drawn to him. *Your boyfriend has such an attractive personality*, the women say, laying their palms across his face as if to check for fever. Immediately awkward, he places his palm across my forehead.

In our first flush, he wouldn't stop photographing me. He had a keen eye for perspectives that drew the eye away from the normal and bludgeoned the viewer into accommodating his view. The photographs captured me at my most unintended, and I hated them. My naked back with the tattoos I regretted, my face, which I had never quite learnt to love, frowning at the camera. Me leaning against the window, smoking a cigarette, my face wearing an expression of displeasure while being captured digging into breakfast at a café that did its Diwali décor a tad too early. There was one of me by the railings of a wooden bridge running across a forest, moments before I slipped into the shallow lake. Another photograph with a black turtleneck pulled up to my face, my eyes shining with the kind of contentment that comes with knowing where home is; he'd slipped this photograph into his wallet. Recently, I noticed he had changed his wallet, and I wondered where that photograph ended up.

Towards the vague end of the party, people assemble in a drunken circle and manoeuvre to make our bedroom into a sanctuary for spaced-out chats and cocaine-fuelled hugs. We're not sure who these people are or what they're doing in our home but we enjoy the false sense of security the evening brings.

'Take a picture of me.'

I grab the camera and frame him. A dark silhouette against the strange purple light.

Later, he uploads the photo on Instagram and titles it: *Limitless.*

I loop my hands around his neck and think of a time when our little tendencies and habits enamoured instead of aggravated one another.

'I don't want any self-doubt after today.'

I'm bored of his romance and proclivity to grab harder each time things don't seem to go his way, grappling with my indifference until I relent. I don't know why I feel this way. All I know is, at this moment, I want to run. Run fast and far—away from the round, smooth bowls of dips and the various accoutrements of our life together. Some mornings, we share one another's toothbrushes; some mornings, I deliberately use his toothbrush, a sense of intimacy more malignant than benign. There is little room for individual mistakes not immediately pulled up for evaluation and consequences. And so, I want to run.

But I lean in, and I kiss him—a nice little show for our guests.

The state of Kunal and my relationship seems to be reflected in what's happening in the country. Things have steadily worsened in the last few years. Bombay is one of the few cities that's allowing marriages under the Special Marriage Act that was being contested in the Supreme Court. We stopped our subscriptions to the local newspapers littered with news of interfaith couples being rounded up and murdered in some districts of Delhi, Haryana and Uttar Pradesh. Horrific images of beheaded men and women with their feet chopped off populated our social media feeds, so we went off that too. It affected our work since so much of it was just blatant self-promotion on socials, but it was becoming hard to function while doom scrolling through the worst panic attacks. A friend of Kunal's tried opening a joint bank account with his Catholic wife, but they were asked to furbish a marriage certificate which was rejected anyway since their state wasn't recognising the Act anymore. Last I heard, they were trying to relocate to Canada. I would, too, if I could, but who's trying to give a struggling artist a permanent residence? I'm not sure if it's a sign of the times, but I can't stop thinking about how living with someone of another faith can only lead to trouble. A part of me wants to fight, and another part is genuinely frightened. Sometimes, my friends talk with the confidence of a thousand safety nets. What does that even feel like?

There's a certain melancholy that refuses to dissipate, no matter how many smiles I put on—letting our friends believe in our closeness, agreeing to everything on phone calls with his mother. When she interrogates me about Kunal's lack of interest in marriage and if it has anything to do with my ambition or temper, I answer her questions with sincerity, alleviating her fears that although he hadn't put a ring on it, it was what I was gunning for. When she buys me expensive lehengas for his father's sixtieth birthday party without asking me what I like, I don't tell her that I hate the glitzy fabric or the extravagant embroidery or that I wouldn't wear anything with sequins or glitter. When she asks me about the regularity of my period cycle, I assume it to be from a place of care, a motherly touch that has evaded me my entire life. I attend family functions at the Willingdon club, smile appropriately, laugh the right amount and say charming things that don't mean much or allow for truth or a real connection. I'm hungry for approval, for security, even if illusory, for his family to save me when mine couldn't.

The further I drift, the more I feel the need to compensate. I convince myself I would never betray Kunal, but when a man or a woman looks at me in a bar or on the street, I momentarily come alive.

One night, as Kunal sleeps, I go through his phone. I peruse photos of a string of his exes, girls he claimed he never dated but had short somethings with. Photos of them smiling into the camera, innocent selfies bordering on sexy, photos of him at various music festivals across the globe, pupils as big as discs. I evaluate how attractive the girls are, with their flat stomachs and glass-like skin. I feel rotten, so the next morning, I propose a date night. We can't settle on a restaurant—we can never agree on anything, not what film to watch or what vinyl to play on Sunday mornings. Finally, we settle on an Asian place neither of us have been to.

The dumplings are thick and tasteless, and an American guy with dreadlocks wrapped in a Tibetan scarf plays covers of pop songs on a ukulele. The restaurant is filled with other couples, similarly bored and dissatisfied, poking at their food, avoiding looking their partner in the eye, waiting for the night to end so they can go home, masturbate separately and sleep.

I try asking him questions about his life, dreams, egging him on to admit that I'm not a part of his future plans, that I don't deserve to be with somebody like him, that I'm not beautiful or particularly smart or even nice and, perhaps, I deserve his indifference. Resigned, he shakes his head and refuses to attend my pity party. I accuse him of still being in love with the last girl he was seeing, the one with freckles, a bright smile and an excited voice. We devolve further into having a theoretical argument about diamonds. He thinks a diamond is nothing but a rock that has no inherent value in society, unlike wheat or bananas, and is a product of a larger marketing conspiracy, like Valentine's Day. I think diamonds are pretty and have long symbolised status and wealth, and if we are to reject their position in society, we may as well reject the artisanal sourdough bread we buy at triple the cost of a mass-produced one, or the creamy Greek yoghurt or the books we read from small-batch, indie presses in London. He falls silent, and I drink a lot.

When I first meet Haider, I don't question my attraction to him, given how he has shades of everything I'm programmed to like; a moody disposition, half-baked opinions proclaimed as universal truths, the need to be the smartest in the room, fear of committing to any one thing—a career, a desire, a woman, a friend, a thought, a culture or even to any one version of himself.

We meet at a talk about mobilising against increasing police brutality against minorities, now popularly referred to as 'vermin'. About a year ago, I was part of a documentary on police cover-ups and staged encounters in Delhi, funded by some money from a leftist political party.

Since they are organising the event, I'm compelled to attend. It also simply feels nice to not be a helpless bystander to everything—my life, my disintegrating relationship, the increasing disassociation I feel from the world.

I first see him standing in the corner of a room. His eyes light up as I approach him, even though his expressions remain unreadable. I drink him in—eyes like liquid soot, the deliberation of his diction, his voice dropping an octave lower when he speaks to me. When he looks at me, he sees boredom, naivety and perhaps a touch of masochism, and he has no trouble taking it all in. I hang on to his every word. He asks me back to his friend's place, and we drink into the night, discussing the state of affairs in the country and what revolution looks like.

His friends are a pair of siblings, wealthy Muslims descending from the royal Awadhis, dressed in expensive silk saris and bespoke suits. Pearls shine around the sister's neck while the brother pours us Japanese whisky. I think about the staggering privilege of sitting in a living room designed to look like a tropical beach house in the middle of one of the poshest neighbourhoods of Bombay while bemoaning the collective loss of heritage, of tradition, of a loosening sense of identity. These Muslims are like me, adept at living double lives, swapping out their salaams for air kisses, their prayer beads for sweating glasses of gin and tonics, London-educated, appropriately lamenting the decline of democracy from a safe distance, frothing at the mouth with opinions picked up from Western philosophers and the BBC.

*What do we do about the lynchings?* the sister asks, and I feel a flicker of irritation at the superficial interest in a matter destroying Muslim families. *We need to mobilise foreign press*, her brother chimes in, his voice slurry and his eyes bloodshot from the whisky. Up close, his skin looks waxy, and I can discern the faintest lines of botox.

The sister puts on an Aretha Franklin record, and her lush vocals fill up the space. I guess we are resigning Lynching Talks until after the record ends.

I watch Haider closely. I'd have been dismissive of the strong, mostly idiotic opinions with any other man, but with him, I'm transfixed. He looks at me with a kind of naked need, an embarrassing hunger, and there's something liberating about caving into it. Later in the night, we retreat into one of the bedrooms while the sister lies down on the felt couch and the brother totters, tipping the bottle of whisky onto the carpeted floor. Their Persian cat sleeps in a corner, her soft paws underneath her.

Haider climbs on top of me and kisses me all over. His hands are over my breasts at first and then snaking down my stomach. I don't remember being touched this way in a long time, and I'm torn between fear and thrill. *I have someone*, I whisper, and he pauses. *Okay, but everything else is fair play.* And he continues to kiss me.

I wake up with my head throbbing, reeking of stale liquor, and I put my dress back on, clasping it at the base of my neck. I rummage for a pen and a slip of paper, scribble my number and leave it next to his car keys. I charge my phone in the cab, the harsh sunlight jabbing my eyes. I see several missed calls from Kunal and a voicemail I don't listen to.

---

The first time I got cheated on, I was eighteen and had been seeing Azhar for a few months, and I was obsessed. I only remember obsessively falling in love, as if the intensity of my preoccupation could be enough to win somebody over for life. The more unsure I was of his love, the more I needed to prove mine.

Haider reminds me of him—they have the same shoulders, a similar tendency to exaggerate their involvement in a mythical cause, same ability to have my moods and intonations revolve around theirs. It's been more than a decade, but I can still recall Azhar's friend calling me and admitting to finding condom wrappers at the foot of his bed and seeing a girl sneak out of his room in the early hours of the morning. There was no reason for her to lie, but I refused to believe her.

I come home to Kunal, vibrating with anger. He says he was worried about me, and I defiantly mock his fears and lie about sleeping over at a friend's. I walk past his accusatory stare into the shower and turn it on, letting the water caress every inch of my body that Haider touched. I brush my teeth vigorously. I feel like my entire aura reeks of him—of stale whisky, excess, desire. I feel a whirlpool of shame descending on me. I'm starving. Kunal leaves for work, and in the dead, cold silence of the house, I heat some leftovers.

I barely pay attention to the food as I search for Haider online. I don't know his last name, but I remember the photo of his dog—a black Great Dane with dog tags that say 'Daze'. I finally find his profile and spend the day refreshing my messages.

---

For several days, Haider doesn't get in touch, and in agony, I debate telling Kunal.

I don't know what triggers this cruel impulse, but everything Kunal does rubs me the wrong way. Our meals together are punctuated by some inane piece of news or television. I'm distracted when he talks to me about his work, only interjecting with callous responses. First, he stops coming up in my conversations, then in my thoughts. I've never been good at leaving people, so I convince myself that if I disappear from the relationship, he'll leave me. I underestimate his desire to avoid the inevitable.

Haider finally texts me and we agree to meet. We sit in a crowded bar, our bodies pressed against one another as old men tip back glasses of beer and smile ravenously at my bare shoulders. Haider towers above me, his long arms hanging by his side, and never breaks eye contact. He calls for whisky for both of us and talks about growing up in Melbourne. He tells me about the first and only love of his life who's still there. He describes himself as a 'militant agitator' and tells me he left his comfortable life as a financial strategist to create a platform for Muslim artists and work with the Left in mobilising from the ground up. He prophesies about the fate of Muslims and what I can do to help. I want him to grab and kiss me, but he never does. I think he knows it, though, because when we stagger out of the dimly-lit bar, he takes me into a firm grip and sticks his tongue inside my mouth. I feel like I am being swallowed whole.

Later, at home, I meditate on objects that belong to Kunal. He uses objects to hide parts of himself from me, from our relationship. A Korg synthesiser, bejewelled with plastic knobs and reverb dials, a leather-bound notebook I picked up for him from a Tibetan monastery with indecipherable scribbles on it, his feelings pointing in different directions—barely legible on his body or face. A spiral-bound notebook with To-Do lists he writes every morning, handwritten letters from a previous girlfriend, deed papers for the house his parents are buying for him. All these objects stay out of sight, a talisman of his life outside me.

Haider gives me no admission into his real life; I don't know much about his family, though I know he has a younger sister who's a teacher and married. He spends most of his time hanging out with the rich Muslim siblings, managing one-off brands to pay the bills and attending exclusive parties sponsored by Vogue or Soho House, where the girl in charge of tickets is a so-and-so he once dated. I know he's obsessed with fame, like everybody else in this city, but at least he's political about it instead of clamouring like every other influencer on Instagram.

I do a shoddy job of concealing my meetings with Haider from Kunal, but it gives me the impression that we're on equal footing. Maybe I'm resentful of Kunal's unblemished family life or his wide circle of global friends, or perhaps the ease with which people gravitate towards him and his silly jokes, so I make cruel accusations, his apologies a knee-jerk reaction to my manipulation.

'Do you love him?' Haider asks me.

'I think I do.'

'Your body is designed to get used to literally anything—any outcome, any season, any wind changing direction. So how special is your love then?'

Is our love special when I am sick and Kunal force feeds me bowls of warm stew? Perhaps, love is his mother's pushiness. Or my father's lack of phone calls. Or is it the moment he looks me right in the eye and tells me he loves me in a way that makes me feel as safe as being in the womb? I was so eager to secure the trappings of a future together, of making sure that I could finally subscribe to a kind of family unit, sublimate my insecurities into setting up a relationship, that I never paused to wonder if I actually loved Kunal, or if he just simply fit this particular phase of my character arc.

Haider drives me back to the apartment I share with Kunal. I can still feel him squirming inside me, and he drives with a blankness on his face—that feeling of completion. Sometimes, he shifts into fourth gear with his fingers inside me.

At home, I swap the heels for comfortable flannel slippers and wipe the red of my lips to reveal a scratch on my lower lip, blood shining like the purple pink of the evening sky. I brush my teeth, rinse my mouth, and sprinkle lavender powder between my thighs and under my arm pits. I sit at the desk with a cigarette and try to explore my guilt. Instead, I come up with a kind of numbness. I should seek professional help but calling Medha is easier.

She seems to have found new purpose and vigour since she started working at the design studio—her boss is a sneaker-head who runs an art newspaper that's distributed to high-end bookstores across the country; she gets discount coupons to a gaming arcade and invites to every new opening in the city, as well as free trips to biennales. She hasn't touched a speck of paint since her last exhibition.

'I can't help myself.'

'You're deluding yourself if you think this dude, Haider, will make you happy.'

She tells me she's exasperated with my need to self-sabotage. I thought things were improving between us, but at times like this I feel she completely fails to understand me. The loneliness feels invited. Like a familiar friend I've summoned, instead of dropping in unannounced. Later, I enjoy the heaviness of my limbs. I sleep endlessly.

'I've got another apartment. It's a kilometre down the road from here,' Kunal tells me, a suitcase beside him.

'But, why do you need your own place?'

'It's just better that way.'

I try to persuade him to leave in the morning. *It's 2 a.m.*, I say, but he's determined and cold. He leaves with a single suitcase, and I watch him from the window, my breath coming up in short gasps, the feeble light of the lamp spilling onto the street like we're the last two pathetic little people on this planet.

First comes the division of things—all the paraphernalia we accumulated in a life built together. He says he doesn't need my help setting up his place, so I don't offer twice. The objects he hid from me take on a telling shine when displayed in his space. He says he doesn't want to speak for a while, and I am thankful. I stop checking my phone for his messages or calls. I delete the numbers of his friends and family. I have blinding migraines, stop eating fish and start drinking every evening. I don't get in touch with Haider the entire time and he makes no effort to get in touch with me. Several weeks pass where I lie in a shocked stupor before I begin to find meaning in daily rituals.

I take brisk walks around my neighbourhood again, reply to texts that have been languishing for weeks, trim my split-ends, and drink detoxifying green juice. The emptiness stays put. The wall of polaroids from Kunal and my travels seems to jeer at me.

Falling asleep is the worst. I dream of Kunal often. Sometimes, he leads me to an imaginary house in the countryside where we watch the leaves turn colour. Sometimes, he sits by a fireplace, a furry dog nuzzling into the crescent of his palm as I watch him from across the room. Sometimes, I scream for him incoherently at an intersection, but he doesn't hear me and continues walking until he turns the corner. Most mornings, I wake up disoriented, reaching out for his warm presence, finding nothing but the cold sheets.

I wish I knew how to make everything stop turning wrong; like the hands of a clock, I could just turn to a better time. I know I orchestrated this, but playing the part of the perfect girlfriend felt weird, eerie, unreal even. I'm not cut out to be a trophy wife. I need to take a risk, shake something up. My eyes burn holes in my skull as I watch hours of reality TV about cosmetically hot people learning to fall in love with one another. I grow strangely fond of this girl on YouTube who makes ASMR videos. I prop a pillow between my legs, curve into a ball and watch her sideways—a heavily contoured face, irises reflecting the fluorescent white of her ring light, her acrylic nails painted a bright yellow and hair tied up in two buns, like a manga character. She speaks into a mic while tapping on various objects—hairbrushes, bottles of water. She whispers to me—*sit back and relax.* I take a deep breath and try to follow her advice—my back muscles loosen as I sink into the bed.

'Use a melatonin pen like a normal person,' Medha says and then talks about her addiction to it, so I switch to lights-out drapes and weighted blankets. Soon, I grow accustomed to the silence of the house, sharpened by the loud noises from the street—a man arguing on the phone, a distant bark, snatches of a soap opera.

I know I'll have to move out of this house owned by Kunal's parents soon enough. I can't imagine moving back into my father's home. I can't possibly give him the pleasure of telling me that he *told me so.* And after cohabiting with Kunal for close to a year, it feels near-impossible to live alone. Last I spoke to my father, he gave me one of his infamous lectures, which I notice he has started doing more and more often. He usually starts with caustic remarks about how my life will amount to nothing if I continue living this way, how I spend too much money, how I'm not a daughter who cares enough about her ageing parents, how I'm too committed to my delusional ideas about writing and not enough to making money, how I talk back, how I don't grab opportunities when they arise, how I'm not praying enough to Allah—the list of complaints evolve with time and his mood. My father's accusations teach me how to be an expert liar. I've often thought that he got this way when my mother left, but perhaps that only made acute what already existed.

It's hard to peg my parents down as good or bad people. I think I'm a good person, but all I really do is overextend and seek approval until the resentment eats me up or the weight of my own expectations brings me down. I think my mother operates in a similar way—constantly providing with an unfailing sense of duty towards those she loves. I think she surprised all of us, including herself, by leaving—the final straw being my father falling in love with another woman.

Gripped with a severe sadness, I finally ring Haider.

He wants to go for a walk. I ask him to meet me in the mauve-lit confines of the bar Kunal and I used to frequent. Inside, I feel a sense of anonymity in a city that seems to be closing in on me. The waiters nod at me politely. Maybe they've seen Kunal come in alone. I feel a sudden rush of pity for him—alone with his pristine synthesisers that he's too afraid to touch and kitschy teacups that his mother still buys him.

Haider walks in with his signature swagger. A strong whiff of cologne wafts up my nose and I immediately want to bury my head in his chest. He takes my fingers and touches them to his mouth, his lips grazing my nails.

'You've lost weight.'

He rubs his hands across my thighs as if examining for defects. There is no immediate closeness I feel with him. I know he can take me for who I am and, later, chisel me according to his own method. It feels good to abandon the weight of self-determination.

And so, I silently take my place beside Haider. I take care of his books, belongings and gaudy objects—the fat bottles of whisky, the packets of store-bought coffee, the blood-stained wrappers of the mutton keema I cook in large aluminium utensils with several onions, hot tears flowing down my cheeks.

Living with Haider is different from living with Kunal. I listen to him rant—anything is an excuse to set him off; a child in pain, a politician's caustic remark, a philosopher whose words hit too close to home. When Haider succumbs to his own depths of despair, he seeks me out for a sense of simplicity and peace that he finds heroic. As for me, I can subsume myself in his life and not have to think of mine. Sometimes, I get the vague feeling, like a mild bout of nausea, that I am being used, but I don't mind.

Sometimes, I think about marriage and if that means finally having my father's approval, but Haider says he can never get married after his last heartbreak. I find a picture of her tucked away with his pants, next to his socks, but I don't bring it up. I stare at her tight curls and bright, slightly manic eyes.

I immediately check the mirror to examine my soft, limp hair, curling feebly at the base of my shoulder, my small, narrow, rather plain brown eyes, thin lips and high cheekbones. I smooth my frizzy hair to my temples.

The weeks Haider goes travelling, campaigning in the dusty districts of Unnao and Maujpur on his great-aunt's ticket, I lie in bed for hours, eyes glazed from the promise of him returning home to me. I play out an imaginary niqah, the happiness in my father's eyes, his hand laid protectively across my shoulder, of the warm glow of accepting faces and duas that bless us with a radiant, married future. Will he still choke me when I am his wife? Will we still fuck against the wall if we are announced man and wife in the presence of Allah? The Holy Book holds no such answers although it does talk about being mindful of my husband's pleasure.

The days pass, the weeks blur together. Slowly but surely, the rot begins to set in.

I get to know the real Haider—the one who lives only for himself. Nothing about Haider surprises me anymore. I am not enthralled or excited at the thought of him. I find myself gripped with acute boredom. I realise his thoughts are stolen from textbooks, and he echoes the sentiments of his family's politics, that his bravado is as brittle as his self-belief, and that he surrounds himself with sycophants, that without the generational wealth and influence of his family, he's an errant teenager in a man's body. I become bored of his limited worldview, his need to undercut everybody else's work and worth. I can't stand to be in his presence; even the sex takes on the savage quality of hatred.

The final indignity comes unannounced yet loud. I'm on his couch, watching a Scorsese film, and he walks in with a friend. They flop down on the sofa, he grabs the remote and switches the channel to a football match, one hand caressing my thigh. I sit still as a stone. Chelsea vs. ManU. Haider pops the corks of two beer bottles and hands one to his friend. I watch their eyes widen with focus as they intermittently yell at the screen; men in blue jerseys and muscular calves moving about the field. I can feel an irrational anger rising within me so I start yelling fabricated words at the TV, alongside the boys, really leaning into my role as a WAG. Initially, it's funny, but at some point, Haider looks pained and asks me to stop. Dripping with venom, I switch the TV off mid-game, causing Haider to hurl his glass at the wall next to it. A stunned silence follows. His friend excuses himself to the washroom. I step out for a walk, slamming the door shut behind me.

I walk well past midnight, and the city falls quiet. I see nothing for miles except cigarette stores shutting shop, scrawny dogs roaming about the empty streets, the rows of Art Deco buildings, bright billboards and tin roofs shielding the homeless sleeping on the pavement. Bits of polythene blow aimlessly in the wind that's risen with a kind of coastal ease when not choked with exhaust fumes. Municipal workers in their dark brown uniforms sweep dead leaves to one side of the street. Sedans with darkened windows drive by me often, as do trucks and lorries with sleep-deprived drivers at the helm. A police car slows down, and a cop stares at me suspiciously. I walk for several hours and finally exhausted, return home to sleep on Haider's couch.

In the dead of the night, I find myself yearning for Kunal's presence, his large wet eyes, eager to please, but I am only fooling myself; I haven't heard from him in three months. I check his socials to see he hasn't updated anything since he moved out, and I cross his apartment several times in the week, half hoping to catch a glimpse of him, half praying I don't.

A few weeks later, Haider's ex-girlfriend comes to visit. Normally, I'd be jealous, but I'm only relieved; any reprieve from him is welcome. Haider banters, flirts and sketches her while cracking lewd jokes. *Do you still sleep naked?* he asks, oblivious to my presence as his voice turns deeper and a fake accent emerges. She gurgles with laughter. We eat some pizza and watch a sci-fi film with bad CGI and a dated climax, and she holds on to him out of terror. They stay up as I go to bed, and while I try to sleep, he blasts music, and I hear the clink of glasses and laughter before it goes silent.

I wake up at dawn, with the first ring of the alarm, and herd my belongings into the single suitcase I carried with me—frayed jeans and old t-shirts, a couple of books, running shoes, the yoga mat, my toothbrush, shampoo, the expensive Italian coffee. I sweep his kitchen from inch to inch, grabbing everything that's mine. As I roll the suitcase out to the living room, I see Haider and her intertwined on the couch, half covered by a blanket. He's naked, and his body looks cold. His hand rests on her ass, turned towards me. He opens his eyes, and heavy, needy energy radiates toward me. I finally realise I feel sorry for Haider. I'm not happy, nor am I sad. I only feel a serenity, a certain calmness of mind, of decisive action. Medha was right. I was deluded. Haider rubs his eyes.

'Haider, I'm leaving.'

He buries his face in her mop of curls, but I know he's listening. His skin has lost some of its usual shine, and in the morning light, his hair looks greyer than ever.

Later that day, I ring Kunal. I don't believe he'll pick up, but he does. He tells me he finally started the edit on his film, about how he's trying new coffee beans from Coonoor and how I should have a cup with him sometime. I listen, and I smile, picturing his soft eyes crinkling with careful joy.

# 9

# MARINE DRIVE

SO, IT'S HAPPENED. NO, THAT'S NOT QUITE right. It's been happening. It's been building up slowly and steadily. And now finally with a resounding force, the constructs of what I, as a privileged Indian, know to be safe, familiar and real have collapsed. Despite my education, access and partial NRI advantages, even my half-Hindu lineage, I have been reduced to what my last name denotes. I think of how having to build a life outside the country has robbed my father of a sense of rootedness, an inability to call one place his own. He's postponed his retirement because he's not sure how to return to today's India. The colony he grew up in now has houses marked with saffron flags and routine morchas taken out by men, frothing at the mouth with chants of '*Hindu khatray mein hai*', '*Jai Shri Ram*' and '*Mandir yahin banaenge*'—the war cries of a lost generation.

I sit on the floor in the middle of the new apartment I've recently leased at a highly subsidised rate from a friend's family. Cardboard boxes pile up around me, taped and marked with labels—books, clothes, kitchen stuff, medical reports, electronics. The apartment's situated in an old building with paint peeling from its walls and a smelly, narrow staircase, but it's on the fourth floor and faces the east, allowing sunlight to filter through rows of buildings.

At night, a hush falls over the street, giving me space and time to reassemble my life after the spectacular failures of the last few years. I lie on the single mattress on one end of the room with a lone lamp by its head. A steady quiet permeates the house even though I can hear the footsteps of the neighbours upstairs. Next to it are some planks of plywood I plan to use to build a bookshelf, a two-burner stove not plugged in yet, some brightly coloured bedsheets Ma sent across with matching pillowcases, the expensive film textbooks from Prague that I haven't opened in a few years and Polaroids neatly contained in ziplock bags. The only thing I've figured out in the last few weeks is the WiFi; the green buttons blinking in the night like fireflies.

I take a few books, create a makeshift desk and prop the laptop on it. I click on trending hashtags populated by the ruling party's IT cell paid to troll on social media and scan doctored videos and smears of saffron across profile pictures—a digital collage of hatred. Social media channels like Twitter, Facebook and Instagram only echo my thoughts back to me, and yet I cannot look away.

I've always had a confusing history—an Arya Samaji Hindu mother and a Sunni Muslim father. They met at his older brother's wedding in Lucknow, and my father immediately fell in love. They both stayed in Kanpur in the 1980s—Ma lived in Gulistan Colony, a predominantly upper-middle class Hindu settlement. My father, the second of seven siblings, held a menial job as a warehouse manager—the only employment his bachelor's degree from Kanpur University earned him. They both defied several societal norms to move to Delhi, where they got a home together in South Extension, an upcoming part of the city not yet hemmed in by jewellery stores and fancy clothing showrooms. A Muslim man and a Hindu woman living together before they got married—it was practically unheard of, but their reality nonetheless.

Rooting through my boxes, I find a wooden photo frame with my parents' photo encased in it, and the words 'love jihad' echo in my brain. Today, it might be impossible, even illegal what was once just difficult.

Nana-ji was a judge with the Lucknow High Court, and Dada-jaan worked in the railways. Ma and her younger sister, true to their Baniya roots, studied at AMU and IIMs, and were expected to hold down corporate jobs that would ensure a comfortable life. Nani was a Sanskrit Ph.D. scholar, whereas Dadi was married at the age of fourteen. After her death, they found seventy-thousand rupees hidden neatly in the folds of her crisp cotton saris—the only material remnants of her legacy.

Ma's English was slick. They had a television at home, and she was taught how to play basketball even if she wasn't allowed to wear jeans outside her home. My father started working at eighteen and did considerably well for himself—a mix of charm and street hustle that helped him rise through the ranks. At my parents' wedding reception, nobody from my father's side showed up except his parents, while my mother's father offered him money to not marry her.

The grandmothers were the first to establish any real bond, extending what they knew best: empathy, perhaps because they'd had to exercise so much of it over the years.

On Twitter, amateur videos of manic mobs marching down barely lit back-alleys surface, their chants of *desh ke gaddaron ko, goli maron salon ko* reverberating off bolted windows and padlocked doors. This country hates me. I see tweets about a spontaneous protest at Marine Drive, in response to what's happening in Delhi. It's almost midnight, but I decide to take a taxi there; part of me is relieved that I am in Bombay, and another part feels like I've betrayed the place where I should be, where the violence is happening.

Ever since the protests against the bills began, I've turned up at the Gateway of India and joined people in the chorus of 'Bella Ciao' and 'Hum Dekhenge' by Faiz, uncertain but spurred by the electricity of the moment. I've watched women in hijabs take the mic and policemen attempt to dismantle protest sites. I've craned my neck to catch a glimpse of student leaders and been taken with their poise and courage in the face of humiliation and distress. Students, activists, leaders from local Muslim parties and other community members pass biscuits and juice around. Some stand with a look of confusion, of disbelief that things have finally come to this, while others show the way, sing protest anthems and put their truth across with conviction and a lack of fear. But it disturbs me, this complete lack of fear, knowing that nobody sleeps in tents and braves police lathis and sanghi venom unless they're determined and here to stay, and I know it disturbs 'them' too.

The matter of 'us versus them' is a convenient matter, a political tool strategically employed and intensified by the powers that be until it seeps into the subconscious of the country. That's one argument. Another is that bigotry always existed and lurked in nooks and corners but is now emboldened and being worn as a badge of honour. There are clear camps and we must pick a side. I'm not a practising Muslim. I can't be immediately identified as one on the street. I don't wear the hijab, and have an ambiguous first name. But I'm immediately consigned to a community, handed the generational trauma I may have had some luck escaping.

At Marine Drive, I run into Kunal. We stay quiet as he holds my hand and makes his way through the crowd. My phone dies while I film the spontaneous gathering of outrage in the hope of posting it online to my meagre followers and mobilising more people. There are dozens of policemen surrounding the growing gathering, putting up barricades. As detention vans line the roadside, the crowd builds, everybody glued to their screens for news of Delhi. Police loudspeakers announce that people should disperse. Some of us sit with burning candles in a quiet huddle. A woman films a policeman's heavy-handedness, so another cop flips his phone out and films her back. I stare at him, daring him to meet my eye, but I'm only a face amongst the hundreds.

I watch several young students being dragged into detention vans on their way to the nearest police station. Phones are snatched midway through filming cops dragging boys by their collars and roughing up women. I'm quick to get up—I'm afraid I could be harmed or dragged into a police station or have a record, maybe an FIR charging me. My head teems with all that could possibly go wrong, and I am as scared as I am ashamed.

At the sidelines of the mayhem, another policeman catches up with me and asks me to vacate the premises. I yell at him about the violence and how he feels about the murder of a policeman in Delhi while he avoids looking me in the eye, shepherding me with his baton to a corner. I know he's just following orders, but my rage feels as vicious as it feels helpless. Kunal, who's been recording everything on his phone, grabs my hand, and we cross the road to apparent safety, my head buzzing with a strange kind of adrenaline. If this is happening in Bombay, what is it like in Delhi?

Growing up, the religious divide was distant rhetoric, emanating faintly as if from a badly tuned radio but permeating my psyche nonetheless. As a kid, I knew I had to fold my palms and do my namastes to Ma's side of the family and cup my hand and offer salaams for my father's side. Little rituals were put in place to appease two sides that had bristled initially at the union. As a child, it was hard to understand the accusations in certain words or the connotations of my dark skin and my Arabic name. Family albums from my first birthday have the words laid out in frosting: Happy Birthday Mehak. I don't remember being called Mehak.

All I remember is being called Sophia by my father and Gudiya by Ma.

I didn't understand the implication of the duality I was expected to carry within me at all times, but children have a way of subconsciously imbibing the moods and expectations of their elders, and so I adapted quickly. Partly to survive and partly to gain validation and acceptance, the lack of which had haunted my parents.

When I visited Qureshi uncle, the local tailor, I would bow my hand in a perfect salaam and refer to Ma as Zeba—the name handed to her by my father's family—the birth of an identity they'd find acceptable. But everywhere else—in the posh confines of art and theatre institutes, elite private schools, South Delhi parties—Ma went by her maiden name, Rima. In these places, we could bask in the glow of being inter-faith, of having a pluralistic identity. I didn't quite register the conspicuous lack of Muslims in my class or my peer group, or even in the books I was reading or the films I was watching. But since religion was a very private affair in my household, I didn't pay it much attention.

The walls of our homes weren't adorned with Ayatul Kursis or idols of Ganesha. Ma would chant the occasional Gayatri mantra, and my father would offer the odd namaaz but each festival, whether Eid or Diwali, was celebrated with equal enthusiasm. We took all the festive bits of religion and integrated them into our lives without paying much heed to society's expectations. Slight fissures would appear on occasion, like when my Nana would call me 'Gudiya' publicly in a bid to establish rapport with his Hindu colleagues or some of his lackeys dismissed a plumber's shoddy work as 'Rehne do, Muhammadan hai'. But judging by what has transpired in the last few months, these seemingly insignificant details have taken on new meaning.

I check Kunal's phone and see that although a huge group has assembled outside the Delhi chief minister's home, there is no sign of the newly elected CM. The violence seems to be continuing in the neighbourhoods of North East Delhi. I see tweets from the kinds of people I've humoured in the past, people who've been largely silent on the issue, saying *I can't believe it. This is not what I voted for.* But this is precisely what they voted for.

I stay the night at Kunal's, asking him to bolt the front door. My sleep, fragile and teetering on its last legs, vanishes. Kunal lies down next to me, but his eyes stay open. When he holds my hands and tells me it's going to be okay, that we can go back to the protest tomorrow, that there's no need for me to feel helpless, that I should catch a few winks of sleep, his kindness wears me down. I thank him for letting me stay over and silently hope he doesn't read it as anything more.

As a child, I'd only heard of the horrors of the Sikh riots of 1984, Bombay in 1992 or Godhra in 2002. I didn't think I would have to live through another such occurrence in my lifetime, but here I am, trying to estimate the loss of life, the number of families torn apart and the magnitude of information and data suppressed. I remember lounging on carpets at family gatherings with the incidents of 2002 playing out in conversations between the adults. I was only ten years old, but I do remember the casual way in which my father dropped the words 'civil war'. At that point, the idea seemed absurd; we had a perfectly normal life, and nothing felt particularly amiss. For a man who didn't come from excessive money or a fancy education, my father did what he could to the best of his abilities. He had me admitted into one of the best schools, helped with my biology diagrams and sketched my geography maps out for me. I fondly remember our first trip to McDonald's and our Friday night dinner ritual, irrespective of how tired he was. I also remember Ma's impatience with my inability to be good at fractions, with a pencil poked right into my hand, and her insistence that I master *Wren & Martin's High School Grammar*. For her, perfect English was the key to succeeding and cracking the Indian middle class dream.

In the shifting sands of childhood, I didn't register the subtle mockery of my father's rusty, distinctly UP English at family friends' homes. It's only now that I notice how my parents' ostensible secularism was much appreciated in certain upper-crust circles, while Abid chachu, a neighbour and a family friend, with his well-groomed beard and Urdu colloquialisms, wasn't extended the same glow of approval. Nor were his wife and their three kids, who attended the local madrassa for after-school Qur'an classes. The kids were often missing from neighbourhood picnics and sleepovers. I loved visiting them and felt the closeness that was apparent between our families. Between plates of mutton biryani and haleem, nothing seemed amiss. Meanwhile, their son and I co-wrote rap songs in his bedroom about defiance or children standing up to their parents and recited them with fervour over dessert. The adults would break into a smattering of applause. From our modest two-bedroom apartment in an upcoming part of New Delhi, with our education and aspirations for social mobility, it felt like nothing could ever go wrong.

The first night at home since the riots, I wake up to a string of texts from Medha. *don't worry if you don't hear from me for a while. don't tell Mom and Dad. just ring my manager. here's the number. love you.* I frantically dial her number, which rings for too long before it goes silent. I call her manager's number that goes unanswered as well. Finally, her manager calls me back. He tells me how she must be asleep. How she lost her friends at the protest, how an autowallah helped her escape as goons surrounded the area and barricaded it from the press. Her friend suffered a head injury, and Medha was in shock. I stay silent. Words feel entirely trite and hollow. The worst I'd experienced was tonight. Am I really allowed an opinion when I trickle into a bar near Gateway after protests with similarly liberal friends for a bottle of wine while Medha was on the ground, getting beaten up? I know she'd been active in the protests for a while but was it foolish to go to the site of violence? Was I allowed my despair when I was cushioned behind the protection of a computer screen, sitting safely in my flat, waiting for the world to collapse?

My separation from my father first began in 2001, when he moved to London for work.

He never had much of a 'service industry bone' in him so after a few jobs that didn't work out and navigating his way through several small-scale businesses in New Delhi, he wanted to try his luck overseas, at the firm where his older brother worked. From the very beginning, my father hated London— it reminded him of his broken English, how conspicuous the colour of his skin was, his last name that could stir shit up if he was found in the wrong neighbourhood. *If I have to live as a second-class citizen, I'd rather do that in my own country,* he would often say wistfully at the odd family dinner.

Ma was a strict disciplinarian, having imbibed her father's often cruel parenting methods. My childhood away from my father was marked with a dense yearning for him and resentment towards Ma's long hours at work and the rotating cycle of nannies. I soon found myself revelling in small rebellions like bunking the double maths period in fourth grade or barricading colony roads to ride bicycles. I developed these mysterious fevers that left the family doctor stumped until he pinned it down to my father's continued absence.

In 2003, Ma decided it made sense for the family to be together, and we moved to Dubai. I had the experience of growing up in a country where being Muslim wasn't something that needed to be hidden or downplayed. My class was populated mainly by Muslim kids—from Syria, Iran, Sudan, Egypt, Lebanon, Iraq and Somalia. In a single day, I'd learn French from a Romanian teacher after a Syrian teacher taught me Arabic, before maths or French tuition at a Sudanese home. Boundaries had blurred and been reduced to the colour of passports.

Ma calls, and I speak to her with one eye back on Twitter. With the break of dawn, the mob of men armed with homemade pistols, petrol bombs, wooden sticks and knives has retreated, leaving a trail of unbelievable destruction behind. There are talks of more protests being planned for Marine Drive and Gateway, but someone circulates a paper claiming that Section 144 has been imposed in the city—it's illegal for more than four or five people to assemble in a public space.

I'm not sure I can do anything except be glued to social media. I'm not sure I can survive another night of this. Paranoid about the faintest sound or movement I feel or hear in my empty flat, chiding myself for not having unpacked sooner, I'm pulled out of my spiral by Ma's anger; she's livid with my online activity.

'Why can't you post anything positive? What's the point of further inciting hatred?'

I feel incensed at her words, and let down. How can she sit so comfortably when a community she was once married into was being assaulted in broad daylight?

'They've had the chakka jam on for so long. Why disrupt the daily life of civilians?'

An entire community's self-respect, identity, lives being somehow less important than people inconvenienced while going to work, picking up their coffees, their cars unable to navigate throngs of women who are simply demanding their right to exist. Ma tells me she watches 'all news channels' because that's the only way she can have an objective point of view about what's happening, that she isn't partisan to one community. I am unsure of what to say, not just because I'm angry but because I'm perplexed. Surely, my smart, educated mother cannot fall for propaganda.

I tune into the news, and still, there is no coverage of the riots; only of inconvenience on account of the chakka jam, of how eighty-three-year-old women have been paid by the opposition to attend protests, about how food stalls organised with impeccable efficiency were attacked and dismantled in the dead of night. Nothing about the dying bodies, the missing children and men, the women hiding in fear of sexual assault and rape. Even some channels that could be counted upon to show more objectivity report these incidents as 'riots' rather than a pogrom, the language of loss barely distilled into catchy headlines.

On Twitter, I watch a video of a man being interviewed while he stands in the rubble of what was once a butcher's shop. He talks about coming back home from his village after the first night of violence, about the overwhelming stench of rotting rubber, maybe flesh. The Delhi air, he says, was danker than usual. In the distance, smoke billowed from the low-lying houses. Then, he crossed a fire brigade truck and a mob of journalists with video cameras and mics. Some stray police vans lined the roads. He heard the journalists mention 'riots' and 'Muslims killed'. He walked right past them, his pulse racing. A policeman stopped him and asked for his identification, which he said he forgot to carry. After some negotiation, the policeman let him proceed. Upon passing through the gate, he saw entire homes reduced to rubble, scorched walls, and bits of petrol bombs lying beneath his feet. The entire area was deserted except for a few Muslim families huddling in corners and investigating the remains of their homes and shops with a look of stunned horror. A maulvi pointed towards the remains of a dargah, an orange flag jammed into its crumbling wall, and a green flag lying torn on the ground. He avoided stepping on some pages of the Qur'an turned black and tattered. Broken pieces of glass everywhere. A few shops down, a small temple was shining in the morning light, untouched by the carnage. He saw houses marked with saffron flags intact and the rest blown to smithereens by gas cylinders, now empty. As the residents tried to salvage what was left of their homes, he walked ahead and arrived at a parking lot. Twenty burnt cars and vans on each side, the windshields hollowed out and tires missing. The police cordoned the area at its many exits, and the entrance to some lanes was barricaded by bricks and concertina wire.

The video then cuts to a man with black sunglasses, bits of burnt flesh clinging to his cheeks. The man says he heard chants of *'Jai Sri Ram'* and felt the building next to his shake after a huge blast, so he tried to run and was hit on the head with a bottle of acid.

Other videos are flagged with a 'fake news' warning by Instagram. In one such video, sounds of a brass band and a wedding procession blare in the background where the groom sits atop a white horse with a garland of currency notes around his neck. *We've lost everything*; an older man, holding his belongings in a sack, speaks to the camera.

I receive a DM from a Muslim music producer from Hyderabad who lives in LA whose work I've been following for a few years—*we've lost this country forever. I'd argue we never had this country, to begin with,* I text back. She tells me she texted her friends in Delhi to ask if anybody could find a safe home for the women and children affected by the violence, and nobody responded. I write with increasing desperation, *who do you turn to when the very systems meant to protect you slaughter you while the rest turn a blind eye?* She leaves me on read; I don't blame her. There's nothing much left to say. The news of the police not allowing residents back into their homes trickles in.

---

I don't remember facing any particular religious slurs as a child, only the usual slurs that focused on my dark complexion or weight or nerdiness. Had I blanked them out, or had something changed? I do remember the relentless fights my parents would often engage in, with me caught in the crosshairs. I remember their slow and nasty descent into calling out each other's families—the prejudice of others and the lack of validation becoming weaponised during domestic battles. Their rage fuelled by errant remarks. 'Baniyas are known skinflints' or 'Mohammedans are intrinsically an unhygienic people'.

I wonder now who equipped them with the language to so surely and deeply hurt. To cast their partner's entire identity aside by way of a slur, by the immediate 'otherisation' of their characteristics to preserve a sense of self. Is it behaviour learnt from the news blaring on news channels? Is it picked up in school when boys rip each other's pants down to check who's circumcised? Is it learnt in college when hijabi women are stopped from entering colleges on account of their burkhas? Or does it start at home, when grandmothers keep a separate set of utensils for people from any community, religion or caste that may 'pollute' their own? It's easy to reflect on these questions today as an adult, but as a child, I simply mimicked these behaviours and carried them with me to classrooms, workplaces and close relationships.

Later that day, I receive a call from my father, who's been supporting me in attending the protests so far, assuaging Ma's worry with diplomacy: *Let the young do what they need to*. But when we speak, he gives me a ten-month window to leave the country. He tells me to come back to Dubai. He cannot live in constant fear that something might happen to his daughter, he says. I can sense the worry beneath his decisive tone. He forbids me from going to protests or posting anything online. I nod along, buying time but unsure of whether I'll abide by his requests.

Leave the country and go where? Starting a life from scratch comes with its own limitations. I chose this country to build a life for myself, to connect to my illusionary idea of 'roots'. Only to be told that I don't belong here. It's cowardly to leave. But, it's also probably the only sensible course of action. It would be good to not stick out like a sore thumb, to not flinch inwardly, to collect in small throngs, drinking Sulaimani chai, tuning in and out of snatches of polite Arabic.

Dubai's divides are sharp and unforgiving. Segregated into 'white' and 'brown' Dubai, separated by an architectural marvel that cost 230 million USD to construct, the world's largest photo frame that enables one settlement to look into the other. On one side lies vast desert land hastily converted into dusty parking lots, low-rise buildings with first-generation immigrants who run one-dirham shops, service centres for Android phones, shawarma stalls. Decrepit apartments are inhabited by Malayali waxing ladies, Indonesian street vendors and Balochistani cabbies. Here, women roam about in hijabs unless they're white, and they, too, are careful not to expose too much leg or cleavage.

As an adult, I realise how the wealth doesn't just cover up, but aids the inequalities. That pay scales in Dubai are determined by the passport one holds. How the law bans abortions. How two men or two women can't be seen in love. How the proportions of life take on truly excessive and absurd contours—like a muzzled cheetah in the bathroom of the Sheikh's wildlife controller, government-sponsored media, authorities hiding the HIV-positive status of locals accused of rape. How the dress code is part of criminal law. How apostasy is a crime punishable by death.

If I could close my eyes, align with my Muslim side and play by all the rules, Dubai would open up to me like a pearl in an oyster.

As dusk creeps in, bathing my room in a soft pink flow, I wait, terrified of the videos that might start rolling in. A few hours pass, and Twitter remains limp—just a handful of tweets about some celebrity's birthday party, the new word game everyone on the internet is obsessed with, a WHO report on a disease outbreak in a town in China, some conspiracy theorists predicting a pandemic, activists speaking about the danger of protesting in the capital, where the police are now using tear gas canisters, along with batons, to disperse the crowd.

I know I should take a break, unplug from the matrix, stop compulsively checking my phone for Medha's calls or social media for news bulletins and eat a homemade meal, perhaps. There's some talk of a protest coming together, despite Section 144, but I receive warnings on a Telegram group about the police keeping protesters in jail overnight. Somebody's saying it's an intimidation tactic; somebody else says to not risk it.

I put my phone away—the sounds of the night closing in on me—and drag the wooden planks from the bedroom to the hall. I lay down a plastic sheet, secure them in place with my legs and begin to sand them down along the grain. The harsh noise of the sand against the wood is comforting, and I lose track of time. I tip the primer into a plastic container, add thinner to it, and run the brush along the grain a few times, then across, then along again. I find comfort in coating the wooden planks and running warm water over the brushes as I wait for the wood to dry. I repeat the steps across all the planks and finally doze off, fatigued, when I am done.

I dream of my first trip outside Bombay after Prague. I am on a train from Delhi to Madhya Pradesh for an assignment. Production has me travelling alone, in the first AC compartment—a coupé with two berths. On my way in, I spot a slew of men in orange kurtas and red tikas, and I immediately conceal my face behind the book I'm reading, shrinking further into a corner, as if that'll render me invisible. Passing through smaller towns and villages, I notice an increase in saffron flags marking some homes and conspicuously missing from the patios and doorways of others. The berth across from mine is soon occupied by a man with a large belly bursting out of the seams of his tight khadi kurta. He looks me over with shrewd eyes and passes an oily smile as I take in the red tika glaring on his forehead. A beefy security guard stands outside in the doorway. The man takes the seat in front of me and I bury my nose deeper in the book I am reading. There is a nameless fear in my belly that I try to calm by breathing deeply.

In true prying-Indian-uncle style, he asks about the book I am reading, where I am going, who I am meeting and what

I do for a living. I answer with sincerity and desperation, one eye on the bell taped to the wall that would summon an attendant in seconds. Am I being too paranoid?

Unasked, he reveals he is a member of parliament from Jabalpur. He seems to take an inordinate interest in the documentary I am shooting and wants to know my affiliations. I try to dodge his questions by confirming that I work with an international channel and only make films on social issues. He registers my evasion with distaste and asks my name. I hesitate before telling him—*Sophia.* I see the light shift in his eyes. His curiosity turns into cold, hard detachment. He asks if he can see any identification. I dig into my bag, calculating how this could play out, and finally hand him my union card. He studies it for a second before returning it with a wry smile. I realise I've begun to tremble, so I excuse myself for the washroom.

Inside the cold-steel washroom with the open pit reflecting the gurgling ground underneath, I splash water on my face and try to assess the possibilities. My phone barely has any signal.

I return to the cabin to find the MP gone and a mother and child in his place. I am too relieved to question it and settle back into my seat.

I wake up late, the sun spilling through the naked windows, lighting up the room and all its corners. I sneeze so loud that my entire body shakes; the smell of turpentine clings to my nose. The bedsheet lies crumpled beneath me, evidence of a fitful sleep; there are some fresh scratches on my arm and I can feel a slight headache coming on. I take the wood out to the balcony to dry. I wrap the plastic and place it on one side. I make coffee and go online; resisting the urge to log onto Twitter, I check my account balance and place an order for a single bed. I locate cheap lighting stores in my neighbourhood and make a mental note to drop in after my run. I make a list of the things the house needs—a rug, perhaps a circular one, an armchair I could place next to the window, plants that require low maintenance, something living to give me company on nights such as the last.

Since my parents' separation, things have changed irrevocably. Ma's gone back to her maiden name, if not in legal documents, then on social media. She does routine havans now to appease gods she didn't believe in earlier. My father offers the ritualistic namaaz every Friday and sends me verses from the Holy Book recited by local maulvis on WhatsApp. Their separation has exacerbated their loneliness—neither has been too successful with love—and they have now turned to religion to find succour.

Being cocooned in the better parts of Delhi and Bombay offers me a kind of illusion of security, of comfort in hobnobbing with the like-minded, a kind of secure anonymity amidst millions. It's only once or twice that I've been refused as a tenant in some part of town because of my surname, or delivery boys from Swiggy or Zomato have refused to deliver whenever I've stayed on the other side of the Yamuna. It's only that one time when the immigration officer at Delhi airport took me aside for a lengthier interrogation while returning from a film festival in Beirut before allowing me to re-enter the country. It's only one ex-boyfriend whose mother jokingly asked him to not take our relationship too seriously, asserting that Muslims are fundamentally different. As a child, I didn't catch on to the subtle display of power my Nana-ji would indulge in by politely showing my father his economic place or what his education could afford him. After almost two decades, it's only now that I look back and feel my father's humiliation.

The protests in Delhi carry on even as things settle down in Bombay. Kunal convinces me to attend a small gathering at his friend's house. Over dinner, we are joined by his friend's father. He refills our wine glasses, pouring whisky for himself, as he talks about how life has been difficult since the protests and, in the same breath, mentions how his colleague's son is throwing a lavish wedding in Srinagar. His wife clarifies they won't be attending for security reasons. Considerably drunk, he recounts his youthful days when he dated Parveen Babi briefly and what a sad fate she suffered. Somebody plays some ghazals by Abida Parveen. I feel myself withdrawing from this gathering of people.

I finally get a FaceTime call from Medha. I tell her I've been bolting my door the last few nights. She tells me about the crazy three days she's had, visiting shelters for the victims of the violence, about activists being shut out, about her fear, about the police being in on everything, about the power tussles between the chief minister and the Centre, about failing democracy and social media and right-wing power. She looks exhausted. I'm unsure of what to say. We're separated by a screen, yet somehow connected.

# 10

# ONLINE

WHEN I CHECK MY PHONE, I SEE A STRING of anxious texts from Medha—*are you seeing the news? they're proposing a month-long total lockdown. stepping out to stock up. saw a woman with an entire dupatta wrapped around her head. terrifying. these masks are fucking uncomfortable. Soph?*

Her texts immediately spike my anxiety and I switch off my phone, slipping it into a desk drawer, and get ready for my work call. There's no mention of a lockdown on the news, just ad breaks about teeth whitening strips and news bulletins on cases of what they're calling Coronavirus spreading through Kerala alongside the American president's visit to the country culminating into a gaudy event. The prime minister, in his signature starched white kurta, beige vest and groomed beard, mouths the words to the national anthem as an instrumental version blares from loudspeakers.

My nerves about my call with the celebrity director obscure the apocalyptic news pouring in. Although I've tried fixing the lighting in my bedroom, the image is still hazy and deepens the shadows under my eyes in the light of the stray lamps in disparate corners. The apartment is sparsely furnished with thrifted cane furniture, a second-hand TV, a functional kitchen and a bathroom where no natural light permeates. I wanted to meet in person, but she insisted we do a video call.

She lays down the rules of our engagement—we are to have a daily check-in call at 10 a.m. where she'll narrate scenes to me as I type them into a scriptwriting software. Then, I will edit the scenes, ensure they're in chronological order, 'cross the t's and dot the i's' and we'll go over them together at 5 p.m. I wasn't expecting the work to be this clerical, but I'm intimidated by her piercing presence, even through the grainy video call, and don't protest. I'm glad to be assisting her; the pay just about covers my rent but I'm assured it'll look good on my résumé.

During our evening call, her eight-year-old son disrupts our meeting, and she doesn't apologise when she ignores me to attend to him. I sit before the laptop, watching my face on the tiny square in one corner, wondering why it looks so grim. Her son interrupts my thoughts with a card trick he fails at. I pretend to be delighted and clap after his performance, mentally counting the minutes to when I can clock out.

*holiday soon?* I text Medha and she says all travel is about to be stopped. I call her out for being a fatalist and text Kunal instead. Perhaps, it's a bit selfish to continue staying in touch with Kunal after having cheated on him so brazenly, but he hasn't protested. We agree to meet at the bar we used to frequent. I think it's pretty poetic, but I know we are here mainly because it's the cheapest one in the neighbourhood. I stick to vodka and soda while he drinks gin and tonic.

'I'm assisting this editor on a new feature film,' Kunal chews on the ice chips.

'What's it about?'

'It's about screenwriters in India and how the industry has changed over the years.'

'That sounds cool. What about gigs?'

'The last gig was about a month ago. Anyway, all parties play trashy House like we're in Ibiza. I want to play minimal tech.'

'Has there been any activity on the protest groups?'

'Nah, they've been silent since the riots.'

'Are we out of things to talk about?'

'I'm also sort of seeing somebody,' he says, pushing his white-rimmed glasses up his nose that glistens with a thin layer of sweat.

'Sort of?'

'It's complicated. She's the other editor on the doc and has a boyfriend.'

'Damn, that's spicy,' I chuckle and beckon the waiter for a refill. He picks up my glass and his expression is inscrutable under the mask.

Kunal leans towards me, threatening to spill his gin and tonic.

'She's into light bondage. Role-play. Exhibitionism. Just a wild time.'

The news of him sleeping with another girl falls lightly but surely on me. Not that I expect us to get back together. It just feels like something sacred has been lost, a promise broken, even though I set the wheels in motion. He averts his gaze as he tells me about her complicated relationship with her boyfriend, how they've been together for a decade, so it makes sense why she might crave excitement. Then, he comments on the impossibility of monogamy. I wonder if he's trying to rationalise my affair, and our break-up.

'I find role-play contrived, honestly.'

'How's Haider?'

'We broke up a while ago. I told you that. Excuse me.'

In the washroom, I stalk her Instagram. She's pretty in a predictable way, and I immediately feel less threatened.

'I don't think you should kink-shame her.'

A shadow passes over his face, and his eyes turn cold. It seems like he wants to ask me something, but the moment passes, and he relaxes into his seat.

'How's your new job?'

I mumble through my answer; I don't want him to know how absurdly overqualified I am for the position, but at least the work is writing-adjacent. He laughs at the jargon I spew. I tell him I haven't been able to write since the grant fiasco; perhaps this will finally frustrate me enough to start writing again. We drink more and flirt; I touch his arm, he touches my thigh.

We step out into the humid night, and the wind carries the fragrance of kebabs mixed with the whiff of alcohol. We wait for the rickshaw on the emptying road, lights from the intersection spilling over us, and I kiss him. A car passes us and an old man, old enough to be my grandfather, shouts out an obscenity. My head spins with the liquor.

Back home, I don't turn the lights on as we descend onto the bed.

When I wake up, I see Kunal's already slipped out and I appreciate his consideration.

Dressed, I briefly look for the discarded condom wrapper but abandon the search after some futile minutes to put the coffee on. When the video call comes on, I smile, the sunlight hurting my eyes. My boss cuts the call short today. There's been an announcement of a fourteen-hour curfew; she needs to stock up on supplies. I'm convinced she's overreacting, but I'm grateful for a few free hours.

Moving into the new home has brought with it a sense of comfort that's rare and precious, something to hold on to during times like these. Just when I thought shit couldn't get wilder, it did.

I put on some soothing music and take three deep breaths, turning inwards, connecting with what's inside me, not craving, not needing, not wanting, not aching, no attachments. Just an inhale, and an exhale.

Can't lay my shit on anybody, can't be an inconvenience, don't think about my parent's broken marriage or the string of failed relationships, the gnawing insecurities and the fear I'll never be enough. Just when I thought I was grounding myself in the present moment, I'm forced to recede behind a screen, forced to think of a future where I move about easily, don't live pay cheque to pay cheque, and finally stop wanting to bolt the minute I'm in a stable relationship. My desires are so banal.

Stay in. Stay in, swallow my pride, swallow my ego, annihilate any sense of self, morph, become a sponge, absorb everybody's bad moods, be the good friend, the solid friend, the stable friend, don't ask for too much, don't reach out when things are hard. People laud me for only reaching out when I've figured things out. It's exhausting. Nobody has time for anybody. We think we do, but we don't. Nobody really wants to listen. So, I listen in the hope that somebody else will return the gesture. Try and be the best I can be so I can feel a sliver of the love I've been chasing as a child. Who fucked me up? Who fucks us up?

Shut up; your interiority means nothing when the world is collapsing. *You've been dealt an unfair hand: you're brown, you're a woman, you're Muslim,* Sonia said this to me on a call a few days ago. Who wants her pity? I read books and listen to music nobody else does, and I date strange people against my best instinct, hoping that the friction will polish me, but it doesn't.

Sometimes, it feels like it does; at parties, in new relationships, or in certain moments that come forth with startling consonance and clarity, it feels like all the pain, disappointment and heartache has been worth it. But the rest of the time? Not so much. I'm going to turn thirty-one in a few months, and I have nothing to show for it except parents who can't stand each other, a family whose foundations were never quite laid right; in the post-apocalyptic world, there's no room for sadness.

Buddhism teaches to not seek a home anywhere but inside yourself, so I accumulate—I accumulate intellect, kindness, dissolution of the ego, friends, lovers, degrees, continents, clothes, lipsticks, recipes, heirlooms, bad hairstyles, mood swings, niceties, playing to the gallery and its attendant exhaustion—I collect it all, bit by bit, like a magpie fucked up on some substance, hoping to kindle an inkling of what home must feel like. I wish somebody would hold me, hold a mirror to me, tell me I'm enough, but that's the game, that external validation game that's both sweet and bitter, necessary and superfluous; a constant push and pull.

My brain has felt broken for a long time. Earlier this year, I Googled a psychiatrist in the neighbourhood after a string of panic attacks where I felt like my heart would crack right through the middle and pop out of my chest if I didn't medicate or seek help.

The psychiatrist was a forty-something woman, slender, with an intense expression on her face, leathery skin and sleek hair, faint veins running into her skull like rivulets. I sat before her, trying not to pay too much attention to the ugly posters with the words, *Depression, Call this hotline for suicide help, Dial this number for domestic abuse.* My panic attack seemed to pale in comparison to the collection of trauma that comes with being alive in this country. We spent ten minutes in silence where she studied me, not moving a muscle, while I tried not to worry about the sweat soaking through my t-shirt, or my chin that always trembled in an ugly fashion whenever I'm on the verge of tears.

Once I started talking, I couldn't stop. I spoke about how, one night, after drinking an entire bottle of wine alone, I turned up at a bar I knew Kunal frequented to watch football matches. How I forced him to talk to me, but he refused, saying I was too drunk. I yelled at him in front of all his friends, so he walked out of the bar. I forced him to come home so we could chat. We suffered through a silent auto rickshaw ride, him vibrating with anger. At home, I don't remember what we argued about, I tried to have sex with him, and he shook me off, disgusted.

He threatened to call the police, and I laughed. He finally left when his friend turned up.

I blubbered as I spoke, and comically big tears rolled down my cheeks. She listened calmly and then asked me if I had trouble trusting people. I stared at her and let out a mean laugh.

Then our time was up. I never went back.

---

After the curfew ends, I pick up supplies I'll need in case there's another lockdown of some sort; Harpic, bar of washing soap—I should've rented a washing machine—dried herbs packaged in plastic bottles, tinned chickpeas, peaches, oranges, pineapples, red kidney beans, tinned everything, rolls and rolls of one-ply toilet paper—they're out of the three-ply—sanitisers, a special herbal solution to wash my veggies in. I pick up many snacks—Mars bars, Kettle chips, baked kale chips, oat cookies with raisins and cinnamon, as if snacks could save me from the end of the world.

'Are you okay?' Medha calls.

'Never been better.'

'You sound manic.'

'I mean it though, I like being at home. I've gotten into a routine. No getting out for unnecessary meetings. No social plans I can't get out of. No strange dates with random men.'

'They're saying it's twenty-one days, but I've heard rumours it could go on for several months.'

'Even better.'

'You definitely sound manic.'

---

I've never thought about death as much as I do now. It strikes me at odd times, when I least expect it—waiting in line outside grocery stores cordoned off with ropes or when I steal a walk through my neighbourhood that now appears to be a ghost town with feeble street lights. While I watch videos of hospitals running out of beds in Italy and celebrities singing the cover of 'Imagine' on Zoom, the wail of ambulances is more prominent than ever before. I only ever think about my own death, though. I can't decide which way I'd want to go—cremated or buried? Naturally, my parents will have their respective preferences. I hope they don't have to endure the cruelty of losing their child first.

I think cremated. Turned to ash and vanished into the ether. There could be a casual affair of some sort after, with good wine and tea cakes and finger sandwiches. No eulogies. I can picture Kunal and Medha holding one another, bereft, silenced by their grief. I better write emails to everyone I love and despise. The ones I hate deserve to hear from me more than the ones I love; I often despise without reason.

Sometimes, I do chores. Chores lend the days, that usually seem to bleed into one another, a sense of meaning. Dishes that pile up, meals that need prepping, corners that I didn't know existed accumulating dust. For once, living alone doesn't feel like the walls are closing in on me every evening. I know that life is cyclical because nature is cyclical. Nature's repetitive patterns, the way the wind blows through the leaves or the way water trickles out of a stream into rivers or the fact that dawn comes after night or spring follows winter, how often I have caved into the arms of another, only to be alone on my bed now during a global calamity.

Amidst the madness, my work's steady monotony lends me a sense of purpose. I smoke the last piece of hash, get bombed and watch a TV show about trying to find Allah in Trump's America. An online quiz predicted I'd lose my shit on day thirty-five; it's day twenty, but the cracks are beginning to show. Being high helps kill time, but I find myself going down rabbit holes on the internet that act as a crash course in the fast decline of civilisation.

The internet is my best and worst friend right now. I only surface from Twitter, Instagram wormholes to glimpse Medha on FaceTime, who's currently Covid positive. I'm racked with worry. I call her three times a day, trying hard to keep my tone steady so as to not add to her anxiety. I can't fly down since air travel has been halted. I try not to cave into sentimentality.

Today, I read her a poem as she nods off to sleep.

*My God, I think,*
*if paradise is to be here*
*it will have to include her.*

As I go down my internet wormhole, slack-jawed and dead-eyed, I make my way through an entire jar of sweetened hazelnut cocoa spread. I only realise it when the spoon hits the bottom of the glass jar with an aggravating noise and comes up empty. I check Flo. I immediately text Medha, who is bored out of her mind in the last days of her recovery from Covid.

*I ate an entire jar of Nutella.*

*Whatever floats your boat.*

*I'm also late.*

*Oh, take a test.*

*Covid?*

*Pregnancy test.*

After that, everything moves quickly. I call up a few pharmacies in my neighbourhood—most lines are busy, and the recorded messages on the calls mix with the wail of the ambulance outside, sometimes distant, sometimes terrifyingly close. Finally, a man picks up; he sounds distracted and out of breath, and there's a din of voices in the background. I feel ashamed asking him to deliver a pregnancy test, so I throw in an order for an oxygen metre and some paracetamol. He asks me if I or anybody in my home is positive. I stay alone, I say, before instinctively wanting to take it back, wondering if that's inaccurate. He tells me they're delivering according to priority—with positive patients or caregivers at the top of the list. I plead with him, panic creeping into my voice, and he curtly tells me I'll get it soon.

While I wait, I draw the curtains and turn the lamps on. In the light, my dark circles don't seem as deep anymore. I strip down and study myself in the mirror. Nothing feels notably different except nipples that seem sharper and darker, which could simply be PMS. I put my clothes back on and calculate whether I was ovulating last I had sex. I regret never paying attention in maths class and pick up the phone to text Kunal. *We need to talk.* I delete the message.

I light a cigarette and take a drag, but the taste is metallic and rotten; my mouth feels dry as a cactus, and I retch. I stub it out immediately. When I smell the smoke on my hands,

I sanitise them, rubbing a soothing, hydrating gel that smells of lavender, and clean out the ashtray in the kitchen sink. I grab a bottle of juice from the fridge and pour myself a glass. The cool liquid soothes my chafed throat and I read the ingredients on the back. Too many preservatives to justify the 'natural' label.

Medha calls, and her face glows on the FaceTime screen. 'It's not here yet.'

I catch a glimpse of a smooth, round butt bobbing naked behind her and hear the tinkling of ice in a glass.

'I'm on a call!'

The butt disappears. I see long, pale legs and the flash of a gold waist chain. Medha looks at me, a bit embarrassed.

'Ajda.'

'Who?'

'We met a week before the lockdown, at this exhibition. She's a curator. Moved to Delhi like, a year ago.'

'And now she's living with you?'

'I'm living with her.'

'What about Covid?'

'Eh. She took care of it.'

'Is she positive too?'

Medha shrugs and looks sheepish, the embarrassment of new love etched across her face. I wait for that pang of irritation, of jealousy, but it doesn't come.

'I'm genuinely happy for you.'

The doorbell rings, and I'm on the toilet a few moments later. I position the sterilised plastic cup after some struggle and piss. I wipe myself, drop the tube in the cup, and drop a few yellow pellets on the pregnancy stick. My hands tremble lightly, more because of the cigarettes than nerves. I don't need to read the instructions. I remember it from eight years ago, all of it—memories of Medha's cool hand in mine, the whir of the fan at the clinic, Azhar's glacial indifference and the glow on my face, despite hormones wreaking havoc on my body. The moment where I knew, in any other circumstance, age, epoch, era, I'd have kept it. The strip turns pale pink, and a faint line begins to form. A single line. I wait a few seconds more, and then the second line forms. I stare at the two lines, the most mundane image ever and look into the mirror; my irises, rounder than ever. I lift my shirt and study my stomach, imagining the baby to be the size of a raisin. I think of whether it's a girl or a boy or if it's simply too early to tell. My body feels foreign, but for once, I like it.

It takes about three months for a baby to turn from a cluster of cells to a foetus with features. I wonder about the detachment of the word 'foetus'. I think of its primitive face with large, dark circles for eyes, a small mouth, a lower jaw, and its throat developing. Blood cells take shape, and circulation begins. A micro heart tube will beat sixty-five times a minute by the end of the fourth week. Each ear begins as a little fold of skin at the side of the head. Tiny buds that eventually grow into arms and legs. Fingers, toes and eyes find form. After the eighth week, the gynaecologist refers to the embryo as a foetus. By the end of the second month, the foetus is about one inch long and weighs about one-thirtieth of an ounce.

My boss has had a rough few weeks. She looks haggard—her greasy hair sticks to her forehead. Her dark brown eyes look black in the light, and without make-up, her skin looks dull. We discuss some scenes in the script—about the protagonist going back to her married home to collect her things. She steers the conversation away from the film and talks about her ex-husband.

'I was never one for marriage. He wanted it, a grand party and everything. Flying in lilies and orchids from Amsterdam, engraving gold bands with our names. Fixing my hair at the mandap. Now, look at him. Meets Aryaan once a month, if that. My friends warned me about him—he's always had younger women flitting about him, attracted to his start-up money. He's kept himself fit, despite age. When we met, he was looking to build a name for himself in the industry. I moved to Bombay for him.'

I'm not sure how to respond to her sudden vulnerability. It feels odd to have access to the private thoughts of somebody famous. Should I tell her I found out I was pregnant and haven't told the father or anybody else yet? That I Googled the names of gynaecologists in my neighbourhood and picked one after reading reviews by new mothers? The one with the most glowing testimonials. I imagine the doctor and I would discuss water births, what vitamins to take, if it was possible to have a child as a single woman in India, that abortions could be gotten up to twenty-four weeks, if I should look into freezing my eggs, how involved should the child of my father be, when I had done everything in my power to make sure he hated me?

But when I talk, I say something inane and only focus on how hoarse my voice sounds. She says I'm a good listener, and at the end of our call, I ask her for a raise. She seems surprised but agrees.

Later that night, as I sleep on my side—spurred by the information I gleaned from a medical website to optimise blood flow to my belly—I dream of the house I grew up in.

It's a small one-bedroom apartment with a hall-like area that my parents have done their best to make hospitable. There's a three-piece sofa set, with freshly dry-cleaned beige upholstery, and a coffee table made of oakwood. On the table lies a book of baby names opened to the page under the letter S. A few names have been circled with a blue pen. Next to the book are Ma's reading glasses, the morning's daily, a half-finished chai, a film of milk coating its surface. The rooms are sparse but comfortable. There's a compact terrace with vines and creepers' tendrils running along the metallic railing. The house has only one air conditioning unit that cools the bedroom and makes it a sanctuary from the oppressive Dubai heat. The kitchen is spotless—the chequered cleaning cloth hangs from the fridge's handle and the kitchen smells of lemons, cloves and ginger. There are plucked marigolds in a bowl kept on a marble-top mantle. There are knick-knacks from their limited travels—a miniature Taj Mahal, Goddess Lakshmi in brass, a scroll of Chinese silk Dad brought back from Guangzhou, tacky fridge magnets from Mauritius, Singapore and London.

I lie on a single bed with fitted sheets embroidered with tiny purple and pink flowers, a mid-sized white teddy bear holding a blue heart that says 'I love you'—the street lamp illuminating half of my face. I feel a wetness on my bed, something against my leg. Thin snakes with triangular faces slither up my legs and hips. I count twenty. It's frightening and disgusting, but I'm turned on. The pleasure of it sends me back to sleep. In the morning, my parents call me from downstairs. They are together. There's a sense of occasion. I go to the bathroom, and while I piss, I notice the wastebasket overflowing with toilet paper, rubber gloves stained with blood and tattered masks. The pile grows larger and larger and blocks the bathroom door. I'm unable to get out.

I wake up drenched in sweat. It's 5 a.m., and it's still dark outside, the gaudy white of the street lights merging with the extravagance of the coastal night sky. I call Kunal; he picks up after a few seconds. We speak over one another.

'Why are you up?'

'Are you okay?'

'I was playing FIFA.'

'I'm pregnant.'

The conversation's brief and to the point. I tell him it's his since I haven't been with anybody else. He's silent. I can picture his small eyes widening behind his glasses, panic setting in. I tell him I haven't made up my mind yet. He reminds me we're in the middle of a pandemic, and the future is uncertain. I tell him that women have children in bushes, in open fields and in transit, the cost of freezing eggs is wildly out of my reach and that I've never felt more sure of anything. He asserts he'll pay for the abortion and I feel a violent urge to ice him out of my life. The casualness with which he approaches money is both liberating and suffocating. His immediate response to any kind of tragedy or seismic shift is to shut down completely or open up and rationalise through logic, science and empirical evidence.

'We're far too young.'

'Ma had me at twenty-six.'

'I just don't imagine us prescribing to that same old tired model. Look at the world around you. You want to contribute fifty metric tonnes annually to the carbon footprint?'

'Stop Googling statistics that'll help your case.'

'You think you're ready for this? Two years ago, you left me for another man, then you left him—'

I hang up before he can finish. He texts me to apologise and says he needs time to process the news.

I Google safe poses and stretch into my morning yoga routine, ending with ten minutes in the corpse pose. My nausea's taken a particularly devious turn, and I crave something salty constantly.

I make the mistake of reading the news—bodies wrapped up in PPE kits from head to toe, a doctor feeding a vial of cow urine to a Covid patient in some government hospital make up the surreal news reports. Many experts predict the current wave will not peak for at least three weeks and that the actual number of cases and deaths is much more than what is being disclosed officially. Most of the population with no documentation, no access to even three square meals a day, much less public healthcare, are reduced to numbers in the undertaker's count. In the face of widespread death, large-scale election rallies carry on, waves of saffron flags towering against the sun. Somewhere, a doctor wears an orange scarf printed with the ubiquitous lotus.

Living in this country, especially at this time, feels like jumping through ascending levels of a video game. Kept job. Level 1 passed. Didn't get Covid. Level 2 passed. Stayed alive. Level 3. *Ding ding ding.*

Medha calls me. Her blonde hair is now dyed blue and has grown into curling wisps around her face. Her eyes shine, and her cheeks are red from the Delhi summer. She tells me she needs to show me something, flips the camera around, and I watch a hazy video play on her laptop screen.

A woman with blonde hair knotted at the top of her head in a messy bun, like all beautiful women know how to do, with an enormous belly, leans against a bathtub filled with cool blue water while a man, presumably her husband, holds her by the waist and rocks her back and forth as she deep breathes through her contractions. Sappy violin strings cut through her heavy, pained breaths, followed by a crescendo of piano keys as she lowers herself into the bathtub. They skip over the ugly parts of her screaming and pushing, and the video dissolves to her holding a slimy baby, its skin blue and purple, while the midwife strokes its tiny skull. I feel like retching and crying at the same time.

'This is cruel.'

'You're seriously considering keeping it?'

'There's never a good time for anything.'

'Here, a friend got mugged by the cops at gunpoint. You want to bring a child into this world?'

Beset with doubt, I stay silent.

---

I have developed a taste for a clean home. It's a more productive way to kill time than smoking pot and much less expensive. It also doubles as a workout. I borrow a hand vacuum from my neighbour, whom I seem to have caught in the middle of an argument. She looks frazzled in her jeans and t-shirt stained with smears of baby food and streaks of turmeric as a pressure cooker whistles in the background. Her four-year-old jumps around her, clinging. I hear the low hum of football commentary. She hands me the vacuum, throws me a terrified look and slams the door shut in my face. I realise I'm not wearing a mask.

The vacuum sucks up tobacco bits, biscuit crumbs and hair strands. The clean linen of the couch beams back at me. I wipe down the laminate kitchen counters, diligently picking out the gunk stuck to the gas stoves. I munch on cucumber as I wipe the glasses and place them back on the shelves, then I wipe down the grease from the tiled walls. The tiles are ugly—yellow with shiny red apples and green stems, years of sediment and dirt caking their grooves. I take the freshly washed clothes and hang them on the stand. Where can I buy baby clothes? I'll need a cot. Perhaps, a compact stroller with black wheels and a rose-gold canopy with dolphins and other cute animals hanging from it. Not the terrible ones that jingle as you push the stroller. The idea of rolling the stroller on the gravelly roads of my neighbourhood makes me wince. Plastic diapers won't cut it, and investing in organic cotton would be too heavy on the pocket.

Almost immediately, I feel exhausted. What kind of a mother will I be? How much can I possibly love this thing growing inside me? Now I understand Ma's need to protect, her constant mollycoddling, her oscillating between wanting me around and pushing me away. Her disbelief at having to live her life in service of me. Her fears when I wouldn't return home for several days, while I was out drinking with my degenerate schoolmates or hanging out at Azhar's studio apartment with its bare walls and unwashed bedsheets, her anger at me for talking back, never checking in on her. Her disappointment when I sided with my father when he made fun of the way she wore her dupatta or her childlike enthusiasm at the family getting together.

Will I be the cool mom? The one who smokes the first joint with her kid, drives them to concerts, never yells and creates a safe space in her home for when tantrums strike? A room with activities like clay modelling, free drawing with crayons, soothing fairy lights, a radio that plays recordings of rain or a waterfall? Something to regulate the nervous system. I know that despite the books I may read on parenting in the age of anxiety, my kid will hate me with an irrational rage from time to time, as I did with Ma.

I wake up with a sharp pain in my abdomen and book an appointment with a gynaecologist for the evening. Breathing through it makes me feel slightly better but Googling it is a bad idea—it can be as mundane as gas or as terrifying as a miscarriage or an ectopic pregnancy.

As I wait for my boss to clock in on the pixelated video call, I receive an email from Kunal about a scheme that allows you to freeze your eggs free of cost in exchange for giving half your eggs away.

'What about co-parenting? Lots of famous people do it, Tiger Woods, for example.'

'I don't think we should be taking parenting tips from the playboy of golf.'

I enjoy the light banter between us. It doesn't need to be complicated or twisted. Having a child alone is not something only wealthy people or characters in films do. Sometimes, I feel like I'm failing feminists but isn't feminism just about living out my choices without any shame? What was the fuss about fathers? The best ones I know, mine included, were absent even when they were around.

My boss is really struggling with the lockdown. Her usually neat hair is a mess, and her son causes havoc in the living room as he runs around with a plastic aeroplane. She tells me her ex-husband forgot to take him for the week, and school hasn't been on for months, so she has to devise clever ways to entertain him. She looks crushed, age evident on her face, and asks me to help her, so I agree on the condition that I seek her advice about something personal. Flustered, she agrees.

I tell her everything. The abortion, the cheating, the failed jobs, the gnawing but sure love for myself I have found for the first time since the lockdown, since the pregnancy. She listens intently. An hour passes, and I stop, coming up for a breath, immediately embarrassed and worried as to if this will be my last day at the job. Before she can say anything, her son interrupts, and she disappears into one of the bedrooms. Through the video, I stare at her living room, now empty, with its French windows, the sticky, dappled Bombay sun shining, and I can hear the low murmur of their voices, followed by a shriek. She comes back to the call, looking rattled.

'I know it doesn't seem like this work is fun, and there are moments where I picture what my life without Aryaan would be like, and the answer to that is—it would be exciting. Maybe more directing opportunities, definitely more hours of sleep, more travel. And then, there are days when the only messages and calls I get are about work; everybody wants something from me. When Aryaan points out something simple he did with his day like learning a new card trick, or he asks me why men can't have babies or if the moon is made of cheese or if ants invented the world's first social network or why I dress up or buy things—I feel closer to being pure and untainted. Without the day's bullshit or decades' worth of work, bills, ambition, failed relationships and projects. I'm not saying that's everything, but it's much more than most things. And what you're doing is brave.'

I listen, unsure of what to say but thankful for her words all the same.

After three months, life returns to a semblance of normalcy. There are more cars on the roads. The grocery stores stay open beyond ten in the morning. Then restaurants reopen with socially distanced outdoor seating.

I step out to meet some friends. I feel delirious from the tight hugs, kisses, feverish catching up on one another's lives, sharing drinks, laughs and the aux cable. They get drunk on red wine, roast chicken with parsley and thyme and play Mono Deal, through which I shamelessly cheat. The din on social media seems to be dying out. My father got the Russian jab in Dubai. There are talks of a vaccine being available in India in a few months. My friend tells me I'm showing, and I'm vaguely irritated, so I tell him how my breasts are growing exponentially. Although I'm glad they're not as sore anymore. The headaches have begun, but nausea has dissipated for now. Another friend of his, a lawyer, tells me children of unmarried women in India are in a legal and moral grey zone and getting mine into schools or colleges will be tough. I say I'll figure it out.

Later that evening, I search for baby carriers online, thinking about how easily design and technology borrow from the natural world without giving anything back. I think of when would be a good time to tell my parents, how they might react. My father would be glad for the lack of a partner, one less person for him to deal with, my mother will be appalled initially but come around eventually. I know these inquiries are premature, I'm as unsure of this as I have been of anything in my life so far, and I'm hoping to present a sense of total self-belief to the world that will enable it within me. I know nobody's asked me to do this, and everything around me is designed to remind me that I'm not ready for this either because I don't have financial stability or a marriage, meanwhile sending me overt messages that time is running out and my eggs are dropping like dead flies.

I consider the possibility of this being a response to getting rid of habits that no longer serve me—cigarettes, toxic relationships, a way to forgive myself. Is it a reaction to knowing that everyone's lives will move on and I'll be here, alone with my thoughts and cleaning routine? Or is it a response to the time I'm living in, the real backwash of which will only be felt when I'm standing on the other side?

For now, I'm content. I'm learning how to sit still. Learning not to worry about the outcome. I don't feel like reaching out to my parents or even Kunal. I'm now more connected to my body than ever before. I know when it's hungry and needs water; I realise how prone I am to neglecting its needs. I realise I'm not doing this just for myself.

The doorbell rings while I'm in the middle of my guided meditation. That's an anomaly. Nobody drops in unannounced anymore. I began meditating a couple of weeks ago, when I felt the first flutter of a kick. I'm surprised to note that it doesn't hurt, but that I can feel it squirming ever so slightly inside me. Besides having to pee every hour, not much has changed in the last few weeks. Kunal texts me twice daily, checking in about how I'm feeling, and whether I'm still convinced.

Everything he says irritates me, but I know it's more to do with my uncertainty than his fear. In one of our heated text exchanges, he calls me hysterical. I block him for a few days after that. Men find it so easy to dismiss any insistence on the part of women as hysteria. Freud blamed repressed memories for it. The Egyptians blamed the wandering womb. The Greeks? Sexual depravity. Ma was termed 'hysterical' in hushed tones at Delhi parties when she arrived in India after Dad's affair. She didn't get in touch with him for a long time. Nobody seemed to think she was grieving, taking space or figuring out what shape her life could take after spending thirty years with one man. The logical conclusion seemed to be that she was neurotic and emotional.

I can barely get out of bed on most days, but despite all evidence suggesting otherwise, I'm still here. I made it. I fix the mould on my bedroom walls; I don't waste my time on weird men who, apart from being rotten, are also dull. I call Ma once a day. I can meditate, admittedly with a lot of fidgeting and sharp exhaling, to the guided pre-recorded voices of husky Scandinavians, dripping with honey and sex. I don't ice Kunal out of this pregnancy, although his behaviour's begging me to. Whose test am I trying to pass? There isn't a god or man or woman or anybody out there who will lay a warm hand on my shoulder and hand me a shiny, laminated certificate with *You Made It* in gold lettering. I have nobody to answer to except myself.

I get the door. It's Medha. She's here in all her perfumed, blue-spiky hair, grinning glory. I stand awkwardly for a few moments before she envelops me in a huge hug, almost crushing my ribcage. I've always been awkward about hugs; I feel like I move away too soon and leave the hugger confused and stranded. When I try to jerk my body away from hers after what I feel is a respectable amount of time, she holds on to me even tighter. Once she finally moves away, she puts her hand on my belly—the tips of her long, slender fingers dotted with triangles in black ink. I ask her if it's to commemorate her Jewish heritage. She rolls her eyes at me; she picked up tattooing during the lockdown.

She drops her bags by the door and surveys my room.

'Turns out you're immune for a few months after you get Covid. I couldn't think of a better time to fly down. Delhi summer's unbearable.'

For the next two hours, she moves about the house like a gazelle in a jungle, clearing bits of paper, stacking my books vertically and organising them by height, drawing back the curtains, folding my clothes and keeping them in the cupboard but not before she lays down old newspaper on the splintered surface. She whips out some soy candles from her bag and lights them, the smell of vanilla filling up the room. I watch her from my seat by the window, feeling a maddening rush of affection. When she finishes, she unpacks and places her clothes next to mine, surveys the fridge, fixes a plate of olives and cheese with sparkling water for me and a beer for herself.

She twists the cap off with her teeth, and I wince.

'It's shocking you still have your teeth.'

'Not as shocking as you literally carrying a child.'

'If you've come here to get mad at me or try to change my mind, know that you're wasting your time.'

She throws the bottle cap at me and it misses me by a few inches. 'I'm staying.'

'I hope you are. How's Ajda?'

She tells me how things moved too fast with Ajda, that the pandemic gave them a false sense of accelerated intimacy. After two months, the little habits that initially were simply annoying compounded and became downright divisive. Ajda didn't believe in Western medicine, so she refused to take any pills for her developing allergy. Living with her meant waking up to her sneezing across Medha's bare chest. Once, she was on her period and sneezed so hard that a blood clot fell to the floor. If Medha insisted that she take a histamine blocker, Ajda claimed it was designed to dull her senses to the ongoing climate calamity.

'I told myself she's European, they don't really have problems, it's a crazy time, I should understand why she needs to care about *something*.'

Apparently Ajda processed her feelings by going into long spells of silence, which was awkward for Medha. Once, when Medha broke the silence with an ongoing monologue about Covid cases, vaccine apartheid, whose turn it was to make zucchini noodles for dinner, Ajda snapped at her—*Don't you Indians ever shut up?*

'Racist.'

Medha downs the beer and immediately uncorks another one. The gold bangles on her thin wrists glisten, and she smiles at me, her eyes filling with a kind of warmth that I only experience when I think of a little pink mouth against my cheek.

We have spinach and ricotta cheese ravioli for dinner. From scratch. She's drinking a bottle of red and I, some water with mint and basil. While she blanches and sautés the spinach, I mix the flour with eggs and salt and knead the dough. We each move around the kitchen in silence, some soft jazz wafting from my laptop in the bedroom. I switch to deep frying bits of garlic and basil in a pan with olive oil while she folds and cuts the dough into perfect squares, filling the centres with blobs of creamy cheese and spinach.

After a few glasses of wine, she sets the plates and looks straight at me, her eyes narrowed.

'Why are you doing this?'

Her blue jeans have smudges of purple and orange paint, her black nail paint is chipped, and her eyes shine with curiosity and slight fear. Maybe she's been steeling herself to ask me this question the entire flight, listening to a baby crying and wincing, attempting to understand why I do any of the things I choose to do and failing.

I wish I had a clear answer. An impressive answer would convince her beyond a shadow of a doubt that I'm ready for this, that I am not only an adult but emotionally mature enough to handle tantrums, potential learning disabilities, bullies at school and exploding expenses. But I come up short.

During the first lockdown, I received news that a cousin I grew up with tested positive in her second trimester. She was rushed to the hospital, where she developed a severe infection and lost her baby. It had been a few years since I had last met her, but I'd grown up in her orbit. I visited her at her college hostel when I was twelve or thirteen and watched her and her friends drinking rum, discussing the Nehrus and organising protests. I was fascinated with their verve, wisdom and urgent need for change. Ma asked me to reach out to her after her miscarriage but I was sure my words would fall short.

My instinct has always been to try and protect the ones I love from harm. I usually can't, and watching tragedy play out warped and hardened me as a child. I realised I'd become a cluster of everything and everyone I've loved and lost; my family, my Nani, with her pearl necklaces, saris that smelt of French perfume and talcum powder, her kind laugh and endless patience, the illusionary ideas of home, of first love, of an artistic career, of the different markers of growing up I was using to define myself, other adult relationships, of wild nights in the streets of Delhi or Prague or Beirut, of experiences words can never do justice to, of losing the first child, of the silly, often deceptive confidence of being young.

Over the years, I've accumulated all the love I have nowhere to put, and it's coagulated in my arteries, liver and tendons, spewing up in bursts of anxiety, sadness and pathological self-sabotage. I'm unsure how I can explain this to Medha, although I know if I try, she'll understand.

'I'm tired of loss.'

That night, as I sleep on my side, I can feel Medha's hand on the small of my back—warm and gentle.

I wait at the clinic, squeezed between a row of women with bellies of various sizes. Everyone wears masks, and the nurses wear shiny blue PPE kits with face shields. There's a line for women meeting with the ob-gyn and a different one for surgeries. No men are in the room except a full-length photograph of the clinic's founder that is framed and hung behind the main desk. I watch the receptionist—she deftly switches between calls, speaking to prospective patients in dulcet tones, an aura of calm around her. She swipes credit cards in the machine and scribbles prescriptions with speed and care. Soon, my name is called, and I walk into the doctor's chamber, glad the room's not dressed in pink or any other colour that would signal fertility or womanhood.

An examination table lies in a corner covered with a clean, white sheet, metallic clamps and lubricant gels. I lie down, my knees drawn up. She rubs the gel on my belly and fires up the screen. As her instrument glides across my midriff, cooling and soothing me, I try to tell to the black and white splotches on the screen. She tells me we're both healthy. I probe her face for a smile, obscured by the mask, and see her eyes crinkle.

---

After today's work call, I stay back. My boss is going through a pandemic emergency drill with her son. Calmly, she asks him, in case she were to lose consciousness and he found her on the floor, what would he do?

First, he protests, laughing and hiding his face in the cushions. Mothers don't feel pain or simply *pass out.* It's an absurd thought. Then, my boss wears her mask, gets down on her knees and lies on the floor, her hair obscuring her face. The son bursts into laughter, his skinny body shaking with glee. A few moments pass before he sobers up, the darkness of reality crossing over his face.

He walks up to his mother and shakes her. Her body moves like a limp, discarded glove. He furrows his brow in confusion, shrugs and walks towards the kitchen. She, defeated and confused, sits up and calls out to him for an explanation.

'I'm getting chips.'

I burst out laughing, and she looks at me as if to say, *he's a fool but I love him so much.*

Things that seem absolutely useless and unnecessary currently: dating, fashion, film journals, films in general, influencers, social circles, fake niceties. Things that have gained importance: music, meditation, calling my mom, neighbours, reading novels, yearning, dogs, kindness when it exists even without the construct of mutual reciprocation, cooking with Medha. I read reports that pregnancies have gone up by about 25 per cent since the pandemic hit. Every day, a new barrier of civilisation collapses. Today, it was clothes as I walked around the house half naked, tipping the remaining bottles of vodka and white wine into the sink. I find myself loving the easy, daily rhythm that an earlier me would have dismissed as boring. Why fix it if it isn't broken? I watch myself intensely, searing this moment into my memory, all my good and bad habits; a reminder of what I could pass on.

Later, I help Medha with a fund application and set up a ring light and the iPhone video in portrait mode. She talks about how queer artists are trying to reimagine a radically different future and how her practice has been ridden with doubt since the last exhibition. How her friend was taken into police custody for drawing a comic panel about the state-sponsored media, and how finding and sustaining a community has become imperative for artists to survive in the current reality. Her next exhibit curates naps as a method of radical resistance against hustle culture. She shoots the camera a big smile, and I switch it off.

'If we had a podcast, we'd be billionaires travelling like Jeff Bezos to Mars.'

'I don't know, we're quite politically incorrect.'

In the corner of the living room, she sets up her canvas on the easel, lining cans of paint against the wall and stacking art zines next to my books on cinematography and lighting.

'Yeah, I mean, we'd be forced to travel to Mars.'

I snort as I laugh. Then, I join her on the balcony, the soft, red glow of the setting sun illuminating our faces, lights flickering on in the building across ours.

# ACKNOWLEDGEMENTS

THIS BOOK WOULDN'T HAVE BEEN POSSIBLE without the love, support and encouragement of so many people. To my editor, Sanghamitra, whose instinctive understanding of my work and faith in my style has allowed the novel to see the light of the day, and to the rest of the Westland team; I'm thankful for their wisdom and generosity. To Ambar, my agent, who took a leap of faith with my book in its infancy. His incisive editorial eye and gentle guidance helped the novel come into its own and gave me confidence in my voice as a writer. To Abhay, who listened to my late-night ramblings about plot twists and character arcs, made me endless cups of coffee, and interrupted my writing with vinyl listening sessions, binge-watching *is it cake?* on Netflix, while tolerating my various pathologies—thank you for always being the best first reader and editor. To Nicole, for being the most intuitive first reader of my work. To Ishanou and Diya, for getting on grainy video calls to entertain wild ideas, for pulling me out of the throes of self-pity and doubt, and for bringing me back to reality during my various manic creative highs. To the friends who stayed patient through every cancelled plan and exhausted phone call and who created a safe space for me to reside in each time I drifted away from the story. To the various workshop mentors and authors whose snippets of advice and attentive listening went further than I could've imagined. To my parents and aunt, thank you for your impossible courage. And lastly, to the reader; I hope this book finds you at just the right time.